Praise for Aimée Thurlo

"Thurlo is a master of desert country as well as fast-moving adventure. Aimée Thurlo has added an exciting new dimension to Harlequin Intrigue."
—Tony Hillerman

"Kudos go to this brilliant writer who is the romance genre's Tony Hillerman."
—Affaire de Coeur

"Aimée Thurlo is skilled at capturing the emotions of love and attraction, and involves the reader in the romance of her tale."
—Publishers Weekly

"An explosive author who can successfully mix the hardboiled and romance genres…"
—PI Magazine

"Connoisseurs of mystery and romance alike will appreciate Ms. Thurlo's intelligent plotting and deft characterizations."
—Melinda Helfer, Romantic Times

"Aimée Thurlo is the queen of the romantic hardboiled novel."
—Mystery Scene Magazine

"Nobody can do romantic intrigue better than Aimée Thurlo."
—Talisman

"A simple writing style and wonderful storytelling skills."
—The Gothic Journal

Dear Reader,

They're rugged, they're strong and they're *wanted!* Whether sheriff, undercover cop or officer of the court, these men are trained to keep the peace, to uphold the law. But what happens when they meet the one woman who gets to know the real man behind the badge?

Twelve of these men are on the loose...and only Harlequin Intrigue brings them to you—one per month in the LAWMAN series, starting with Cisco Watchman, Aimée Thurlo's sexy Navajo detective.

Be sure you don't miss a single LAWMAN— because there's nothing sexier than the strong arms of the law!

Regards,

Debra Matteucci
Senior Editor & Editorial Coordinator
Harlequin Books
300 East 42nd Street
New York, NY 10017

Aimée Thurlo
CISCO'S WOMAN

Harlequin Books

TORONTO • NEW YORK • LONDON
AMSTERDAM • PARIS • SYDNEY • HAMBURG
STOCKHOLM • ATHENS • TOKYO • MILAN
MADRID • WARSAW • BUDAPEST • AUCKLAND

To Kath and Keith Wilson, our new friends across the pond. We hope you can read this. It's written in American.

ISBN 0-373-22377-3

CISCO'S WOMAN

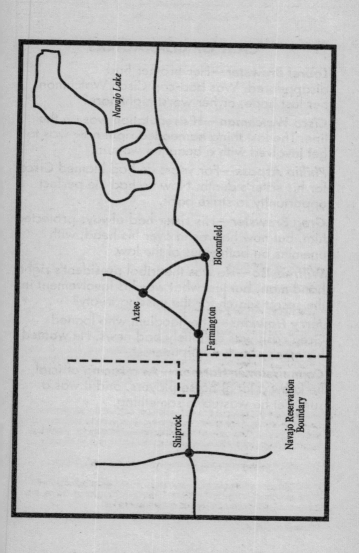

Navajo Lake

Bloomfield

Aztec

Farmington

Shiprock

Navajo Reservation
Boundary

CAST OF CHARACTERS

Laurel Brewster—Her brother had disappeared. Was bad-cop Cisco Watchman her last hope, or her worst nightmare?

Cisco Watchman—His reputation was on the line. The last thing he needed right now was to get involved with a beautiful woman.

Phillip Aspass—For years he had blamed Cisco for his sister's death. Now he had the perfect opportunity to strike back.

Greg Brewster—His sister had always protected him, but now he was in over his head, with enemies on both sides of the law.

Wilfred Tso—He was the tribal president's right-hand man, but just what was his involvement in the secret search for the missing treaty?

Jerry Hawkins—The hoodlum who loaned Greg cash was definitely bad news. He wanted his money back—with interest.

Commissioner Harmon—As a racing official, he knew a lot of horse players, and it was a sure bet he was up to something.

Dear Reader,

Cisco's Woman is a story I've wanted to tell for a long time. The heroine in this book has severe asthma, a physical ailment I've lived with all my life. This is a story that's very personal to me. I'm grateful to Harlequin Intrigue for allowing me to tell this story my own way. Without playing down the difficulties my heroine must face, I wanted to show that having a physical limitation doesn't mean a person is helpless. Victory in the face of adversity is all the more precious.

Laurel Brewster was easy for me to create. Though this book is a work of fiction, a lot of my own trials and triumphs are woven into her. My vision of Cisco Watchman evolved more slowly. A loved one's ailment can place a terrible burden on a relationship. I knew Cisco would have to be a man whose courage would allow him to face both personal and professional uncertainties with valor. Cisco came alive for me when I decided to use my husband, David, as a model. I created Laurel and Cisco's strong loving relationship from the inspiration of my own twenty-six years of marriage. I know I could never have accomplished as much as I have in life without my husband's unwavering support.

I hope this story will touch your heart and that the characters will linger in your mind for a long time to come.

All my best,

Aimée

Prologue

Detective Cisco Watchman stood in front of Police Chief Joseph Begay's desk, trying to shut out the tirade aimed at him. Chief Begay's mood seemed to match the violence of the thunderstorm raging outside.

As the short, barrel-chested chief continued pacing, his voice drowning out the deluge, Cisco's glance shifted to the rain-splattered window. It was a wet summer for the rez. The steep arroyos would soon be bursting with runoff, and the soaking of ready-to-mow alfalfa fields would start. A season of sorrow seemed destined to unfold, unless the recent barrage of thunderstorms slacked off soon.

A flash of lightning suddenly illuminated the office with its peculiar off-color brightness. The building shook as an explosion of thunder overwhelmed all other sounds. Cisco watched Chief Begay absently run his finger over the turquoise bead that hung from a leather strap attached to his gun belt. Cisco suspected the bead had been part of the Shooting Chant, and now was protection against lightning and any illnesses caused by its strikes. The old ways and the new shared common ground on the reservation, an uneasy truce having been forged between them long ago.

Behind Cisco, the chief's door remained open, just as Begay had intended. Cisco couldn't remember the squad room ever being so quiet. Even the occasional ring of a phone was quickly silenced, answered in hushed tones. The perk of the squad's coffeepot was clearly audible halfway across the enclosure, despite the falling rain outside. Everybody was on edge, waiting for the expected outcome, the ousting of a rogue cop.

Cisco felt the power behind Begay's glare as it probed and searched him for any sign of weakness. "You're a disgrace," the chief said, continuing his tirade. "Taking those bribes makes you no better than the scumbags we're here to stop."

The knowledge that so many had chosen to believe in his guilt—fellow officers who had worked with him and should have known better—still stunned him. "I *am* innocent," Cisco said steadily.

"Yeah, right. Do us both a favor, okay? Save it for the lawyers. I have no time for your excuses."

Cisco clamped his mouth shut. He'd expected the going to be tough, but until that very moment, he hadn't fully realized how much the respect of his fellow officers meant to him. He could feel the cold anger of the men in the squad room. They would all come down hard on a dirty cop. It would be particularly bad for someone like him, who'd barely associated with any of them off the job. He'd never had any close friends in the department. He'd decided long ago that it was better that way, for him and for them. But having few allies meant there was no one to stand by him now, when he needed support. Knife-edged loss was cutting up his gut as he was forced to accept being branded a traitor to the department.

The chief raised his voice again, ensuring that everyone in the communal office heard clearly. "You're beneath contempt. As of now, you're on suspension, but I expect dismissal and formal charges within a week. Turn over your badge and your service weapon. Then get the hell out of my sight."

Cisco reached for his badge and dropped it on the chief's desk. He then snapped his holster open, slipped out the nine-millimeter pistol and placed it beside the badge. Without them, he suddenly felt naked. Somewhere along the way he'd stopped being anything but a cop. He lived and breathed the life.

As Cisco turned and walked out of the chief's office, gazes quickly darted elsewhere, and the normal flurry of activity returned to the squad room. Cisco kept his shoulders squared and his back straight. As he passed by the desks on either side of the center aisle, silence spread around him in an ever-widening circle, like the spirals of a violent dust devil.

As he approached the door, Cisco's brother-in-law, Phillip Aspass, left his chair and stepped toward him. Phillip hesitated as he neared and stopped short of Cisco, careful not to block his path. Two other officers, Benjamin Kelliwood and Curtis Blackhorse, came to stand behind Phillip, lending their support wordlessly.

"First you bring tragedy and sorrow to my family," Aspass said, his voice low but tainted with bitterness. "Now you dishonor our department. It's too bad this didn't happen two years ago. Had my sister seen you for what you truly are, she would have thrown you out of her home. Then maybe she would still be alive today."

Memories crowded Cisco's mind, and pain from a wound that would never heal penetrated his heart. He took a step toward his brother-in-law, who held his ground, assuming a defensive stance.

"What happened to my wife was an accident," Cisco growled. "You know that." He stared at the man for a moment, then glanced coldly at the two behind him. Pushing back the anger that clouded his thinking, he broke eye contact.

This was pointless. Phillip would have to come to terms with the past himself. The others who backed him were eager for a fight. He wouldn't give them the satisfaction. It was time to go, because he had a job to do.

Wordlessly Cisco turned and opened the door. The truth about the bribes would come out in a few weeks—he'd see to that much himself—and these officers would have to eat their words. Yet the hard reality was that little would change for him even then. He would remain alone, a dark shadow trapped behind impenetrable walls of ice.

Chapter One

Laurel Brewster waited for the traffic light to turn green. The warm breeze, carrying the scent of a neighborhood rose garden, wafted through the open window and ruffled her reddish brown shoulder-length hair. It was turning out to be a beautiful summer day, despite the earlier downpour. Mrs. Allen, her neighbor, was outside working in her flower bed, pulling weeds where the earth was soft. Farther down the street, Emily Gonzales was hanging up laundry, taking advantage of the sun. Everything looked comfortingly familiar and commonplace, as if nothing could ever be wrong in the safety of the small city of Farmington, New Mexico.

Yet something *was* terribly wrong. She couldn't shake the anxiety that nagged at her. It enveloped her like the stench of meat rotting in the desert heat. Something was going to happen, and soon.

Laurel shook her head, trying to banish her premonitions of gloom. She wouldn't give in to these strange feelings. Her brother, Greg, had gone away for a few days—that was all. He wasn't her little brother anymore. Greg was twenty-four years old and perfectly capable of taking care of himself.

Laurel sighed. Who was she kidding? Even when they were both old and gray, Greg would still be her baby brother. Some habits were just too hard to break, and looking out for him was one of them.

This time, for whatever the reason, her brother had skipped town. Even judging on facts alone, there simply was no other explanation that made sense. No one seemed to know where he was, not even his boss. She'd received a very irate call earlier from the head of the security firm that employed him. If Greg didn't show up for work by tomorrow, he'd be fired. She'd been worrying about him ever since. He had never been *that* irresponsible.

Laurel parked in the small driveway of her two-bedroom cottage. Preoccupied, she unlocked the front door and went directly to her office. Maybe Greg had called and left a message. As she entered the room, her eyes went to the answering machine. The red 0 glowed back at her.

Suddenly she heard someone move behind her. Thinking her brother had returned and come over, Laurel smiled as she turned her head. Before she could complete the motion, her arm was quickly twisted behind her back, and she was shoved forward.

She staggered and fell, bumping her head against the side of her desk. Reeling from the pain of the blow and aware she'd surprised a burglar, she struggled to her feet. The intruder had already run from the room. As she reached the office entrance, she heard the back door slam.

Laurel fell back against the wall, using it for support as she tried to catch her breath. Asthma again. Angry at the chronic condition that seemed to surface at the worst possible times, she went to her desk drawer and retrieved the spare inhaler she kept inside.

She gave herself a quick puff, then dropped down unceremoniously onto her chair, glancing around. Nothing seemed to be missing from her office. A second, more thorough examination, however, pointed out the mistakes of her initial estimate. The memo pad she always kept next to the answering machine was gone, and her caller-ID device was missing, too.

Her breathing restored, Laurel reached for the desk phone to call the police, but stopped before her hand touched the receiver. She'd use the cellular in her car instead and avoid tampering with anything here and disturbing evidence.

Laurel walked out to her car and reported the break-in, letting the dispatcher know that the would-be burglar had already made his escape. Assuring the woman that she didn't need medical attention, Laurel remained in her car, waiting for an officer to arrive.

The minutes seemed to drag by. Finally she saw the police cruiser coming down the street. To Laurel, it felt as if several lifetimes had passed. Patience had never been one of her virtues.

Leaving her car, she met the officer as he stepped out of his vehicle. He was a middle-aged man with kind eyes and a slightly protruding belly. She smiled, relieved. If her guess was correct, he wouldn't be as apt as a younger cop to ask why she hadn't followed the man outside to try to get a better look at him. Laurel disliked explaining her asthma to a stranger. But from the looks of this officer, she concluded that a foot pursuit wouldn't have been his choice, either.

"I'm glad you're here," she said, and gave him a quick rundown of her experience.

"Did you get a look at the intruder?" the officer finally asked after she'd finished telling him all she remembered.

"No, I'm afraid not. Everything happened in the blink of an eye."

The officer placed his hand on the butt of his pistol. "Stay out here. I'm going inside to take a look around. It's just a precaution at this stage, but I'd like to make sure it's safe before you go back in."

Laurel watched him cautiously enter the house and then disappear from her view. The minutes seemed to stretch out endlessly as she waited.

Finally he came back out. "You can come inside now. I'd like you to take a good look around and make a list of everything that was taken."

Laurel walked in with him and, for the first time, methodically studied the living area. Nothing was missing here. The living room was as cluttered as ever. She wasn't a slob, not really, but she had long adopted the pile method of filing, and at times her entire house looked like the aftermath of a paper-mill explosion.

Laurel walked past her couch, currently half-covered with three stacks of folders, maneuvered around the computer packing case set against the wall and stepped into her bedroom. More files and sketches lay on the carpeted floor next to the bed. Two drawers were half-open, attesting to her quick change of clothing before going to visit Kyle, her brother's roommate. A can filled with pencils had tipped over onto the floor.

"Looks like someone searched this room."

She smiled wanly. "No. This is normal, I'm afraid."

The officer gave her an owlish blink that spoke volumes. "Can you tell if there's anything missing here?"

Laurel took her time, searching for the few things of value she had, like her cameo pendant. It was her only reminder of her mother, who'd passed away when Greg and she had been just kids. It was in her top drawer, next to some earrings and a turquoise-and-silver chain. "Everything's here."

Finally Laurel returned to her study and searched the room again. "The only things he took are my caller-ID unit and a message pad I keep by the phone machine."

"How much is the phone unit worth?"

"About sixty bucks." She shook her head, puzzled. "This is really weird. My laptop computer would have been about as easy to carry, and it's worth more than two thousand dollars. It's almost brand-new."

He studied the room. "All your computer equipment looks expensive."

"I'm a graphic designer—I use it for my work. I have clients all over the United States," Laurel added proudly.

"Stuff like this is easy to fence nowadays, so there's only one explanation that makes sense. You must have surprised the thief before he got a chance to load anything up. He must have panicked."

"Will you be able to catch him, you think?"

"We've got another patrol car searching the vicinity for anyone suspicious, but I wouldn't hold my breath. A sixty-dollar loss isn't going to get high priority, and we're backlogged as it is." The officer walked to the desk corner, where the phone and answering machine sat. "I can try and lift some prints and run a check. If any match a known felon, we can follow them up. But like I said, don't have high expectations."

After getting the officer's okay, Laurel turned on her equipment and made sure her computer programs hadn't been sabotaged. A few minutes later, she felt some of the tension wash out of her body. Everything seemed in order there.

The officer, having retrieved some equipment from his vehicle, stood by the windowsill, studying the wood frame closely. "Do you always keep this open?"

"Yes. My evaporative cooler does a lousy job unless I vent out the hot air in the house, and since the humidity's been up, it needs all the help it can get. Until now, crime's never been a problem in this neighborhood."

The policeman shook his head. "I know these coolers are effective in the Southwest, but I've never liked them. I prefer refrigerated air, like we had in the Midwest where I grew up." He studied the sill, then began to work the area with his fingerprint kit, searching for possible prints. "I recommend that from now on, you only leave the window unlocked and open when you're home."

"Count on it."

The officer took Laurel's prints for comparison purposes, then packed up his equipment. Lost in thought, she stared at the spot on her desk where the caller ID had been. Something niggled at the back of her mind, but try as she might, she couldn't define it.

"I'm through here," the officer said, giving her his card. "If you notice anything else is missing, or if you see anyone or anything suspicious, call us immediately."

Laurel walked him to the door. "Thanks for coming."

A few minutes later, she was back in her office when she heard a knock. Thinking that the officer had returned, she hurried to answer it.

When Laurel opened the door, a tall, handsome Navajo man was standing there. He towered above her five-foot frame and was as far from the overweight police officer who'd just left as a bulldog was from a mountain lion.

"I'm Detective Cisco Watchman, from the tribal police," he said, his voice low and sexy. He reached into his dark brown windbreaker, held up a gold badge in a leather wallet, then quickly stowed it back in his pocket.

Laurel barely had a chance to glance at the ID, but it didn't matter. It was difficult to tear her gaze away from the obsidian pools focused on her. There was a coolness there that chilled her to the marrow of her bones.

Vaguely aware that she'd been staring at him, Laurel cleared her throat. "What can I do for you, Detective? Surely the tribal police isn't investigating my break-in. Farmington isn't on the reservation."

"No, ma'am. I'm here to ask you a few questions about your brother. I haven't been able to locate him."

Her heart began hammering at her throat. Why was a man who appeared to be as hard as tempered steel searching for her brother? A Navajo tribal-police detective, no less! "What do you want with Greg?"

"I need to speak with him on a police matter."

There was something too intense about this man's gaze. It unsettled her, making it hard to think clearly. Laurel glanced down and found herself staring at the open collar of his light blue shirt. The coppery skin it revealed was smooth, all except for a pale slash that extended down beneath the fold of his shirt. The scar looked as if it might have been made by a knife.

"May I come in?"

She hesitated, then nodded and stepped aside. "I just had a break-in. I'm still trying to get my bearings. If I seem to be a little slow on the uptake, that's why." A plausible reason, though not really the truth. The fact was, Detective Cisco Watchman had a presence few men possessed, and something more, an intangible quality that was mesmerizing and vibrantly male.

The man walked across the room with a grace she hadn't expected. His movements were fluid and purposeful, as if he was unaccustomed to wasting energy on useless motion.

He stopped beside the couch, searching for a place to sit. Moving over next to him, Laurel picked up the stack of files that occupied one of the cushions, set them on the floor, then gestured for him to have a seat. "What business do you have with my brother, Detective? You never said." She cleared the chair opposite him and sat down.

"You're right, I didn't. Do you know where he might be?" He smiled at her.

If he'd packed a sensual wallop before, it had just tripled. The smile changed his face, gentled it somewhat, though its warmth never really reached his eyes. Questions remained in her mind, but her heart was dancing.

Laurel disciplined her thoughts quickly. She had probably just been spending too much time in front of the computer. She'd been too busy to date for months. She glanced back at him. No, it wasn't overwork; this man simply exuded a blast of sensuality that was staggering.

Although she was sure he must have been aware of his appeal, he certainly didn't act cocky. Of course, that probably meant he'd grown used to his effect on women. The thought sobered her. She certainly wasn't about to be charmed by a sexy smile, particularly when it came to giving out information about Greg.

"You want my help," she commented, making sure to keep her tone matter-of-fact. "But I see no reason to give it when you won't even answer a simple question for me."

"My business with your brother is between him and me. Surely his whereabouts aren't a secret you need to guard. Or are they?"

Laurel forced herself to give the detective a calm smile. "The bottom line hasn't changed. You're still hoping to get an answer from me, but you refuse to grant me the same courtesy. I think it's time to rethink your strategy."

Cisco Watchman leaned back against the cushions of the couch and regarded her for what seemed to be an eternity. She'd done business with tribal members before, and knew that to interrupt him now would be a mistake. It would be seen as rude, if nothing else.

Laurel sensed he was testing her, but she couldn't figure out if he was trying to gauge her knowledge of Indian customs or her respect for them. Or maybe he was just hoping she'd grow uncomfortable with the silence and start talking. Several minutes went by. When he finally spoke again, he'd relaxed visibly, and she knew he'd made up his mind about her, though she had no idea what he'd concluded.

"Your brother is a guard for Huntley Security. His last assignment was guarding a tribal document that's on display at the Farmington convention center."

Laurel felt her skin prickle with unease, although the detective hadn't told her anything she didn't know. "Has something happened to that document?"

He paused as if measuring his reply. "Everything seems normal, but I need to ask your brother some questions."

"You mean about the security arrangements?"

"That, and other things, as well. *Now* will you tell me where he is?"

Cisco had tried to meet her halfway, though she sensed that trust in any degree came with great difficulty for him. Suddenly she felt terribly guilty about the fact that she had no information to exchange for what he'd shared with her. She took a breath and gave him the honest answer he'd earned. "The truth is, I don't know. I've been trying to find him myself."

"You never had any intention of honoring your part of our bargain, then," the detective observed flatly. Something dark and dangerous flickered in his eyes.

"I *can* help you. As soon as I hear from him, and I *will*, I'll let him know you need to talk to him." It was the best offer she could make. Laurel now wished she hadn't stooped to playing cat-and-mouse games with this proud man. Although her motives had been good, she didn't like the way it was making her feel right now.

"When's the last time you heard from him?" he probed immediately, as if sensing her regret.

"Four days ago, Detective."

"How often do you usually speak?"

"Almost every day. We're close."

Laurel noticed the subtle change in his expression, like ripples marring the glassy surface of a still pond. She suddenly had the feeling he'd done more than routine checking into their past. Yet a bare-bones dossier filled with background information would never explain the loyalty that had grown over the years between Greg and her, turning them into a real family.

"How do you explain his absence? Is this something he's done before, or has he been acting differently lately?"

The question was simple enough, but the answer was tricky. If she told him the truth, that Greg had definitely been acting strangely, there was no telling how he'd interpret it. Having a police officer searching for her brother in order to question him didn't sound good.

Cisco's eyes remained on her, his expression guarded. Although he seemed totally relaxed, she could sense the tension in him. He was a man with a purpose.

"I'm not sure how much to tell you," Laurel answered truthfully. "I get the feeling you're searching for some kind of scapegoat, and I won't let you do that to my brother." It had been a shot in the dark, nothing more. A test for him. His surprised reaction told her she'd hit the mark.

"Have I said something to lead you to believe that?"

"Call it woman's intuition."

"As I said, all I want is to ask him a few questions. What happens after that depends on his answers."

"Then when I hear from my brother, I'll let you know." Laurel went to the door and opened it. Stepping back without looking, she abruptly collided with Cisco.

Desire, strong and intoxicating, sizzled through her as she felt his hard body against hers. He grasped her forearms, steadying her, but didn't move back. His grip was strong, but there was a marked gentleness in it, as if he were acutely aware of his strength and cared enough to temper it for her.

Trying to ignore the way his touch set her heart drumming, Laurel forced herself to move away. "I'll be in touch."

"I *will* find your brother," Cisco said softly. "But he'd find it easier if he came forward on his own."

Though his voice had remained smooth and soft, there was an iron-willed resolve about it that frightened her. It was then that she saw clearly what a threat he was to Greg. That made him her enemy, as well.

"If you have something specific to charge him with, then say so," Laurel snapped. She waited, but he remained silent. "I thought not. Then goodbye, Detective Watchman."

He held her gaze a moment longer, as if he were trying to look into her soul. "You're very protective of your brother. But he's a grown man. Are you so sure that he needs or wants your shelter?"

The question, so smoothly spoken, cut her deeply. She'd asked herself the same question many times. But it was hard to let go. She'd taken care of Greg all her life. Worry for her brother, combined with anger toward Cisco Watchman, made her hands shake. She tried to take a deep breath, but her lungs felt constricted.

"Please leave now," Laurel managed to say. Her voice sounded a little winded to her, but with luck it wouldn't be noticeable to anyone else. She wouldn't permit herself to have an asthma attack, not now, in front of this rude stranger.

Cisco turned away and walked casually down the sidewalk.

Laurel slammed the door and hoped the sound would make him jump. But she hadn't banged it out of anger. It was her way of ensuring it would actually latch while she went to search for her inhaler.

A moment later, she found her purse. Her inhaler was at the very bottom, next to the breath mints. Damn. One had become lodged in the mouthpiece. She pried it loose, then quickly used the spray.

It would take a minute or two for her breathing to return to normal. Laurel waited, her thoughts racing. She didn't trust Detective Cisco Watchman. More to the point, she didn't like him. Well, maybe she did like him, but it was in all the wrong ways. In fact, considering the circumstances, that attraction was totally inappropriate, and she had no intention of letting a few stray erotic thoughts get out of hand. She could handle herself, and Cisco Watchman, too. From what he'd said, there was no doubt in her mind that the stakes were much higher than he'd intimated.

CISCO WENT TO HIS PICKUP, started the engine and backed up about a hundred feet along the curb until he was under the shade of a large cottonwood. This was the perfect spot for a stakeout. He could see his subject's home clearly but still remain out of view from her windows.

The Anglo woman puzzled him. His gut instincts about people were usually right, and at the moment, they told him that Laurel Brewster would be nothing but trouble, personally and professionally. She'd read him better than anyone had been able to in a long time. Suspecting that the snow-job meter of a cop was highly attuned, she'd gauged her answers carefully. She hadn't lied, but she was holding back something important.

Cisco leaned back, ready to wait her out. In the background report he'd read on Greg Brewster, his sister, Laurel, had been listed as the person closest to him. He had no doubt that the man would contact her sooner or later. All he had to do was wait. Either Greg Brewster would come to her, or she'd go to him. And when it happened, he'd be right there to make his move.

Chapter Two

It was midafternoon. Laurel stared at a photo of Greg and her taken last Christmas. Her brother was in serious trouble; she had no doubt about it now. Although she had no idea where to even begin her search, she had to find him . . . before Cisco Watchman did.

As always, she'd do her best to protect Greg. That responsibility had fallen to her many years ago, right after their mother's death. Their father, unable to cope with his grief, had withdrawn from both of them at the time they'd needed him most. Laurel had only been twelve, but she'd been the one eight-year-old Greg had turned to. She'd realized that unless she took care of her brother and herself, no one else would do it for them. The closeness that desperate need had fostered between them had blossomed over the years into the fierce loyalty that existed now.

A disturbing uneasiness wound through her as she recalled how Cisco had left under protest. That type of man didn't give up easily. Laurel walked to a window and glanced up and down the street. There was no one in sight. Still unsure, she opened the door a crack and glanced out.

A beat-up cream-colored pickup was parked back up the street, almost out of view. She could make out Cisco Watchman's face well enough to positively identify the man behind the wheel. Scowling, she closed the door.

First and foremost, she had to get rid of him. If Greg decided to come here, Cisco was the last person she wanted him to encounter. She had to find a way to get the detective to leave. But how?

Laurel considered everything she'd learned from his questioning. He was investigating something to do with the treaty on display at the convention center. That ostensibly explained the tribe's involvement outside their jurisdiction. A thought slowly dawned on her. Unless the tribal police were almost bankrupt, Cisco was certainly not driving an unmarked, police-issue vehicle. That old pickup looked ready only for a decent burial.

Laurel picked up the phone, got the number for tribal-police headquarters from the operator and dialed. Using her best no-nonsense tone, she demanded to speak to someone in authority. After several seconds, she was given the desk sergeant on duty.

"I'd like to file a complaint about one of your officers. He's harassing me, and I want it stopped. I live in Farmington, outside the reservation, and at the very least he has no official jurisdiction here."

"What's the name of the officer?"

"He introduced himself as Detective Watchman."

There was a long wait, and Laurel wondered if they'd been disconnected. Finally the sergeant spoke, "I'm going to connect you with the tribal attorney in Window Rock."

"Can you tell me—?" Before she could get the rest of the question out, the officer had placed her on hold again.

Laurel drummed her fingers impatiently on the arm of the couch. Finally another voice answered.

"This is Wilfred Tso. I represent the Navajo Nation. What is your name, please?"

"I'm Laurel Brewster. Detective Watchman arrived at my home this morning, asking me about my brother. I answered his questions, but now he's parked in front of my house, and I don't think he plans to leave. This is harassment, and I want it stopped right now."

"Yes, I'm sure you do. *Have* you seen your brother recently, Ms. Brewster?" Tso asked in an officious tone.

Laurel shook her head in disbelief at the abrupt way he'd switched the subject. "That's *not* why I'm calling."

"Yes, but we do need information about your brother. Where would we be likely to find him when he's not at home or work?"

"You're totally missing the point of my call."

Ignoring Laurel's protest, Tso continued pressing her for information about Greg. "Where does he go on vacations, or when he wants to get away from it all?" he persisted.

She felt her skin prickle. Why wasn't anyone willing to tell her why they were looking for Greg? It had to be connected to the treaty somehow, but Cisco had claimed it hadn't been stolen. Of course, maybe he'd been lying.

Realizing she was getting nowhere with the tribal attorney, Laurel hung up.

A quick call to the convention center verified that the Navajo treaty was still there on display, so that ruled out a theft investigation. Lost in thought, she toyed nervously with an earring.

His employer and the Navajo police were obviously extremely interested in finding Greg, so maybe someone else was, too. That could explain why the man had broken into her home and taken her caller ID. The origin of each incoming call would be stored in its battery-powered memory. Maybe the crooks had decided to check all the numbers stored in the device, hoping to find out where Greg was staying.

Good thought, except Greg hadn't called. Her answering machine had registered no new incoming messages, either. For the first time, she was glad Greg hadn't contacted her.

The trouble Greg was in, however, was spilling over into her own life. She had to locate her brother and learn what was going on. She'd start by checking the Cowboy Club out on East Main tonight. She knew he hung out there from time to time after ending a midnight shift. Good-ole-boy bars filled with smoke were difficult for her to visit, but in this case she had no choice.

Laurel spent the afternoon clearing her desk of work projects that were scheduled for completion. She wanted nothing to interfere once she began her search for Greg.

Around dinnertime, Laurel picked up the phone again. She wanted to get started, but before she could do anything else, she had to get rid of Cisco.

"Farmington Police Department," the voice said.

"I'd like to report someone watching my house. I think it could be a burglar waiting for me to leave."

LAUREL CHANGED her clothes. Her best chance of avoiding unwanted attention at the Cowboy Club was to wear a pair of loose-fitting slacks and an oversize shirt. The outfit, though comfortable, hid her body's contours very effectively. She was looking for her brother, not hunting "cowboys."

By the time Laurel stepped back into the living room, she saw a patrol car cruising down the street. Laurel opened the front door and peered out. Cisco's pickup had disappeared. Maybe he'd become bored, or perhaps he'd seen the patrol unit and decided it was time to make himself scarce. Either way, she noted with satisfaction that there was no sign of him or his car.

A moment later, a Farmington police officer came to her door. Laurel greeted the officer and came clean about Detective Watchman's visit. "I see no reason why a member of the tribal police has to watch my home, do you? Isn't this out of their jurisdiction?"

The question elicited the right response. She'd always heard that police departments zealously guarded their own turfs.

"I guarantee we'll find out what that's all about," the officer said flatly.

As the patrolman left, Laurel glanced at her watch. Almost six o'clock. Time to take one of her asthma pills to make sure she'd be able to deal with the smoke in the bar.

Laurel went to the kitchen. The pills weren't meant to be taken on an empty stomach. As she made herself a quick sandwich, she switched on the small television set she kept on the breakfast bar. With any luck, the local news would carry a story about the display at the convention center. She had a feeling it would be to her advantage to learn more about the treaty.

As she took her last bite and was reaching to turn off the set, Laurel saw Cisco's photo appear on the screen. The reporter revealed that the Navajo police had suspended Detective Watchman, pending an investigation. Cisco Watchman was reputed to have ties with an unnamed racing official from Farmington, and was suspected of having taken bribes to conceal evidence on several occasions.

The news took her completely by surprise. If he was suspended and under investigation, Cisco should have been trying to keep a low profile. Why had he come after Greg, when he was up to his neck in his own troubles? Either way, at least he was out of her life now.

Laurel picked up her purse and walked out to the car. The drive to the East Main bar took twenty minutes. Though it was not even 7:00 p.m. by the time she arrived, the parking lot was already jammed.

She parked at the north end, beneath a streetlight. It was a bit farther from the door than she would have liked, but it would be better after it got dark. As she stepped out of the car, she moved the inhaler from her purse to her hand. Better to have the puffer handy in case she had problems once she stepped inside.

Laurel was crossing the parking area when she noticed two men in baseball caps standing by the front steps, watching her. The tall, burly one—wearing a black T-shirt that seemed two sizes too small for him—gave her the creeps. His underweight companion was watching her just as intently, but somehow lacked the menace the first man projected.

She forced herself to glance in their direction, letting them know she was aware of them, but didn't make eye contact. Just a few more steps, and she'd be inside.

"Wait a second, momma. Aren't you Laurel?" the burly one asked, pointing a stubby finger at her.

Surprised that the man knew her name, she stopped. "Do we know each other?"

"I met you at your brother's place one evening. Don't you remember? You were leaving as we arrived in my friend's 4x4."

She bit back the obvious *Thank God* that popped into her mind.

"I remember." Out of the corner of her eye, Laurel saw the second man approaching. He didn't look intimidating, but there was a lack of emotion on his face that reminded her of a rattlesnake eyeing its prey.

"We're looking for him. He owes me and Lachuk here some money."

The thinner man, Lachuk, began circling behind her, and a warning bell went off in her head. "I have no idea where Greg is."

Laurel tried to walk past the burly man in front of her, but he deliberately moved to block her path.

"Then it looks like we're going to have to negotiate with you instead."

"I have about twenty bucks on me. You're welcome to it."

Something about the way he laughed at her offer made her skin crawl. Laurel took a step back, but her escape route was now blocked by Lachuk, who grabbed her arm.

Instead of trying to pull away, Laurel attacked. She elbowed him hard in the stomach, then kicked the man ahead of her in the shin. She darted past him, but before she was out of reach, he grabbed her wrist and pulled her back.

As Laurel slammed against the wall of his chest, she twisted and sprayed him directly in the face with her inhaler.

The man yelled and reached for his face, letting her go. She ran toward the bar again, but the one called Lachuk caught up before she could reach the door. He grabbed her hair, yanking her head back painfully.

Though his grip had been sure, Lachuk suddenly released her with a gasp. Laurel broke free and saw Cisco Watchman slam his fist into the man's jaw. The burly man in the T-shirt attacked then, but Cisco spun, kicking out hard, and sent him sprawling to the pavement with a blow to the chest.

Laurel started to thank Cisco, when she saw the dangerous flicker still shining clearly in his eyes. She suddenly realized he'd enjoyed the challenge.

"Where's your car?" he asked.

Laurel pointed. "Why—?"

He grabbed her hand and quickly propelled her to it. "Your keys."

It wasn't a question. "I'm not giving you my keys!" she protested.

He glanced back. "They're getting up. We're almost out of time. I *know* I can lose them in a foot race. Are you certain you can, too?"

She reached into her purse and tossed him the keys. "You drive."

Laurel checked her seat belt as they sped out of the parking lot. She glanced back and noticed the men scrambling into a big black pickup with a blue sign on the door.

"Hurry," she urged Cisco, then found herself regretting it a minute later when her little sedan rose to a speed it had never reached before. She forced herself to turn and look back. "They're not following us. Slow down and pull over."

"They aren't the type to admit defeat that easily. This road has several stoplights farther down. It wouldn't be hard to catch up to us."

She remembered the way Cisco had taken care of the pair back at the bar, though he'd been outnumbered. He was twice as dangerous as the other two.

"I want to thank you for stepping in to help me. I was certainly surprised to see you. How did you happen to be in the area?"

"I followed you."

"You *what?*"

Cisco repeated himself calmly.

"Okay, that's enough of this game. I demand to know what's going on. I already know you've been suspended, I saw it on television. What's your real interest in my brother? And why are you following *me?* What exactly do you hope to learn? This is harassment, pure and simple."

"You didn't think so five minutes ago," Cisco said, his voice rich with masculine sensuality.

Laurel tried to swallow, but her mouth had gone dry. "Look, I appreciate what you did, but unless you tell me what you're up to, I'm going to report you to the police. You showed me a badge, but if you've been suspended, I have a feeling you're not supposed to carry it."

"Oh, anyone can carry the one I showed you. I bought it at a toy store." He smiled at her. "And why bother the Farmington PD again? You tried that already. Lucky for you, it didn't work."

His confidence was unshakable, and she found it unexpectedly annoying. "They have your description and they'll be looking for you."

"It won't do them any good. They don't have the manpower to search every street, and I know all their procedures. All I did last time was park in an empty driveway with a hedge and duck down until they passed by. Then I went back to your neighborhood. I knew you were about to make your move. And of course I was right."

She saw him check the rearview mirror carefully. He'd been watching since they'd left the bar. Cisco obviously hadn't discarded the possibility that the two goons who'd attacked her would try to lay a trap for them. "What's going on? If I'm going to have to watch myself against guys like those two back there, I *need* to know."

"I know that your brother has quite a few debts. When those two accosted you, they mentioned that your brother owed them money. That's probably true."

Laurel felt her heart sink. "I know Greg has every credit card on the planet stretched to the limit, and he's making a big car payment. He's always strapped for money. But I still don't understand *your* involvement in this. You're on suspension. You shouldn't be doing any police work at all right now."

It seemed at least five minutes before he replied, and Cisco's comment was preceded by what sounded like a curse in Navajo. "You do deserve an answer, but what I'm going to tell you is not to be repeated. Agreed?"

She nodded, knowing that she needed to encourage his trust all she could. Cisco Watchman was her only source at the moment.

"This morning in Window Rock, before I was suspended, I overheard our top legal adviser talking to the tribal president. They were speaking freely, unaware that I was right outside the window taking a break. The tribal attorney told the president that he'd discovered the treaty on display at the convention center is not the original our tribe loaned your city. He claimed the document there is a forgery. I know that treaty well, so I decided to check it out myself. The attorney was right. What's there on display is *not* the real treaty. Your brother was assigned to protect the document, and as far as I can tell, he's the only person who had close access to it. But he's disappeared, along with the real treaty, and I need to find him."

"But you're on suspension, remember? It isn't your job anymore."

"You're wrong. Protecting that treaty is a task that has fallen to my family for years. It has nothing to do with my being a cop."

"I can assure you my brother wouldn't steal anything from anyone. I practically raised him myself after our mother died. I know him."

"I'm not saying that he stole it. But his disappearance tends to indicate that he knows something about what's going on. I have to find out what that is. I staked you out because I figure that eventually you'll lead me to him."

Considering how quickly he'd dispatched the two men at the bar, there was one thing she was certain about. She didn't want a man like Cisco finding her brother without someone else being around to protect Greg. He was no match for Cisco Watchman.

"We have to work together," Laurel said firmly. "With men like the two at the bar after Greg, I can't afford to search for him alone. You, on the other hand, won't know where to look for him unless I help you."

"Sorry. I don't work with civilians."

"You said this had nothing to do with being a cop, and technically, since you're on suspension, you're a civilian, too. Are you going to refuse to work with yourself, as well?"

The glacial look he gave her could have frozen the San Juan River. She forced herself not to react at all, pretending great interest in the passing scenery.

As the silence stretched out, Laurel cast a furtive glance at Cisco. He was grasping the steering wheel so tightly that his knuckles were white.

"Think about this," he said in slow, measured tones. "Do you really want to get more involved than you are? The danger is there, you've already seen that. I can't guarantee I'll be there to protect you next time.''

"I'll take my chances." Laurel smiled, sensing his discomfiture. She was certain that very few people ever challenged Cisco. She was surprised to find she was enjoying her confrontations with him very much.

Another long silence followed. Laurel sat very still, waiting. She couldn't explain it, but despite his warning, she was certain that as long as he was around, no physical harm would ever come to her. The fact was, he *had* come to her rescue back at the bar, though he could have chosen to sit back and let her handle her own mess. Whatever trouble he was in with his department was his own problem. At the moment, she needed every advantage she could get to find Greg.

"How far are you prepared to take your duties as my partner?"

"I beg your pardon?" Laurel stared at him, taken aback by the question.

"You're pardoned, but I still need to know how you're defining our partnership. There's no telling how many days we'll have to spend together, *partner,* before we find your brother. Days and *nights,*" Cisco added, his voice husky.

Laurel could feel her body tingling in the most disturbing places. His sizzling virility surrounded her, tantalizing and tempting her. She took a slow breath, wanting to make sure her voice came out steady. "Our partnership will be very *professional* and extend only to the search for my brother. After we locate Greg, you'll go your merry way, and I'll go mine." Though it was certainly a pity, that was the way it would have to be.

"Fine by me."

As she shifted in her seat, Laurel saw Cisco studying her. She pretended not to notice the discreet yet incredibly thorough look that took in every inch of her body. A curl of warmth ribboned through her in response.

"Where to, first?" Cisco asked at last. "You're the expert on your brother."

She considered the question carefully. "When Greg's disturbed about something, and the sky's clear like tonight, he usually goes up to Farmington Reservoir. There's a high spot on the north side that overlooks the water. He loves to sit there and unwind."

Laurel gave careful directions to Cisco, then sat back in her seat, brushing away her own doubts. She'd opted for the best course of action. Though their partnership was far from ideal, it was necessary. This was no time for second thoughts.

Twenty-five minutes later, they began their slow walk around the lake. Except for the thrum of bullfrogs and the gentle lapping of water on the shore, the place seemed deserted.

As darkness slowly enveloped them, Laurel gave the man beside her a sidelong glance. Even here, amid the peaceful symphony of nature, he remained vigilant. At random intervals, he'd stop abruptly and listen, though the only sounds other than the lapping water she could hear were the wind rustling through the low junipers and the occasional cry of a bird swooping low over the water searching for insects.

"He would have been sitting here by this rock if he was around." Her shoulders slumped slightly as she indicated the empty spot. "Oh, well. I didn't expect it to be easy."

"Don't be discouraged. This is only the beginning of our search." His gaze took in the entire skyline, now a deep Prussian blue. "I can see why your brother likes coming here," he said softly.

He crouched by the shoreline, dipping his fingers into the water. "Have you ever noticed how during the summer, a fine pollen collects on the surface of pools and lakes like this one? Navajos call it water pollen, as if it were produced by the water itself." He allowed the pollen-laden water to trickle into his palm. "Some would say this is a good sign to mark the beginning of our search. Pollen symbolizes the water's light, its power of motion, its life."

"What does the pollen found in other places say to the Navajo people?" Laurel was intrigued by the glimpse he'd given her into his world.

"Pollen is the emblem of all things good, of peace, happiness and prosperity. It's supposed to bring these things to those who believe."

"What do you believe in?" She glanced at Cisco, entranced by the way his eyes gleamed like the lake before them. As his gaze met hers, she felt a shiver of excitement.

"I believe in myself. I'm a cop. At least, I used to be," Cisco said with conviction.

Laurel's pulse raced. There was something unique and disturbing about Cisco. It was as if he experienced life on a totally different plane. He was a man accustomed to living on the edge. Yet despite that, or maybe because of it, he'd taught himself not to let any part of nature's beauty escape him. Right now, he seemed to drink in the serenity around them like a man long accustomed to thirst, using it to refresh and renew his spirit.

Despite that sensitivity, however, there was an aloofness about him that puzzled Laurel. It made her wonder if any living being could ever truly move him as deeply as the land.

"What's the matter, partner? Having second thoughts about our association?"

He touched her face lightly with the tip of his finger, and the contact made her tingle all over. Laurel mentally shook free of the sensation and focused on his question. "I don't regret it, no, but I would like to get to know a little more about you," she said as they headed back to the car.

"Like what?"

"Well, for starters, I know you said you're bound by duty to search for the treaty. But don't you think you should be out clearing your name, too?"

"That will come, in its time. All the charges against me are false."

He said it so confidently, Laurel was almost ready to believe him. But he'd misled her once before about the treaty. Perhaps he was simply accustomed to twisting facts around to suit himself. That made him unreliable at best. The problem was she needed him in order to find Greg. She'd made a bargain with the devil; she didn't doubt that for a moment.

A half hour later, they reached the car. "Where to now?" he asked.

Laurel shifted, facing him more squarely to study his reaction. "Once we find Greg, what will you do? What if he doesn't have the answers you need?"

"I'll continue my search elsewhere," Cisco answered flatly. "Now I have a question for you. Are you prepared to deal with whatever *you* learn?"

"I *know* what I'll learn."

"That certainly answers my question."

She focused back on his question about Greg's possible whereabouts and considered the matter. "There's a cabin up by Navajo Lake, among the pines, about one hour from here. It belongs to Greg's former girlfriend. He may have gone there. Irene hardly ever uses it, except on weekends, so she let Greg keep the keys. Just head east. I'll let you know where to go once we cross the dam."

"No problem."

His tone was so matter-of-fact it frightened her. "Now you're holding back, I feel it. What else do you know that I don't?"

"Volumes, on a variety of subjects."

"You're evading."

"That's one of the things I do best. For the most part, it's a survival instinct." He glanced into the rearview mirror. "And you better hope I'm very, very good at it."

"Why?"

"We're being followed."

There's one of the things I do best. For the most part, I'm a survival method. He glanced past the rearview mirror. Wish you and the brothel were very very good at it."

"Why?"

Wire being followed.

Chapter Three

Laurel turned around and saw the sedan directly behind them slow and turn down a dirt road. "It's not that black pickup. And besides, they've turned. So much for paranoia."

"The other sedan. We've picked up a new tail. He's directly behind us now."

"Who is he?" She turned around, but the driver stayed far enough away to avoid being identified.

"I don't know, but he's following us and I intend to make sure all I lead him on is a wild-goose chase." Cisco let off the accelerator and cut sharply to the right. They slid sideways onto a gravel road.

Laurel grasped the seat to keep from bouncing into Cisco. "What are you doing? You should have stayed on the highway where there were more people."

"We can't afford to have a tail now." An instant later, he cut to the left down a dirt road carved between two open fields. Halfway down, he spun the car sideways again and headed across open country.

The last jolt sent her upward, slamming her head against the roof. "Are you nuts? What's this car look like to you? A tank?"

"Next field, we'll cut across the other way and head back to the highway. The heavy sedan following us won't stand up to this terrain. It will bog down in the soft dirt and either get stuck or rip out the oil pan. Your car won't have a problem. The shock absorbers are real stiff, giving us more clearance. This is the only way I can make certain we won't lead anyone to your brother."

The thought sobered her. At least the ground was mushy because of the recent rains. Otherwise, the inevitable cloud of dust triggered by their passage would have led her straight into another asthma attack. Experiencing the equivalent of a 9.9 on the Richter scale of asthma now might have unsettled Cisco to the point of dissolving their uneasy partnership. Asthma could be overwhelming to those not used to dealing with it.

"We've lost him," Cisco answered as he turned down a narrow track between fields. "I'm glad it wasn't those two goons from the bar in that 4x4 truck. They'd have run circles around us. Now I can slow down and take it easy on your car."

"Thanks. Considering it's the only transportation we have at the moment, that's downright sensible of you."

They reached the highway after ten of the longest, bumpiest minutes she'd spent in her life. "Just head for Navajo Dam. It's a forty-minute ride from here."

IT WAS TEN O'CLOCK when Cisco parked beneath the cover of some tall piñon trees about a quarter mile down from the cabin. Something was wrong. No night insects sang out in the darkness, and there was a peculiar scent in the moisture-laden air.

As they moved forward, Laurel Brewster surprised him. Most city dwellers moved with the stealth of a flock of geese in a shopping mall, but she scarcely made a sound except for the harshness of her breathing. Laurel sounded winded, like someone badly frightened, but she continued to press toward the cabin.

Her loyalty to her brother impressed him. He had a feeling she would have walked into the afterworld itself, the eerie land of the dead in Navajo beliefs, to help Greg. Cisco found himself wishing someone felt that way about him, but then discarded the thought quickly. He had his life just the way he wanted it. Nobody in particular worried about him, and he had no one to worry about, either. That gave him freedom, and that's what he wanted. He'd paid his dues.

The warmth of a woman, and the demands of friendship, just added complications, and life was uncertain enough without looking for more problems. In that respect, Navajo beliefs were right on target. But unlike some on the rez, he found no solace in chants that were said to restore order. He'd known too much pain to have faith in anything except himself.

Cisco led the way, following the deep tracks of a Jeep or 4x4 pickup until they came to an area with thick underbrush. The vehicle that had made the tracks was no longer there.

He turned and placed one finger to his lips, his instinct for trouble working overtime. Crouching, Cisco tried to find telltale marks that would give him some idea of where the vehicle had gone. As a sliver of moonlight filtered through the pines, the dull gleam of a jagged metallic object directly to his right caught his eye.

He focused his gaze on the object just as Laurel stepped around him. Recognition came to him in a heartbeat. Hurling himself against her, he tackled her, breaking their fall with his shoulder.

Laurel gasped for air and stared at him as if he'd lost his mind. To her credit, she didn't scream.

"It's okay," he whispered. "You almost stepped into that bear trap."

Her eyes widened in horror as she saw the vicious spring-loaded metal teeth that would have snapped shut around her foot. "Why would anyone put a bear trap so close to the cabin? It's dangerous!"

"They weren't after bears."

As her breathing became more irregular and shallow, Cisco saw Laurel pull out an inhaler from her purse and use it. He hadn't expected this.

"Don't give me that look," she shot back in a harsh whisper. "It's my problem, not yours, and I can handle it. Now, let's get going."

Cisco made a mental note to ask her about it later. There was no time to discuss her condition right now. "Stay behind me, and as much as possible, walk in my tracks."

"You've got it."

Cisco noted with relief that her breathing was nearly back to normal. As he stepped carefully toward the cabin, all his senses were fine-tuned. He was aware of everything, from the night song of the crickets to the rustle of leaves in the underbrush. He was also acutely aware of the woman behind him. He could feel her presence, hear every step she took no matter how faint a noise it made. He could sense her apprehension, as well as her determination to keep going.

Cisco fought to banish Laurel from his thoughts. There was danger here for both of them; he couldn't afford distractions. He moved slowly toward a break in the tree line. From there, he'd be able to get a clear look at the cabin he'd only caught glimpses of until now.

As a breeze blew past them, he identified the upwind scent that clung and mingled with the smells of the damp earth. It was stronger here, and there was no mistaking the acrid odor of gunpowder. As if to confirm his senses, Laurel nudged him and held up a spent cartridge. He took the rifle shell casing silently and studied it for a second. It hadn't been out here for more than twenty-four hours.

Cisco edged around the trees and gazed at the log cabin ahead. No lights were on, and it was quiet. In the brightness of the full moon, he could see that bullets had splintered the roughly hewn wooden back door. The small window had been smashed, though from the glass on the porch he surmised that someone had shattered the pane from within, returning fire from inside the cabin.

He moved in line with the back door, which swayed back and forth slowly on its hinges with the gentle breeze.

"We've got to go inside now! My brother could be in there, wounded!" Laurel whispered harshly.

"Be still for now." Cisco listened for another minute, then indicated with a gesture that she should remain where she was. Reaching for a small pistol hidden inside his boot, he crept forward.

He moved in a crouch, ready for action. No one was visible at the window or door as he made his approach. When he finally reached the cabin, he flattened against the wall, watching through the door for movement within. No sounds came from inside. Moving quickly, he darted past the door and entered the cabin, diving behind the closest available cover, an old sofa.

He remained concealed, glancing around the blackness of the room, searching for signs of life as his eyes became accustomed to the interior. Whoever had been here was now gone. Only the evidence of a gun battle remained.

Cisco stood up slowly and crept into the bedroom. From the unmade bed and the bullet gouges that lined the wall, he knew the attackers had taken their victim by surprise here, probably attacking late at night.

Suddenly he heard footsteps behind him. Cisco spun in a crouch, his gun aimed at the door.

Laurel saw the weapon trained at her chest and stopped cold in her tracks. "Easy! It's just me," she whispered.

"I told you to stay put."

"Why? There's no one around. It's too quiet. Besides, you've been in here for a while. Had there been trouble, I would have heard something."

"I've only been inside the cabin three or four minutes. Did you stop to consider that trouble might not have had a chance to find me yet?" Cisco snapped. "Don't ever creep up behind me like that again!"

Laurel nodded, her gaze taking in the room. "Any sign of my brother?" She wanted to keep her voice steady, but the best she could manage was a strained whisper.

"I haven't seen anyone. If your brother was the person attacked here, I can tell you that he defended himself well. I haven't found any traces of blood yet, so I don't think he was hit. But I want to look around some more." Cisco retrieved a penlight from his shirt pocket and turned it on with a flick of his thumb. He focused the beam to a wide angle.

"Can you tell when this happened?"

Cisco reached down and picked up a splinter of wood that had been blown from the wall by a striking bullet, then held it up to his nostrils. "Recently. This wood still smells freshly splintered, though that's in part due to the rising humidity. And you've noticed how strong the gunpowder smell is. Gunpowder scents linger for a long time, but to stay this acrid, it means the battle happened less than twenty-four hours ago."

She looked into the half-open closet. "These are Greg's clothes. From the pile of laundry on the floor, I'd say he's been here for two or three days."

Cisco retrieved several shell casings and studied them. "He had a nine-millimeter pistol and a .308 rifle, so he was well armed."

Laurel walked out to the living area. The walls were pockmarked, and glass from the windows lay around on the floor like jagged spears. Although they both searched carefully, there were no traces of blood anywhere.

"He left here in one piece," Cisco said.

She met Cisco's gaze boldly. "Now you see he's not guilty. If he had stolen that valuable treaty, he would have been long gone, not hanging around waiting to be gunned down. And if the people who attacked him had been cops, we would have heard about the raid on the news."

"Your loyalty is commendable, but you have no real reason to jump to conclusions."

"Meaning, you still think my brother's got something to do with the theft of the treaty?" Laurel shook her head. "How is that even remotely logical? You told me only a few people know the treaty was stolen. None of those people would be trying to kill Greg over it. They'd just want the document back, wouldn't they? So why is someone trying to kill him?"

"I agree he's running for his life. But I can think of several explanations for that."

"Like what?" she demanded.

"He could have found out something he's not supposed to know. Or maybe he was working with the thieves and now wants out, or—" Cisco stopped speaking abruptly and crouched down beside the well-worn sofa and the packing crate that served as an end table. "Here's a leather briefcase. It looks like the one the tribe uses to transport the document."

Using his light to lift the handle, Cisco slid it out into view. "It's the same case. The tribal seal was pried off here." He pointed to the top half, where a square outline of glue remained.

Laurel's heart felt leaden. "Are you going to open it up and find out what's inside, or shall I?"

"Impatience can get you into trouble."

"At your rate, old age will do it first," she snapped. Reaching over, she flipped open the center catch with her finger and pulled the top up.

Laurel stared at the contents. Before she could figure out what she was looking at, Cisco scooped up the case and hurled it into the bedroom. Grabbing her arm, he dragged her along as he sprinted out the cabin door.

"What's—"

He never slowed down, his grip on her hand firm.

They'd run only a few yards when the cabin suddenly exploded with a deafening thump. The impact hurled them to the ground like rag dolls. Laurel crawled behind a boulder, following Cisco's lead, and turned to look back at the cabin. The entire back wall had disappeared, replaced by a thick curtain of flames.

The heat took the breath right from her lungs. She reached for her inhaler, never taking her eyes off the fire. "What happened? My brother wouldn't have done that! He's never messed with anything bigger than a firecracker."

"You're probably right. I figure your brother set the bear trap to surprise unwanted visitors. The bomb in the briefcase has other earmarks."

"What's going on? This doesn't make any sense to me."

"There are dangerous people running around who obviously want your brother out of the way, permanently. My guess is that they left this behind, hoping to finish him off if he came back." Cisco watched the flames beginning to die down already. The recent wet weather had soaked the log cabin, and there wasn't much to burn in the clearing where it was located. Fortunately it wouldn't be spreading into the forest.

Thunder rumbled ominously in the distance. Laurel scanned the horizon, wondering how she'd managed to step right into the worst nightmare of her life. She led a quiet life, both because of her health and the fact that she liked working alone. But now the only family she had left was fighting for his life, and everything she'd ever thought about herself was being challenged.

She stared at the cabin, then at the man beside her. "This clinches it. One way or another, I *must* find out what's going on."

Cisco glanced down at her inhaler. "Are you sure you're capable of going the distance if things get physical?"

"Yes. Asthma means I have to take certain precautions, but it has never held me back from doing whatever I had to. Finding the answers we need to help Greg will entail using my brain a lot more than brawn. If muscle is needed—" she shrugged "—*you* take care of it."

"Do I have a choice?"

"No. Your best chance of finding Greg is to stick with me, and we both know it. Look at it this way. It's a balanced partnership, since we each need something the other can provide."

"That briefcase tends to support my theory that Greg is involved in the theft. Are you sure you still want to uncover the truth?"

"This may have convinced you he's guilty, but I've known him from the day he was born, and I'm just as sure he's not. Greg doesn't always think things through. He can follow orders and he's honest, but independent thinking just isn't what he does best. My guess is he made a judgment call that backfired. That's very much in character with my brother, believe me. There's no way anyone can convince me he could get himself into or out of this kind of mess on his own. If there ever was a time when he needed me, it's now. You're Navajo. I would think that you would understand family responsibility."

Cisco's eyes flashed with cold anger, then as quickly as that emotion had flickered there, it disappeared. His expression was suddenly emotionless, as if he'd hid his thoughts behind a wall of ice.

Laurel knew she'd struck a nerve, but there was nothing she could do about it now. It was too late to take the words back. She watched him for a moment, hoping he'd explain his reaction. As time dragged on, however, he remained silent, staring at the diminishing flames of the cabin. A drizzling rain began.

"What now?" she asked finally.

"You tell me. If he couldn't use this cabin as a hiding place anymore, where would he go? To that ex-girlfriend's house?"

She considered Cisco's question. "Greg wouldn't put Irene in danger, any more than he'd show up at my house. He's probably on the trail of the missing treaty. He'd take his responsibility to it very seriously," she said pensively. "Before I can predict where he would have gone, I'm going to need more information from you."

Confident that the rain would keep the fire from spreading, Cisco rose and began leading the way back downhill to the car. "What do you want to know?"

"For starters, who around here would be interested in a historical document like that treaty? Is it worth a lot of money, either to a collector or by ransoming it back to the tribe? Is its absence particularly advantageous to anyone? And last of all, who will benefit most by its recovery?"

"All good questions." He mulled it over. "I don't know of anyone offhand who'd benefit by the treaty's absence, though there are certainly some politicians who might use its loss against the current Navajo leadership, or might want to take credit for its recovery if the theft was made public. As far as marketing it, I think only a historian or collector would find it valuable.

"Treaties aren't really collectibles, not in the sense that any one individual could actually have an abundance of them," Cisco continued. "Each tribe has a copy pertinent to them, and the government's originals are kept in the national archives. They're never one-of-a-kind items in that respect. There are other tribal antiquities that are worth far more."

"Then its greatest value is to the tribe. We should find out which tribal representative is most likely to be approached, should the thieves want to ransom it back to the tribe."

"What exactly do you have in mind?"

"I believe my brother is going after the real crooks. Who else would have wanted to kill him? They, in turn, will probably want to deal the treaty back to the tribe through some individual. If he can figure out who they'd contact, then Greg will undoubtedly do his best to stake out that person."

Cisco shook his head slowly. "I follow your reasoning, but what you ask is difficult. To even guess who their contact would be, I'd have to approach people who won't want to talk to me."

"Because of the bribery charges leveled against you?"

"Partly, but it's more complicated than that. And for the record, there are no charges against me. If there were, I'd be in jail. The department suspended me because of allegations, not evidence."

"Then what's the problem? Can't you find anyone at all who'd be willing to talk to us?"

"You're asking a big favor, woman, even if you don't realize it. I'd be responsible and held accountable for your actions and behavior though you'd be out of your element. I'd have to be willing to place a great deal of trust in you."

"Despite the fact you're accused of corruption, you're asking me to help you find Greg and accept your word that you'll deal fairly with him," Laurel answered. "It's *your* turn to show some trust in me."

She allowed the quiet in the car to remain undisturbed. For someone in his profession, trusting a relative stranger even partially was bound to be extraordinarily difficult. But she'd run out of obvious places to search for Greg. They needed to start working together as a team.

CISCO COULD FEEL her gaze on him. Laurel was a beautiful woman and strong, though life had dealt her a difficult hand. He wondered what it was like for her to be forced to pace herself in ways she would not have ordinarily chosen.

Placing limits on one's own abilities was never easy. He knew that only too well.

Yet despite her circumstances, Laurel didn't give in to weakness or self-pity. He admired the way she seemed to take life by the horns, not shying away from anything, though at the moment, it was making her one giant pain in the neck for him.

Cisco allowed the silence to stretch even longer as he headed to Laurel's house. So many shadows clouded his past. He wanted to trust her, but wasn't sure if he still knew how anymore.

He forced his mind back to the question she'd asked. "Even if I was willing to try, finding a source among the Navajo now, with all the controversy surrounding me, is going to be tough."

"You've been tried and convicted in people's eyes." She paused. "Like my brother," she added.

Cisco thought of the ones who should have believed in his innocence, including Phillip—his brother-in-law—Benjamin Kelliwood or Curtis Blackhorse. Yet instead, they'd been only too eager to condemn him. Although she scarcely knew him, Laurel had been willing to give him the benefit of the doubt. That had meant more to him than she realized.

At the moment, he had to admit it felt good to have at least one ally. Yet he shouldn't have had to leave the rez to find a friend. The knowledge knifed at his gut.

"You're not taking me home, are you?" Laurel asked, annoyance and then disappointment in her tone.

"For now, I am. It's late. We spent about an hour up at the cabin, and it's an hour's ride back to town. By the time we get to your place, it'll be eleven-thirty or so. There isn't much else we can do tonight." Cisco glanced at her out of the corner of his eye. What an appealing blend of fire and softness she was. "Aren't you tired?"

She conceded grudgingly, "Yeah, I am. But there's so much left to do!"

"I know that feeling, but I've learned that you have to know when to back off and get some rest. Otherwise, you're no good to yourself or the case."

Laurel shifted to face him more squarely. "Does that mean you and I will go talk to someone about the treaty tomorrow?"

"I'll try to arrange it, but I can't guarantee anything."

"You mentioned that your family has the job of keeping the treaty safe. Maybe we can talk to one of them."

He nodded thoughtfully. "My uncle knows everything about the treaty and those associated with it. His honor, in part, is dependent upon the document's safety, as mine is. I believe he would talk to us freely. But, of course, I can't speak for him. No Navajo can speak for another."

"I'm curious. How did the task of protecting the treaty fall to your family?"

"It's a long story."

"I have time," Laurel answered softly.

He glanced at her eyes and, for a moment, felt as if he were being drawn into a world of soft brown velvet and fires as hot as the desert sun.

"My great-great-grandfather was a tribal leader," Cisco resumed, his eyes on the road. "He was one of the warriors who counseled Manuelito during the years the U.S. Army was hunting us down and again at the time of the treaty in 1868. My ancestor spoke for peace throughout the conflict, because of the overwhelming odds facing our tribe. He had traveled back East to Washington and knew the strength that could be brought against the Dineh, our people.

"But Manuelito wanted to continue the resistance. He demanded that we fight for what was legitimately ours. Then the Dineh were defeated, and after years of captivity, the treaty was finally signed. Because my ancestor had seen the need for peace, the document was given into his care. Having it entrusted to him was an honor, as well as a duty.

"The years turned into decades. Later, the tribal council took over the task, and then the tribal chairman, now called the tribal president. Despite that, my clan is still seen as the treaty's traditional guardians. Although I'm the youngest member of the clan, I'm the most qualified to step in now."

"What about your brothers and sisters?"

"I don't have any sisters. My two brothers live away from the rez and have disassociated themselves from everything here. All they ever wanted, as far back as I can remember, was to leave. One is teaching history in California, the other manages a cattle ranch in Montana. They don't write or call. They've done their best to forget who and what they are. It's not my place to remind them."

Cisco parked at the curb in front of her house. "Come on. I'll walk you to the door."

"Would you like something to eat or drink?"

Cisco knew he should see her inside, then leave, but somehow he couldn't make himself take his own advice. "A sandwich would be great."

"Good. I'm a night owl. There's plenty of food in the refrigerator, and most of it is perfect for late-night snacking."

Cisco walked to the door with Laurel. He was glad for the chance to stay awhile. There was nothing waiting for him at home except empty rooms. In truth, there were times he dreaded going there, and to forgo Laurel's company for that alternative didn't make much sense to him right now.

He caught the unguarded look in her eyes and saw she was equally glad he was going to stay a while longer. The thought wound through him, dangerously warming the ice water some said coursed through his veins.

Laurel picked up some letters from the mailbox on the porch, then opened the door. "Let me check my answering machine. Maybe Greg called."

He watched her flip on the light switch, then walk down the hall. A moment later, he heard her strangled cry. Recognizing the terror that rang clearly through that one sound, he ran to her side.

A body lay crumpled on the floor, a few feet before her. The blood soaking the carpet around it formed a horrific crimson aura that spoke only of death.

Chapter Four

Cisco heard Laurel's breathing becoming harsh. "Are you okay?" he asked.

"I've got to see his face," she managed to say, crouching beside the figure. The man's head was turned sideways, and as she saw his vacant stare, tears suddenly began streaming down her face.

"Is it your brother?" Cisco asked, helping Laurel to her feet.

"No. Thank God! Forgive me, Kyle."

"So you recognize him?"

"It's Greg's roommate, Kyle Harris. But why would anyone do this to Kyle?" Laurel paused, her voice choked as she added, "Unless the killer thought it was Greg! They're the same size and have identical hair color. In the dark, you couldn't tell one from the other, at least from behind."

"We know money's not the motive for this murder. The victim still has a wad of bills in his hand."

"He also has the house keys I gave Greg," she added, pointing to the floor. "We better call the police."

"Yes, but not from in here. And don't touch anything!"

Laurel moved over to her desk and saw the handwritten IOU note initialed by her brother. "Kyle came to tap my petty-cash box. Greg must have needed money and sent him—'' Her voice broke.

"Need my spare inhaler," she croaked, reaching for the drawer where she kept it.

But Cisco grabbed her hand. "Don't touch the desk. Use the one in your purse."

With a nod, she went into the hall and retrieved her bag from atop the bookcase where she'd set it on her way to the office. Quickly she reached for the inhaler inside.

Assured Laurel would be okay in a minute or two, Cisco took the opportunity to study the crime scene, making sure not to disturb anything or move around any more than necessary.

As his gaze focused on the victim, he automatically took a step back. He had no wish to touch the dead in any way. He didn't really believe in contamination by the *chindi,* the evil in a man that remained behind after he died, yet some things yielded only partway to logic. Beliefs held for centuries were more tenacious than knowledge gained through education.

As Cisco glanced around, he searched for signs of the murder weapon. His guess was that the victim had been struck from behind by a blunt object. His skull was partially caved in. About three feet away, between a sorting table and a filing cabinet, he saw what he was looking for.

Betrayal and outrage drummed in cadence within him. The lug wrench was his own! Cisco could see the broken corner on the tip he'd created by using it as a pry bar once. The wrench hadn't been missing last time he'd looked in the toolbox behind the seat. Then he remembered his truck back at the bar. The stickers for the Intertribal Ceremonial and the National Karate Championship would have made it easy for someone to spot. Verifying ownership would have been easy once they broke in; by law, the registration had to be kept in the vehicle.

Hearing what sounded like a gasp, he turned around to look at Laurel. She had slid down to a sitting position, her back to the wall. Although she was still holding her inhaler, he could see that it wasn't working as it had before. Her breathing was raspy, though not wheezy, and her chest was heaving.

"You're not wheezing," he said, puzzled. "But you look like you're really having trouble."

She reached for a pad and pencil inside her purse and scribbled a fast note: "Wheezing—enough air passing through lungs. No wheezing—major problems. Have to go to ER now! Can't wait for paramedics."

Cisco could see apprehension and acceptance mingling on Laurel's face. She didn't know if she could count on him, but she had to. She'd been through this before—that much was obvious—but he sure as hell hadn't. Quickly he lifted her off the floor into his arms and carried her to her car.

Cisco pressed down hard on the accelerator, driving as fast as the road would allow. If he picked up a patrol unit, then he'd report the murder. Right now, he had enough problems, and at the speed they were traveling, he didn't dare take his hands off the wheel to use the cellular.

"I'll be all right," she whispered weakly, apparently for his benefit.

"I'll hold you to that." Cisco glanced over and saw Laurel nod her head slightly.

He had no idea how long it normally took to get from her house to the hospital, but he was certain he'd beaten any ambulance's time by a good margin. As he pulled up to the emergency-room entrance, Cisco saw a car parked in front of the doors with the driver waiting inside. The closest empty space was fifty yards away. He leaned out the window, flashed the phony badge and ordered the man to move. Without hesitation, the driver vacated the space and moved farther down.

Cisco glanced at Laurel. Blue was one of his favorite colors, but not on people's lips. He wondered how she managed to stay so calm.

She smiled and mouthed *thank you*. Suddenly he felt like a knight in shining armor. Hurrying around to open her door, he lifted Laurel into his arms and carried her inside.

LAUREL WAS SURPRISED when Cisco came into the examining room after the doctor had left. He smiled tentatively at her. "They normally don't let anyone but family in, but I wouldn't take no for an answer. It's one of the things I do best."

She could see the trace of fear that lingered in his eyes. What surprised her, however, was that he'd stayed. Over the years, she'd learned how men handled seeing an asthma attack for the first time. Generally they'd either be filled with pity or show an almost desperate desire to get as far away from her as possible. The truth was, she didn't blame them. Her asthma made them feel helpless, and she could understand how they'd detest that emotion. She felt the same way.

"I'll be okay," she managed to reply. "Thank you for what you did." After pausing to catch her breath a moment, she continued, "What I really have to do now is keep my mind off my breathing, so it can get back to normal."

"It's too bad that the best way I can think of to distract you would definitely make you breathe even harder," Cisco teased.

She smiled at him, astonished that he could joke with her about it, then glanced at the nurse, who was busy checking the IV. "Breathing hard doesn't always mean I can't breathe."

He chuckled. "Good, I'll remember that. I assume I'm being given a rain check."

Laurel smiled, teasing back by neither confirming nor denying.

The medications took effect slowly, but gave her blessed relief as the minutes ticked by. An eternity later, her lungs finally stopped feeling as if someone had poured cement into them. They began to expand, and breathing became easy once again.

"You're going to be okay now," Cisco said, noting the change with a satisfied smile.

"Yes," Laurel answered softly. "I'll be hyper, since that's what these IVs do, but I'll be fine."

"Then it's time for me to go. I still have to call and tell the police what happened at your home. I didn't want to leave until I was certain you were out of the woods."

"You were wonderful. Thank you." The words seemed inadequate. Cisco had helped her and, most of all, he hadn't made things worse by asking her dozens of questions she couldn't have possibly answered at the time. Even now, he was helping her focus away from the problem.

Laurel watched him leave, lost in thought. As she heard his footsteps fade away, her mind drifted back to the events that had preceded her asthma attack. She'd seen the expression on his face when she'd stepped back into her study after using her inhaler. He'd been looking away from the body, focused on something else. Whatever it had been had disturbed him deeply, filling him with anger.

Try as she might, however, she couldn't recall what had held his attention. She could only remember the blood, and feeling grateful and guilty at the same time that the victim had been Kyle, not her brother.

CISCO PHONED IN THE TIP about the murder anonymously. The last thing he needed now was to be detained by the police. He had a very bad feeling about this. Someone was trying to frame him for this murder, though he wasn't sure who or why.

Once the doctors okayed it, the police would be talking to Laurel. And after that, they'd be looking for him. He had to get moving and try to find answers fast. Using Laurel's car, he returned to the Cowboy Club, where he'd left his pickup. A thorough search of the cab confirmed his suspicions. His lug wrench wasn't there. Someone had removed it and used the tool to frame him for the murder of his prime suspect. Their only slipup had been killing the wrong man.

As he glanced around, Cisco remembered the two men who'd accosted Laurel. They weren't his enemies, at least not ones he recognized, and the name Lachuk didn't ring any bells. His thoughts shifted to Laurel and the way she'd had to fight to keep from being kidnapped by the pair. Possibly they'd hoped to use her to draw her brother in. He remembered the black 4x4 pickup with some kind of blue sign on the doors. He wished he'd had a clearer look at the logo.

Those two men, however, hadn't been the ones following them in the car later. The driver in the sedan had been someone else entirely. At least three people were interested enough in Greg to confront or follow his sister.

As he speculated, another interesting theory came to his mind. He and Laurel had both assumed that Kyle had gone to her home on behalf of Greg and had been followed. Yet perhaps whoever had killed Greg's roommate had been in the house already, waiting. Laurel had mentioned that she'd had a break-in earlier that day. The burglar could have taken a spare key.

Could the murderer have been the guy who'd followed them in the car, or maybe Lachuk and his big pal? One thing was clear: Laurel was in danger from more than her asthma.

Cisco's gut twisted. He'd never had a high tolerance for scumbags who preyed on others weaker than themselves. Laurel was no match for these men, but his involvement would more than equalize the odds. He'd make damn sure of that.

LAUREL GATHERED her purse and inhaler and walked slowly to the reception desk to settle the ER bill. It was a routine she'd grown used to over the years. As she placed her credit card back in her wallet, she saw two men approaching. She stiffened and took a step back.

The man leading the pair quickly pulled out a badge. "I'm Detective Gonzales, and this is my partner, Detective Cooper," he said. "We need to ask you some questions."

She looked closely at the badge to confirm it represented the Farmington police, nodded, then went to the waiting area out in the main lobby and sat down. "I don't know how much help I can be, but I'll try my best."

"I know you've had some medical problems tonight, but we need to speak to you while everything is still fresh in your mind," Gonzales said.

"I'll never forget tonight, Detective, believe me."

He nodded, then continued. "We've identified the man found in your home as Kyle Harris. Any idea who he is and what he was doing there?"

She answered their questions about Kyle and her brother, admitting Greg had disappeared but not telling them about the treaty. After all, she really didn't know any of that for sure. What she had was hearsay, and she thought it wise not to volunteer information that had not been requested. At the moment, keeping Cisco's trust seemed more important than speculating for the police—that is, if she hoped to find Greg.

"Can you verify where you were prior to discovering the body?" Cooper asked.

"Yes, I was with Cisco Watchman. He's a detective with the Navajo tribal-police department."

Cooper and Gonzales exchanged glances. "I believe that officer has been suspended, if I'm thinking of the right guy," Cooper said slowly.

"I heard that, too." Laurel nodded. "Mr. Watchman came to me on a private matter, however." Once again, she noted the glances they exchanged. Unless her guess was wrong, however, she didn't think they knew she'd filed a complaint against Cisco earlier. Homicide detectives would have had no reason to be in on a call like that.

"Where's Watchman now?"

"I have no idea. He drove me here, but I haven't seen him for an hour or so. I just got released, so I haven't had a chance to look around for him."

Gonzales handed Laurel his card. "My pager and office number are on there. When you hear from him, tell him we need to have a talk. He knows the drill. Any idea why he's suddenly making himself scarce?"

"We barely know each other, so he really had no reason to stick around." Her arm hurt from the IV, and she was in no mood for cat-and-mouse games. At the moment, all she knew was that Cisco had been there for her when she'd needed him. These two cops were doing exactly the opposite.

"I'm sorry, Ms. Brewster. I know you've been through a great deal tonight," Gonzales said as if sensing her mood. "But there are many questions about this case that need to be answered. And, of course, the faster we wrap this up, the better off you'll be. You have a vested interest in this. If nothing else, your home is now a crime scene," he added pointedly. "You can't stay there until the forensics team says it's okay to return."

It was an obvious observation, but one she hadn't faced squarely until now. Where would she sleep tonight? She certainly wasn't ready to go home, even if they'd open it to her. "Is the body...?"

The detective shook his head. "No, that's at the morgue by now. Our crime-scene unit will be through in a few more hours, but it would probably be best if you stayed away until tomorrow."

She nodded slowly. "I'll be at the Traveler's Motel. It's decent enough for a night." She shuddered as the image of Kyle's body flashed in her mind. "Or two."

Gonzales gave her a long, thoughtful glance. "I have a feeling you're not telling me everything, and that's a bad idea. You could be in danger."

"Me? How?"

"Let's not forget that a man was murdered in *your* home. You could have been the real target, not Kyle Harris. Why don't you tell me everything you know, and we'll determine if you need protective custody."

Laurel shook her head slowly. "Thank you for your concern, but I neither need, nor want, police protection," she said, knowing that she'd just raised their suspicions even more. "What I'd like is for you to find Kyle's murderer."

Cooper leveled his laser-sharp gaze on her. "We already have some theories about that. Could it be you surprised a stranger in your own home and things got out of hand?"

Anger coiled inside her. "That theory is absurd, and I won't dignify it with a comment." She turned away abruptly, dismissing Detective Cooper without speaking another word.

Holding her head high, Laurel walked slowly to the entrance, then suddenly stopped. Cisco had her keys, and even if he had returned them to her, she had no idea what he'd done with her car. The last thing she wanted to do at the moment was scour the vast parking lot in the dark. She considered her options, then decided to call a taxi and go straight to the motel.

As she turned to go back inside and find a phone, she heard a car pulling up behind her. She turned and saw Cisco behind the wheel of her four-door compact. He leaned over, opening the door on the passenger's side.

Laurel slipped inside, and a minute later, they had left the hospital behind. "The police want to question you," she said.

"I'd figured that, but I prefer not to waste time trying to explain things I haven't found answers to myself. Right now, my energy is better spent pursuing this case."

"You still feel that the treaty is at the heart of it?" She saw him nod. "I agree. It's the only thing that makes sense."

He stopped at a red light, glanced into the rearview mirror to see if they were being followed, then turned to look her over. "Where shall I take you? Do you have a friend you can stay with for the night?"

She shook her head. "No, I won't endanger anyone else with my presence at their home. I'll spend the night at the Traveler's Motel near the shopping mall."

"That's not a good idea."

"I'm sorry you don't approve, but this is my decision to make," she said flatly.

"Then I'll stay there with you, at least for tonight."

The prospect of sharing a room sent a thrill coursing through her that had nothing to do with their professional partnership, but she brushed the feeling aside quickly. "You most certainly will *not.*"

"You may be in more danger than you think."

"I'll be around others at the motel, and I have no intention of opening my door. If anyone bothers me, I'll call the police."

Cisco remained quiet.

"You're not heading in the right direction. The motel's back that-a-way," Laurel said, pointing.

"I thought you wanted to talk to people in the know about the treaty."

She sat up. "I do."

"Then unless you're too tired, I know someone we can speak to tonight."

"I'm not at all sleepy, but it's almost one in the morning. Are you sure it's not too late?"

"The man I have in mind is my uncle. He'll be up at this hour for sure. He seldom goes to bed before two or three in the morning."

"Tell me about him," Laurel prodded.

He nodded. "My father's brother raised me after my dad was killed in Vietnam. He was twelve years older than my dad, and his kids were already grown, but he took me in and treated me no differently from my cousins. I trust him implicitly. We'll both be safe there, and you can ask him whatever you like. Nobody knows more about the treaty than he does."

Once they reached the reservation, Laurel realized that Cisco wasn't taking them into Shiprock. He turned and drove up what seemed nothing more than a rut in an open sector of desert west of the rock formation everyone in the area knew as the Hogback. "There's nothing out here," she commented.

"Not yet. It'll take us another twenty minutes." He gave her a quirky half smile. "This is the shortcut."

Despite the desolate surroundings, she felt safe with Cisco. There was something about him that spoke of strength as great as the mesas to the north and east. For no reason she could name, she felt certain that anyone who threatened her would have far more to fear from Cisco than she ever would.

They reached the isolated gray stucco house shortly before one. The home was dark, but a light flickered within the blanketed doorway of the eight-sided log hogan to their right.

She opened the door to get out, but Cisco leaned over and stopped her. "No. It's considered rude to go up to the door. We wait here until he invites us."

"But how will he know we're here?"

"He knows. Sounds carry easily out here. He heard the car coming long before we ever saw his place."

Laurel leaned back in her seat, studying the sagebrush-littered land around them. It seemed peaceful, yet so terribly isolated she wondered how anyone could choose it as their home. "Does he have any family here with him?"

"No. My aunt died years ago, and his daughter lives over by Holbrook, in Arizona. But he likes it here. He told me once that when he looked across the canyons, he could see the history of the Dineh. Everything he is and stands for is linked to this land."

Before she could ask more, Laurel saw a man step out of the hogan. His back was ramrod straight, and from his stride he seemed in as good physical shape as Cisco. "Is that your uncle?"

Cisco smiled at her as if guessing her thoughts. "He's in his seventies, I suppose. Out here, no one counts years."

The man waved, gesturing toward the house. Cisco walked with Laurel to the door. "There's no electricity out here, but if you need or want anything, feel free to ask. Accepting hospitality is a mark of a good guest, and it's his pleasure to offer it."

Standing at the doorway to the home, Cisco smiled at her. "This is my uncle," he said to Laurel, not giving her his uncle's name.

Laurel nodded. She didn't offer to shake hands, remembering from having done business with Navajos, that they disliked touching strangers. She could feel Cisco's uncle watching her as she stepped inside.

"Names have power, so I won't ask you for yours and wear it out by using it. But I will call you Autumn," he said. "Your hair is the color of leaves in October."

She smiled. "I like that."

Navajo rugs rested on the bare concrete floor of the simple home. At one end of the small room was a potbellied stove, and at the other, a bed. Between the two, a pair of chairs and a three-legged stool were positioned around a tiny wooden table. The man gestured for them to sit in the chairs.

"Are you hungry? I have fry bread you both might enjoy. And some of my herbal tea?"

"That sounds good." Cisco turned to Laurel. "My uncle's tea is popular around here. He makes his own blend. It's very good."

"Then I'll have some, too," she answered, smiling first at Cisco, then her host.

The old man left the room through a blanket-covered doorway and returned moments later carrying a big china plate filled with food. Placing it before them, he sat down on the stool. "Enjoy." He waved for them to start eating. "Now tell me what brings you two here. This is not a social visit, I gather." His gaze was attentive, shifting back and forth between them.

Although his eyes were clouded with the smoky blue that indicated the beginning of cataracts, Laurel had a feeling that little escaped this man.

"You've heard what's been said about me?" Cisco asked.

The man nodded slowly. "People talk, but I know you better than that. You will prove your innocence."

"Yes, I will." Cisco's voice reverberated with conviction in the confines of the two-room cottage. "But now, Uncle, we both need your help." He explained what he'd discovered about the treaty and Laurel's connection to it, then gave his uncle the highlights of what had happened so far.

The man's gaze focused on Laurel with approval. "Loyalty to family is something that's rare in these changing times, but a valued trait nonetheless."

He stood up and checked the two kerosene lamps that lit the room. "Ask whatever you wish."

"Tell me what you can about the treaty itself."

He nodded once. "Listen and learn," he said. "It was May in 1868 when we started talking about a treaty to end the war between the tribe and the United States. But that marked the beginning of new sorrows. Most of our people were being held down south at Bosque Redondo far from the Dinehtah—our land—and were slowly starving to death. And instead of going home, the government wanted us to relocate to Cherokee territory. We could not go. When the

Dineh were first created, four mountains and four rivers
were pointed out to us, and we received instructions that it
was there we should live. First Woman gave the land to us,
to the Dineh. We couldn't live anywhere except the Dinehtah, the land that was home to us.

"Eventually we convinced the white man's government to
let us come home. That was the start of the Long Walk.
Tsohanoai, the sun bearer, appeared in the sky, and our
journey began. The way was very hard, and the Dineh were
weak from years in captivity. But we persevered, mile after
mile. By the time we saw sacred Tsosil, what you call Mount
Taylor, we had lost everything but our spirit, but we were
home.

"That treaty represents our tribe's suffering, our triumph and, most important of all, lessons learned in blood.
To our clan, ensuring its safety is a duty and a matter of
honor."

"Could it be that an enemy of your clan tricked my
brother into divulging details about the security so that the
treaty would be made vulnerable to thieves?" Laurel asked.
"Or maybe my brother handed it over to someone who
convinced him he was a representative of your tribe."

"An enemy of our clan?" Cisco's uncle looked at her in
surprise. "It is possible, but I think unlikely."

"Is there anyone within the tribe who would benefit from
discrediting your clan? The accusations made about your
nephew, though seemingly unrelated, might have been
planned as a way to further demoralize him and your clan."

"I am an old man. I don't have powerful enemies, not
anymore. Is it possible that you do, nephew?"

Laurel saw the seed of doubt flickering in Cisco's eyes. At
least he was finally considering other possible suspects besides her brother.

Silence filled the room like a palpable presence. It was
clear he had no answer, at least none he wished to share with
them. At long last, Cisco's uncle stood. "It is late. I hope

you will both accept my invitation and spend the night here."

Laurel looked at Cisco and realized he'd expected that invitation to come. That's why he'd brought her here instead of the motel. Normally, being tricked into anything would have made her furious, but circumstances lately were far from normal. She was honest enough to admit that tonight, after all that had happened, she hadn't really wanted to stay alone anywhere.

Cisco glanced out of the curtainless window, toward the mesa just east of the house. Laurel watched, sensing his restlessness.

"I'm going to take a look around. I want to make sure nobody followed us." Cisco turned to his uncle.

"You expect danger?" The old man's eyebrows rose.

Cisco shook his head. "Not really. I was careful. It's just a precaution, nothing more."

"Who do you think would have followed us here?" Laurel asked, her stomach doing flip-flops.

"Many people are after us. It won't hurt to be extracautious," he answered nebulously.

"Before you go out there, nephew, there is something I want you to have." The elderly man slipped off the leather thong around his neck. Light from the kerosene lamp played over the surface of the beautifully carved stone fetish he held in his palm. "This was given to me a long time ago by a medicine man. It's an armadillo. The spirit of the animal resides within the carving," he said, glancing at Laurel.

He slipped the thong over his nephew's head and placed the carving inside Cisco's shirt next to his skin. "Armor, and boundaries of safety, are part of its medicine. That is the shield that protects its owner. It now belongs to you. If you treat it with respect and open yourself to it, it will help you."

"Wouldn't you like to keep this with you, Uncle? You've worn this for as long as I can remember."

"It should now be yours. I know you no longer share all my beliefs—you have your own reasons for that—but it's time for you to receive this gift. You are fighting for yourself, for us and for her," he added, referring to Laurel.

Cisco adjusted the leather thong and, with a nod, walked to the door.

Laurel watched Cisco step outside, a dark shape against an even deeper darkness. Even the moon had briefly disappeared behind the clouds now.

"Don't worry. He will be back." Cisco's uncle smiled at Laurel, as if entertaining a secret that pleased him. "I'm glad you have come into his life."

She hesitated, then spoke. "I'm not sure you understand. We're working together out of necessity. That's not exactly the ideal planting ground for even a casual friendship," she added with a sheepish smile.

"It is enough." The old man stood and walked to the door. "I must retrieve another lamp from the hogan. I will be back shortly."

As he slipped out into the darkness, Laurel sat back, surprised by how comfortable the chair actually was when she wasn't anxiously perched on its edge. A special warmth ribboned around her, coaxing her to relax. She took a deep breath, surprised at how clear her breathing had become. Finally she was perfectly safe. There was a rightness about being here that soothed her spirit.

She stretched lazily and, after a few minutes, stood and wandered to the door, wondering what was taking Cisco and his uncle so long.

Suddenly a rifle shot rattled the windows. Terror, deep and primal, gripped her as she crept to the door, staying low, and peered outside. False shadows cast by moonlight dared her to venture out of the house. Instinct warned her to stay inside.

"God," she whispered into the silence of the room. It was more a prayer than a curse.

Chapter Five

Laurel stayed to one side of the door, her back flat against the wall. She listened carefully, but even the night insects had stopped their rhythmic song. Silence engulfed the desert like a shroud over the dying.

Her body began to tremble, and she took a deep breath. She had to go outside to find out what was going on. Laurel edged out, peering into the darkness, searching for any threat that might be hiding behind a rock or bush.

She heard a faint rustle to her right, like the sound of a gentle breeze stirring a patch of leaves on the ground. Too subtle for footsteps, she reasoned. Creeping out, she ducked behind the stunted pine near the front porch and waited for her eyes to adjust to the darkness.

As she started to move forward, she felt a hand on her shoulder.

Laurel spun so quickly, she stumbled and fell back against the trunk of the pine.

"Easy," Cisco's uncle said softly. "You should not be out here."

Fear made her heart race. Words to the question foremost in her mind jammed in her throat, making it impossible for her to utter a sound.

"My nephew is right over there," he said, pointing with his lips, Navajo-style. "I told you he would be okay."

She glanced in the direction he indicated and saw Cisco crouched by the right front tire of her car. "It wasn't a rifle shot, just a tire blowing out? But how? The car was parked!"

Cisco remained in the shadows, but spoke in a normal voice. "It *was* a rifle shot. Your guess was correct. Go inside. I'll be there shortly."

Laurel followed Cisco's uncle into the house and dropped down heavily onto her chair. "I guess trouble followed us. Maybe we shouldn't have come."

"The sound was unsettling, but no one was hurt. You are safe here. This is the one place you two can and should come to whenever you need a haven."

His voice, so sure and steady, calmed her, though she was at a loss to understand why. "Why would someone shoot out my tire? Surely they expected me to have a spare, or to be able to get one."

"A warning," Cisco answered, coming silently through the doorway, careful not to silhouette himself in the lantern light.

"Did you recognize whoever did this?" his uncle asked.

"I never had a clear look," Cisco answered carefully.

"Was that necessary, or do you have an idea who it was anyway?" Cisco's uncle insisted quietly.

Laurel saw the look the men exchanged. The silence between them spoke volumes. She had the distinct feeling that both knew who was to blame, though neither was ready to voice an unsubstantiated accusation.

"What happened out there?" she asked, her gaze on Cisco. "Don't shut me out now."

"When I stepped outside a while ago, I saw the outline of a man holding a rifle about a hundred yards away. Instead of shooting me, he turned his aim and shot out your tire. It was very clearly a warning." He stared pensively at an indeterminate spot across the room. "I went after him, but I couldn't catch up. He drove off before I ever got near."

"Who knows that your uncle lives here? Nobody followed us. We were both being careful."

"Only Navajos know of this place," Cisco answered. "As you saw, it's not exactly easy to find, even when you know where you're going."

"Enough of this for now." Cisco's uncle led Laurel down the hallway and pointed to a small room. "You can sleep here tonight. My nephew will stay in the outer room, and I will sleep in my hogan."

"No, please," she protested. "I don't want to put you of your own bedroom. I'll sleep on a blanket in the outer room or even in my car."

"No," he said in a quiet but firm voice. "You have been through enough." He took several blankets from the closet. "I will see you both in the morning," he said, and walked out of the house.

Cisco went to the window, stood to one side and watched as his uncle crossed halfway to the hogan, then stopped. He took out a small pouch, recited a Navajo chant, then sprinkled a pinch of cornmeal into the air.

"What is he doing? Is that a Navajo prayer?" Laurel had joined Cisco at the window.

"Actually it's more of an offering to First Woman, one of the Dineh's gods. It's a way of making sure the gods won't interfere with the good that may come to the one making the offering. It's a bit different from the prayers of the Anglo world, which are simply petitions for good."

Cisco's explanation was without emotion, as if he was explaining how to change the tire, and Laurel wondered what had stripped him of the beliefs he knew so much about. Something told her it was deeply personal, whatever it was.

"Are you sure it's safe out there for him?" Laurel asked, wanting to change the subject.

"Yes. The warning was given. That was the sniper's only intent for now. But my uncle's eyesight isn't so good. That's why I wanted to make sure he made it over there okay."

Once his uncle was inside the hogan, Cisco returned to the main room. "You better get some rest. If you need anything, let me know."

Laurel walked slowly to the bedroom. It was sparsely furnished, just an old wooden closet and a cot. She sat down on the edge of the mattress, trying to force herself to relax. Sleep would not come easily tonight. Maybe some fresh air would help.

As she returned to the living room, she saw Cisco's outline in the half-light of a single kerosene lamp. He stood to one side of the open window. His unbuttoned shirt hung loosely from his shoulders, stirring open with the breeze. She felt the impact of his physical presence all through her body. For one wild moment, she felt the desire to run her hands over his smooth, muscular chest.

Laurel tore her gaze away and cleared her throat, not wanting to startle him.

"I knew you were there," he said quietly.

"Do you think it's safe for me to go outside for a while?"

"You need something from your car?"

"No, I'm wound too tight, that's all. I was hoping that a bit of fresh air and maybe a small walk would do the trick and help me fall asleep."

"I'll go with you. A walk might do me some good, too."

He started to reach for a lantern, then set it down again. "The clouds have blown north, so the moon's out. We won't need to take one of those. I know every inch of this place."

He led the way outside into a world of shimmering grays and kaleidoscopic shadows that changed shape as they danced with the breeze. Laurel felt vibrantly alive. All her feminine instincts were attuned to the man now beside her. Her heart hammered wildly as the warmth of his body seemed to wrap itself around her like an embrace. She folded her arms across her chest and rubbed them, almost as if hoping to bring the sensation closer and make it more real.

He slipped his arm around her waist and drew her closer. "Are you cold?"

"Not now," she answered.

"Maybe we should go back inside."

"Not yet, please."

She looked into his eyes, searching for answers, wanting to understand him, but what she saw reflected in his gaze only confused her more. He was a man at war with himself. He wanted her, but he still held himself firmly in check. A storm seemed to rage just beneath the cool eyes.

"You're a man of secrets," Laurel said. "But be careful. Those take a toll. Staying behind the mask you've chosen to wear requires constant control. Since you don't want anyone to see the real you, you laugh when you really want to cry and walk away when you would rather stay. In the end, you cheat yourself most of all."

Cisco turned to face her, and for several moments it was as if the whole desert stood still, waiting for what would come next. Laurel scarcely breathed.

His arm slowly tightened around her waist. As he drew her into him, his eyes never wavered from hers. There was an unspoken challenge in them, as if he were daring her to try to move away.

She had no intention of going anywhere. Every feminine instinct she possessed was crying with the desire to know his kiss, his touch.

He took her mouth slowly, gently, barely grazing her lips at first. Her mind was spinning, and she clung to his shoulders for support. His strength, the sheer power of his rugged masculinity, enticed her to surrender to the crazy swirl of emotions spinning through her.

Then he deepened their kiss. His tongue invaded her, thrusting harshly past her lips. His kiss, driven by hunger and need, became rough.

The fires sweeping through her almost made her legs buckle. She pressed herself against him, needing to give more as badly as he seemed to want it. Consumed by yearnings she'd never known, she curled her fingers on his chest as their bodies melted into each other. The warmth of his breath on her cheek, his heart beating against hers, left her trembling with passions raw and wild.

Inexplicably he eased his hold and moved away. "It's time to go back."

A desperate longing for something she couldn't, or perhaps wouldn't, name surged through her. She would have paid any price at that moment to keep him from ending the wonderful sensations that had coursed through her. But the moment was gone.

Cisco gestured wordlessly back toward the house and fell into step beside her. He'd withdrawn from her emotionally. She could feel it as keenly as the empty ache slowly spreading through her.

They returned to the house a moment later. Cisco walked to the window where he'd stood before. Laurel watched him and shivered with a cold that seemed to come from her very soul. As she turned to go back to the bedroom, she saw the fetish on the wooden table. A sliver of moonlight filtering through the window reflected on its surface.

"How come you left the fetish here?" she asked, puzzled.

"I wasn't in need of protection," he answered, then added, "though perhaps you were." His eyes were brilliant and focused only on her.

With effort, she tore her gaze away. She'd been told she had expressive eyes, and tonight she feared they'd reveal much more than she wanted him to know.

Laurel walked over to the fetish and touched it lightly with her index finger, forcing her mind away from Cisco. "It's so very beautiful."

He picked the fetish up in his hand, held it for a moment, then slipped it around her neck. "A loan," he whispered, "to protect you while you sleep."

His breath filled her mouth like a lover's kiss. Excitement made her pulse race.

When he stepped back, Laurel felt desolate and totally alone again. She coiled her fingers around the carved stone, feeling the warmth of Cisco's hand still on it.

"Take the fetish with you tonight. It's all that I'm free to give you," he said, his voice taut.

A sweet ache filled her as she nodded and walked back to her tiny room. It seemed impossibly empty. Allowing her clothes to fall to the floor, she crawled onto the cot. The fetish felt warm against her breast. Pressing it to her, she drifted off to sleep.

CISCO REPLACED THE TIRE with one his uncle had provided, rather than use the spare, which was designed only to get the driver to the nearest station and not for rough terrain. As they drove away from his uncle's home, Cisco glanced at the woman beside him. She looked more beautiful than ever with the morning sun playing on her hair and face. He wanted her. It was crazy, of course. What would he have to offer this *bilagáana* woman? This white woman would look upon the world he knew best and think it was foreign.

He cast her another sideways glance. She still wore the fetish he'd loaned her last night. It was as if she'd made it so much a part of herself that now she was scarcely aware of it. The realization surprised him. It was clear that Laurel wasn't like anyone else he'd ever met. His world might have been strange to her, but she was still willing to open herself to it.

As they left the reservation behind, Laurel rubbed her eyes and sat up. "I'm not much of a morning person, as I'm sure you've noticed," she said with a sheepish grin. "I hope you'll forgive me for being lousy company."

"I have no complaints." He liked the way she blinked back the sun and stared sleepily at him. He suddenly pictured her waking up in his arms. His body grew heated as he envisioned her close to him, their naked bodies pressed together.

He forced the thought out of his mind. "I can't drive you directly to your house," he said, focusing on the case. "I'm going to need to pick up my truck, and it's still at that Farmington bar."

"No problem. We can go there first, then I'll drive myself back home. You might want to follow me back to the house. The Farmington police want to talk to you, and you can't avoid them forever."

"They'll have to wait. I have other duties that take precedence now." As they reached the Cowboy Club, he pulled next to the curb and parked behind his truck. "Do you have a pencil and paper?"

She took out a pad and pen from her purse. "Here you go."

He drew a crude map. "I'm no artist, but this should allow you to find my home if you need to talk or reach me. My phone number's written there, too, but don't trust the line. It could be tapped. If you decide to come over, chances are I won't be there. But you can leave a note, and I'll get in touch with you as soon as possible." He paused, gathering his thoughts. "One more thing. Expect the Farmington police to keep you under surveillance. You're probably their only lead at the moment, so it's their next logical move."

Laurel nodded, placing the map back in her purse. "Thanks for the warning. I'll be on the lookout for anyone watching me. Now I better go see what the police have done and if they've found out anything new."

"You'll be okay?"

"I don't look forward to going home," she replied candidly. "I'm not sure it'll ever feel the same there for me, but it *is* home. I've got to go back and deal with it."

Cisco slipped out of the car and helped Laurel into the driver's seat.

"Good luck," he said, closing the door for her.

As she pulled the little sedan back out into the street, he gazed at it thoughtfully. Laurel was an incredible blend of pride and vulnerability. Being around her filled him with an incredible rush of passion and tenderness. Yet even when his need for her seemed almost overwhelming, the urge to protect her, particularly from himself, added to his control. He hadn't felt that jumble of mixed-up feelings since . . . those days so long ago.

Right now, he hated having her go back to her home by herself. Had it been his choice, he would have returned with her and made sure she was safe.

But at the moment, circumstances dictated his actions, and he had a duty to perform.

LAUREL DROVE HOME SLOWLY, knowing that she had to go back, though more than anything she'd wanted to stay with Cisco. She tried to tell herself that her wish to remain with him was only because he knew how to fight what they were up against better than she did. But that wasn't true. The fact was she was wildly attracted to Cisco Watchman. Unfortunately this was a complication she had no time to indulge.

Angry with herself, she pulled into her driveway and strode past an officer just coming out.

"Wait right there, ma'am," he said.

Ignoring him, Laurel went inside. Suddenly another officer intercepted her.

"Ma'am, what is your business here?"

"This is *my* home. I need to know when I can move back in."

"Whenever you wish," he answered, relaxing. "We were getting ready to leave. I just wanted to make sure you were authorized to be here, since we hadn't locked up yet."

Laurel watched as the men packed up their equipment. After they'd left, she stood alone in the living room, staring down the empty hall. She had no wish to go farther into the house. Her home no longer felt as safe and cozy as it had been once.

She took a deep breath and forced herself to walk to the back rooms. Her office had been left in shambles. A chalk outline marked the carpet, and around it bloodstains formed a crazy macabre pattern.

It took several minutes for her to stop shaking. Trying to push back the horrific images flashing in her mind, she began the clean up process.

Two hours later, after working tirelessly to restore order to her office, the feel of death still hung in the air. She'd rolled up the bloodstained rug and set it in the backyard. Tomorrow, she'd arrange to have someone pick it up and haul it to the dump. She'd also cleaned and waxed the tiled floor, and even taken down the blood-splattered curtain. But it would take more than that for her to ever feel comfortable here again. The furnishings could be replaced, but the memories would haunt her forever.

As her gaze drifted over the silent phone, her thoughts turned to Cisco. He hadn't called. To find Greg, she'd need to work closely with him, even if working with a partner was something that didn't come naturally to Cisco.

The more she thought about it, the more she realized she couldn't trust him not to try to edge her out of the investigation. It would be entirely up to her to see that didn't happen. As a plan formed in her mind, she packed up her small laptop computer. She'd drive to Cisco's house and wait for him there.

It took a while for her to find his home. There were no street signs, just landmarks, but after two hours of searching, she finally found it. It was in a remote area south of Shiprock, part of a newly developed housing cluster that seemed to be close to nothing except the mesas. Cisco's home was a small adobe at the end of a half circle of six homes. It wasn't as isolated as his uncle's home, but it was still far from the residential neighborhoods she was accustomed to.

She started to park in his driveway, but then changed her mind. It was safer to stay out of sight. She drove halfway down the street, then parked beneath an old peach tree that partially shaded an empty driveway.

As the minutes passed, the heat forced her to leave the car. She had just found a cool sitting spot on the north side of an adobe detached garage when she saw a Navajo police car approaching.

She crouched down quickly, hoping her presence wouldn't be noticed. The officer slowed down as he went by Cisco's home, but appeared not to notice her or her sedan.

Once the officer disappeared down the road, Laurel sat back, determined to wait as long as necessary. Opening her laptop computer, which had been inside her purse in a padded carrying case, she began to work on a project for one of her clients.

Less than fifteen minutes later, she spotted a second patrol car going by. This unit had a dented fender. The tribal officer followed the same procedure the first one had, slowing down as he drove past Cisco's home.

She watched curiously. Either this section of the reservation had some superb police protection, or Cisco was hotter than ever. She remembered the policemen at the hospital looking for Cisco, and she opted for the latter.

Too nervous to work and feeling her lungs tightening, she closed down the laptop and reached for her inhaler. As she opened her purse, the mail she'd picked up earlier—before they'd discovered Kyle's body—fell out onto her lap. Laurel fished out her inhaler, used it, then glanced through the

mail. It seemed strange doing such a mundane task after
what she'd been through. As she saw the third letter, however, she suddenly realized that nothing would be mundane
in her life again until Greg returned home.

Laurel stared at the envelope, her heart racing. She recognized Greg's almost illegible scrawl immediately. Kyle
must have placed the note in the mailbox on Greg's behalf
just before he went into the house. There was no stamp or
postmark anywhere. With shaking hands, she tore open the
envelope.

The note was short, but its contents made her stomach
lurch. In it, her brother explained that he'd become a lia-
bility to some important people, individuals whom he wasn't
at liberty to identify at the moment. Certain he'd be framed
for the theft of the treaty, he'd run.

A tear spilled down Laurel's cheek as she grew to understand how trapped Greg had been by circumstances. The
knowledge he'd possessed had made him a target despite his
innocence. He'd feared his enemies would come after her,
too, had he remained in town. Now he warned her to be
wary of strangers and lock the doors even during daylight
hours.

Sorrow engulfed her. Both Greg and she were alone, more
so than they'd ever been. Everything was going wrong. She
glanced back at Cisco's home. His expertise would be the
key she needed to solve the case and help her brother. She
wouldn't allow anything to deter her from what she had to
do.

Laurel stood and brushed the dirt from her slacks. As her
gaze drifted, she spotted Cisco approaching. He was walking along a shallow arroyo, moving surreptitiously across the
low ground. He stopped, turned and appeared to listen, then
moved on, making his way toward his home.

She figured from his actions that he was working hard to
avoid detection by someone, but from her vantage point, she
couldn't see anyone else around. As she edged closer to the

house, she saw another police car, this time with two officers inside, coming up the road. She ducked quickly behind a cluster of junipers, cursing their needles, and remained there until the vehicle completed the half circle, then disappeared back down the road.

Once the road was empty again, she made her way to Cisco's house. As she drew near, she saw him go to the back door and step inside.

Laurel reached the open area surrounding his back porch a moment later. She stayed where she was for several long moments, watching. Finally gathering her courage, she darted forward, crossing the ten-yard distance as quickly as she could.

Reaching the back door, she tried the knob. The door swung open. She took a few tentative steps inside his kitchen and glanced around, ready to call out. Suddenly an arm snaked around her shoulders, and a knife was pressed to her throat.

Chapter Six

She gasped, and the high-pitched wheeze sent a chill up his spine. Cisco withdrew the four-inch blade from against Laurel's throat with a shaking hand and set the knife on the counter. Fear shook him as he realized how easily he might have harmed the one person he wanted most to protect.

Frustrated and angry, he spun her around in his arms. "Are you crazy? Why do you keep sneaking up on me? Haven't you learned it's dangerous? Most people use the front door. Why didn't *you?*"

"I saw you sneaking in, taking the back way. I figured you had your reasons and that I should do the same," she said, readjusting the shoulder strap on her purse and reaching for her inhaler.

"That's a dangerous strategy. If I'm sneaking in, that's because I think someone's after me. Why didn't you call out? I had no way of knowing you weren't an intruder!"

"I would have called out if you'd given me another second!" Laurel protested, stepping back. "I don't get a thrill out of having a knife pressed to my throat, bud."

"Then don't *ever* sneak up on me again," Cisco said, his voice too controlled and soft to pass as natural. Realizing his hand was shaking, he curled his fingers into a fist. The knowledge of how easily he might have slit her throat still preyed on his mind. He seemed to have a penchant for this, hurting people he cared about.

"From now on I'll yodel if necessary."

He scowled at her. Now Laurel was making light of it. Maybe having her trust him wasn't a good thing after all. That's why she was now refusing to acknowledge how close she'd come. She simply couldn't see him harming her in any way.

The realization filled him with a fierce protectiveness. She was right about one thing: he would have just as soon died than harm a hair on her head. "I have a feeling you didn't come here to visit. But before you explain, where did you park, and is there any chance you were tailed?"

"I don't think anyone followed me, and I parked in the empty driveway of the house down the street. I learned that trick from you."

He grinned. "Good."

"You weren't followed, either, by the way. I was on higher ground, and I could see farther up the arroyo."

"Someone was there." Cisco brought out a cold soft drink from the fridge and, with a gesture, offered it to her.

She opened the lift top and took a swallow. "What makes you so sure that you were being followed?"

"I didn't actually see anyone, but believe me, someone has been tailing me today. I *felt* them there." He saw the skepticism on her face. "No, it's not paranoia. A cop develops certain instincts. You watch without even being aware that you're watching, and you're always listening. Twice I caught a glimpse of a shadow, nothing more, about a hundred yards or so behind me. He always stayed far enough away to hide his identity, but he has the tracking skills of an experienced hunter."

"Wouldn't an enemy want to force a confrontation?"

"Maybe he's biding his time." He walked to the sofa in the center of the room and offered her a seat.

Laurel shook her head and walked around, studying everything.

He watched her in silence, wondering what was going through her mind and what his home would reveal to her. It felt strange to have her here. "Stay away from the windows," he cautioned.

"You've got blinds. Nobody can see through those when they're closed."

"Motion sometimes shows through because of the way the light plays on the slats. The last thing we need is a visit from the tribal police right now, so be on your guard."

She walked to the bookcase and looked closely at a small snapshot of a woman with long black hair and dark, mysterious eyes. A Mona Lisa smile added to her ethereal quality. "Who is she? She's gorgeous."

"My wife. She died a few years ago." He'd tried to make it sound matter-of-fact, but Laurel's gaze cut past his defenses.

"You still mourn her," she said flatly. It was an observation, not a question or judgment.

"No, not mourn, just remember. She's gone, I've accepted that."

Though a million questions flickered in Laurel's eyes, he remained silent. Finally she looked away.

"It can't be easy to have known love and then find yourself alone."

"It isn't, but we all learn to cope with whatever life hands us. Choice is a luxury few of us ever really have." He crushed the can in his hands, then lobbed it across the room into a wastepaper basket. It landed neatly with a clank. "I don't want to talk about this anymore. The subject is closed."

"Why do you have to be so guarded?" she asked gently. "By now you must know I pose no threat to you. Do you think it's just not macho to show feelings and be human?"

"I am human, and also a man who has been alone too long. Perhaps it is *you* who should be more guarded and careful."

The smile she gave him told him she didn't believe him for a moment. If the woman didn't realize her effect on him and the effort it took for him to control his passion, then it was time she found out.

He crossed the room and drew her into his arms roughly, taking her mouth in a hot and hungry kiss. His lips ground into hers, forcing them apart.

He'd expected resistance, but she offered none. Instead, she parted her lips and drew his tongue even deeper into her mouth. Fire shot through him, and he groaned with the exquisite pleasure her kiss gave him.

He knew they were both playing with fire, but it felt too good to stop. Her gentleness and sweetness were breaking away the walls of ice that protected his heart.

He tore his mouth away but continued to hold her, his hand beneath the curtain of her hair. She trembled against him, and her response made him half-crazy. He was as hot as a furnace, his manhood stiff and pulsing.

Reluctantly he released her and stepped away. "You see? You're not as safe around me as you might think."

"Safe?" She shook her head. "I never made that mistake. But I do know that you're not the type to hurt someone, not unless it's in self-defense or in the line of duty. I'm judging you solely on your actions. Even now," she added softly, "you protected me, though it went counter to your own desires."

Cisco turned away, focusing on a spiderweb in the far corner, struggling to bring his body back under control. She was the most exasperating woman he'd ever met. Didn't she realize that when a person danced too close to the flames, it was hard to walk away unscathed?

"You want me to fear you, but I don't understand why," she insisted. "Why are you so determined to stay alone? You push everyone away. You're even distant and cautious around your uncle."

"If you believe that I'm trying to protect you, then assume I have my reasons."

"Tell me this much at least. Is it my asthma that causes you to draw away from me? Are you put off by what you've seen?"

"No. What stands between us is something I can't talk about. It belongs to the past, to the life I shared once with my wife." He leaned back against the cushions. "Are you going to tell me what brought you here? I'm now assuming it wasn't an emergency," he said sharply.

His tone had the effect on her he'd intended, but what he hadn't expected was his own reaction to the hurt on Laurel's face.

She took the fetish from around her neck and held it out to him. "This is one of the reasons. You loaned it to me, but with all that was happening, I forgot to give it back."

Cisco took it from her hand. "You didn't have to come all the way out here for this. You could have given it to me next time we saw each other."

"I wasn't sure how long that would be," she replied honestly.

He smiled. "So it wasn't the fetish."

Doubt, then embarrassment flickered over her features. "I also want to show you something I found." She opened her purse and retrieved Greg's letter.

Cisco read it quickly. "So it's as I suspected. We have to keep digging into the death of your brother's friend. Someone killed him, thinking it was your brother. Following the murderer's trail will lead us to whoever has the treaty now, and to the answers your brother needs in order to return safely."

"But where do we begin?"

Cisco walked to the radio and turned it down low. "The news media," he explained. "It's the bane of the department, but in this case, we may find them useful. We need to know what the police have uncovered.''

As the soft strains of a country-western ballad filled the room, she took a seat on the chair across from him. ''Do you think that the man tailing you is the same one who shot out my tire?''

''It's possible.'' Cisco took a deep breath, uncertain how much to tell her. It wasn't as if she'd be able to do much about it.

''Please stop being so closemouthed. What are you afraid of? Do you think I'm going to run out the door and start quoting you to every person I see? Show some faith in me,'' she insisted softly. ''It'll make things easier on both of us.''

Cisco regarded her thoughtfully. It had been a very long time since he'd confided in anyone. Maybe it was about time he did. ''My brother-in-law blames me for the death of his sister, my wife. Now that I've been branded as a dirty cop, he's freed of the loyalty he would owe a fellow officer. That makes it easier for him to seek revenge. Other cops would be more than eager to help him, too. Now that I think about it, the vehicle that fled from my uncle's hogan could have been an unmarked unit.''

He pursed his lips so tightly, they formed a thin white line. ''There are others, as well, who'd love to take a piece of my hide. Criminals I've arrested in the past, victims of a crime or victims of the law who for one reason or another blame me—any one of those could describe the person tailing me.''

Hearing the hourly news announced, he turned up the radio's volume slightly. A prerecorded interview was being replayed, and according to the Farmington police spokesperson, a partial print had been lifted from the lug wrench found at the Kyle Harris crime scene.

''Has the print been identified?'' the reporter asked.

''The partial suggests the wrench could belong to a tribal police officer currently on suspension. That's all I can say for now.''

"Will an arrest be made soon?"

"The print is *not* conclusive. There must be ten points of concurrence to make a definite match, and there are less than that number in evidence. At the moment, we're asking Detective Cisco Watchman to come in for questioning."

When the newscast went on to other stories, Cisco shut off the radio. For a while, he allowed the thoughtful silence between them to stretch.

"Now you really are on everyone's Wanted list."

"'Wanted list'? That's a diplomatic way of putting it."

"Here's a thought for you to consider. Even if that lug wrench was yours, I could provide *you* with an alibi. We both know you were with me when Kyle was killed. Unfortunately I'm not sure if the police will take my word for it. Finding out that Kyle had taken money from my petty-cash box confused their thinking. They ran one of their theories past me at the hospital. They wanted to know if it was possible that you and I surprised what we thought was a burglar and acted before Kyle could identify himself. I let them know in no uncertain terms that I thought they were crazy. Still, an alibi from me might persuade them that a conspiracy of silence exists between us."

"You may be right." Cisco rubbed the back of his neck with one hand. "I think our best bet for now is to avoid both police departments. Let's continue investigating on our own and see what we can turn up." He glanced out the front window, then went to the other windows, peering out cautiously at each.

"We need to find out exactly who Lachuk and his pal are," Cisco continued, "and how they're connected to your brother. It's too much of a coincidence that those two were looking for your brother at a time when everybody else is out searching for him, too. I checked in the lobby phone books while you were recovering in the emergency room, and couldn't find Lachuk anywhere. What do you know

about either of them? I think I remember the big guy saying he'd met you before."

"He'd driven up one time just as I was leaving Greg's
place. I didn't pay much attention to him at the time, but
now that I give it some thought, I think he was the passenger, not the driver. It was that same black truck, the one at
the bar. I remember thinking it was the kind of pickup Greg
would have loved."

She paced restlessly. "I bet Lachuk owns the truck and
was the driver. Maybe I can call information and get Lachuk's phone number. It's possible he's just not listed in the
book. You can have an unpublished number that's not necessarily a private, unlisted number."

"Don't call from here. If the cops are looking for me,
they could have my phone tapped. We can try later, from
another location. It's a good idea and just might pay off,"
Cisco said.

"There was a sign on the truck's door. Do you remember seeing it? Maybe it was from the business where Lachuk works," Laurel suggested.

Cisco shook his head. "All I remember was the color,
blue. The angle was wrong for me to make out the words,
and at the time, I was too busy to worry about it. Maybe
we'll see a business truck while driving around, and it'll
spark your memory. Lachuk could be working for some
auto dealer or repair shop, or an off-road specialty shop,
considering the vehicle. It's too bad I can't use any cop
sources or remember a license tag. We'd track him down in
a minute."

"So where does that leave us?" Frustration was evident
in Laurel's tone.

"We can't go cruising aimlessly down Main, hoping we'll
run across those two. The only logical step for us now is to
go talk to your brother's co-workers, particularly any he
associated closely with."

"There are only two guys besides Kyle he socializes with after hours. One is a guy who works as his partner on special assignments. The other is a bachelor who has a lot of the same interests Greg has. But I doubt that my brother would have confided in either of them. That's not his way. He talks about hunting and fishing, sports and stuff like that, but never about anything even remotely personal. Because he's a security guard, he's especially careful not to talk about business."

Cisco shrugged. "Maybe your brother had too many beers one night and let something slip out. It happens."

"Okay. I'll give Bobby a call as soon as we leave here. I know he's in the book. Greg would often call him from my home and meet him at the Cowboy Club to play pool or dance with the ladies."

"It would be better if you didn't contact him at all ahead of time. That'll just give him a chance to make an excuse or prepare his thoughts. Interviews are better when they're off-the-cuff."

"All right, but I better look up Bobby's address. Do you have a phone book?"

"There's one on the table by the wall." Cisco moved to the back of the room and peered out the blinds. "We should go as soon as you finish. The units that are driving by sometimes have two officers to a car, which means they're doing this on their own time. We don't generally have two-man patrols unless we expect trouble making an arrest."

After she was finished, Cisco led the way out the back door, glancing around carefully. "Stay behind the house and keep your head down as much as possible."

They walked out into the desert fifty yards or so, then made a wide loop behind two houses before heading for the third.

Cisco spotted her car as they rounded the middle house and headed directly for it. Forcing himself to keep his pace moderate for Laurel's sake, he took her toward the cluster of stunted junipers where she'd been standing earlier.

They were almost at the car when two Navajo men in civilian clothes stepped out from behind the junipers. "It's over," the tallest one said to Cisco, pointing a baseball bat at his chest. "We'll let the woman go, but we want you to come with us."

"Who are you?" Laurel demanded.

"Police officers who know this doesn't concern you. Get in your car and drive away."

Cisco met Benjamin Kelliwood's stony gaze with one of his own. "I never saw you in the role of vigilante."

"We're going to keep you under wraps for a while, that's all. You'll be safer with us than out among the people, or in Farmington."

"Why do I doubt that?" Cisco countered smoothly.

"We know about the man who was killed in her house," Kelliwood said quietly, pointing to Laurel with his lips, Navajo-style. "We need to know what part *you* played in his death. After we've had a chance to get some answers from you, and if we're satisfied you're telling the truth, we'll let you go home."

"What if I can't convince you?"

"We're cops, not killers," he said sharply. "You're the one who has forgotten that, not us. Our job is to make sure justice is served. If you're guilty of murder and taking bribes, we'll take you in."

Curtis Blackhorse grasped Laurel's arm and started urging her toward her car. Laurel bent back one of the juniper branches, then released it suddenly. The branch whipped around and caught Blackhorse across the face, sending him reeling back, cursing loudly as he rubbed his eyes.

Almost in unison with Laurel's defense, Cisco attacked. He spun and kicked out at Kelliwood, who staggered backward from the blow to his chest. He crashed into the other blinded officer, who grabbed hold, wrestling him to the ground with a war cry.

In a split second, Cisco shoved Laurel behind the wheel, then jumped through the open window in the rear. "Go!"

Before the two officers got back on their feet, Cisco and Laurel were on their way. As she pulled out onto the main road, Cisco scrambled into the front and gestured to her right, pointing to a car in the distance. Red lights were flashing from the vehicle. "Here comes another patrol unit. Avoid it."

"How? It's coming down the road from the direction we need to go."

"Go down this dirt track, then into the arroyo. Wait there. He won't see you from the road."

She drove off the road quickly, but balked as she saw how deep the arroyo was. "No way. We may make it in there, but we won't get back out. It drops off too fast, and it's still muddy on the bottom."

"You'll be okay. It's not as steep as it looks. But you better hurry—a white woman is kind of distinctive out here, particularly if they've got your description and are on alert."

Laurel accelerated carefully, but the drop was sudden and jolted them both hard. They landed with a soft thump at the bottom. "The ground is soft and muddy. I knew we shouldn't have come into here. I hope you know I'm not very good at pushing."

"We'll be able to get back out. I know this terrain, believe me."

After the patrol unit passed by, Laurel pressed down gently on the accelerator, moving forward cautiously.

"Go straight and up the side about a hundred feet ahead. The brush there will give you traction. But *don't* let off on the gas pedal, or we'll bog down. Go at a slow, steady pace."

When Laurel's gaze took in the slope ahead, she stopped the car. "I have a better idea. You drive us out. That way, if we're trapped, it's your fault."

"Meaning, you won't ever let me forget it?"

"Something like that."

"One thing first." Cisco stepped out of the car and splattered the license plate with mud from the arroyo. He then covered the fender area around the wheels with the reddish sludge. "Now we're ready. With this, and the splattering from your spinning tires, it will *look* like a car from the rez."

Cisco took the wheel. The path back uphill was precarious, but soon they were back on the highway. "Why don't you give me directions to your brother's friend's house? I'll drive. Then if we see another patrol car, you can duck down. They won't give a Navajo man a second look. But you'll attract attention, whether or not they see me in the vehicle with you."

"Okay. Drive out of the reservation first. Then, once we're in Farmington, I can guide you to Bobby's house. He's the bachelor I was telling you about. Fred's going to be harder to catch alone. He works erratic hours and he's got a huge family at home."

As Cisco headed out of the Navajo reservation, his thoughts drifted to the encounter with Blackhorse and Kelliwood. He didn't care much for the ideas that were forming in his mind.

"Are you going to tell me about those guys?" Laurel asked. "They meant business."

"I know."

"Do you think they know about the treaty?"

"I'm not sure. But neither of those boys is dirty. It's possible they just wanted to harass a 'bad cop' and bring him in. Or maybe they do know about the treaty and think I know where it is or have information about it they can use.

They could be doing some on-the-side investigative work for someone. They *were* out of uniform."

"Who could have put them on the job?"

"Maybe our tribal president or his chief attorney. Could be they've formed a search team."

"So did those guys really care one way or the other about Kyle's murderer? Or was that just a cover story for my ears?" Laurel turned to Cisco, searching his eyes for answers.

"I don't know. I find their interest in an off-rez murder of an Anglo a bit hard to accept, but I suppose anything's possible. Maybe I should have gone with them peacefully and found out."

"I think we did the right thing attacking those police officers so we could escape. And please wake me up when this is over. I never thought I'd ever be saying anything like that." Laurel sighed, then sank deeply into her car seat.

They entered Farmington forty minutes later from the west on Highway 550, then drove to a residential area south of San Juan College. As they neared the house, they came upon an intersection where children were playing baseball, using an oversize plastic bat and ball. The kids moved grudgingly as Cisco eased through the infield.

"It's the small cottage at the end of this street," Laurel said.

Cisco parked by the flat-roofed frame-and-stucco cottage, noting a red pickup in the drive. "Looks like we might be in luck."

Laurel started to get out, but Cisco pulled her back inside. "This isn't the rez," she protested. "If we wait for him to invite us in, we'll bake in this car."

"Something's not right here."

"What do you mean?"

"I saw someone peering out the curtain in the living room. Unless I'm mistaken, he was holding a handgun."

"That doesn't sound like Bobby."

"Let me go up and take a closer look around," he said. "Stay here in the car. I'll be right back."

Cisco was walking around the side of the house when a neighbor suddenly spotted him. The woman stood by her clothesline, her eyes riveted on Cisco.

"Hey!" she finally shouted when Cisco ignored her. "What do you think you're doing?"

He'd hoped for stealth in his approach, but that was out of the question now. With a burst of inspiration, he crouched by the gas meter, pretended to write something on a pad, then with a wave, walked back to the car.

To his surprise, Laurel was standing by the sidewalk. "We better go up to the front door," she urged. "That wasn't a handgun, it was a portable telephone. Near as I can see, he hasn't used it yet. But if we can't get Bobby to relax, he may call the cops on us. From his window, he could give a clear enough description to set half the force after us."

"We may end up with more trouble than just facing the cops if we go up to his door and stand there like sitting ducks."

"If we want to talk to Bobby, it's our only choice, and we better act fast."

"From his actions so far, I'd say he's running scared. That makes him twice as dangerous."

"And more likely to have answers. Don't worry. Once we get close enough for him to see my face clearly and hear my voice, he'll recognize me."

"We hope." Cisco added softly.

Chapter Seven

As Laurel walked up to the door, she saw the curtain being drawn back a bit. She knocked, calling out to the figure inside. "Bobby, it's me, Laurel."

A heartbeat later, a tall redheaded man opened the door without unlatching the chain. "What do you want?"

"I need to talk to you," she said. Aware that Bobby's gaze had fixed on Cisco, she quickly added, "He's a friend, helping me look for Greg."

Bobby hesitated, then finally unlatched the door. "Come on in quickly."

Laurel slipped inside, followed by Cisco. The second they were in, she saw Bobby relock the door. "What on earth is wrong, Bobby?"

"I'm in a little trouble. Actually a whole lot of trouble. There's some people I have to avoid running into right now." He looked down at the phone still in his hand and placed it on top of the sofa.

"Does this have something to do with my brother hiding out somewhere and Kyle's death?"

"It could. Greg and I do owe money to the same people, but I don't know exactly how Kyle would fit into this."

"Do you have any idea where Greg is staying?" Laurel turned to glance at Cisco and, following his line of vision, saw him staring at the revolver on the coffee table beside the sofa. It was within arm's reach of Bobby. "Good grief, Bobby! What the heck is going on?"

"I'm doing my best to stay in one piece until I get out of town," he snapped. "If you came here hoping I can tell you where Greg went, you're wasting your time. He didn't say a word. The people we owe money to play rough, and neither of us is dumb enough to broadcast our plans."

"Are you saying that the only reason Greg is on the run is because he owes money?"

Bobby rolled his eyes. "Let's just say he wants to keep his fingers, toes and kneecaps, okay?"

Cisco moved imperceptibly toward the coffee table, positioning himself closer to Bobby's gun. If the security guard panicked while Laurel was there and did something stupid, it would still be possible to disarm him. "Have you noticed anyone belonging to my tribe hanging around with her brother lately?"

"You're not just helping Laurel find Greg, are you?" Bobby's gaze fixed on Cisco. "What's your part in this?"

"Her brother and I have business to discuss."

"The treaty, right? That's what you really want to know about. Is somebody planning on stealing it or something?"

"What makes you say that?" Cisco asked, his eyes narrowing with wariness.

"Greg never told me much. He never talked about work. But I knew he was responsible for guarding that document, and something was making him squirrelly as hell. Some honchos from the Navajo tribe were constantly hassling him. 'Did you do this? Did you check out that? How are you going to protect it from vandalism?' Stuff like that. Of course, what he was worried most about was owing Sammie Ortega money. Sammie's not a patient man."

"How much was he in hock to Sammie for?" Cisco asked.

"About five grand, give or take. Mostly from losing at poker or craps. But Sammie's payment plan is what gets you. Twenty percent of the balance payable each month, cash, plus fifty percent interest. Miss a payment, and...well, you'd better not miss a payment."

Laurel's eyes grew wide. "Greg was in that much trouble?"

Bobby nodded. "He'd promised Sammie that he'd have the balance he owed, in cash, a week ago, but something must have gone wrong."

"What?"

"Greg had some kind of deal going, but it fell through. He never gave me any details, though."

"Would Fred Davis know?" Laurel asked. "I know he worked as Greg's partner on special assignments."

"I have no idea. You'd have to ask him, but he's out of town. He takes his family up camping in Colorado every year at this time. He won't be back for another two weeks." Bobby glanced at his watch. "As riveting as this conversation is, I'm going to have to rush you off. I've got to get out of town. Don't ask me where I'm going."

"I wouldn't advise leaving now," Cisco said. "You're only going to make things worse for yourself. Your testimony could benefit some investigations going on right now. The police..."

"Yeah, yeah, but good guys come in last. Look at Kyle. He was as straight-up as they come. I have no idea why anyone would have wanted to kill him. Kyle never gambled, borrowed money or even ran up a tab on his charge cards. He was as tightfisted with his paycheck as could be. But now he's dead." He peered out the window. "I can tell you this much—Kyle's murder has nothing to do with Sammie. I'm one hundred percent sure of that."

Bobby walked to the door, obviously anxious to end the conversation. "If you want my advice, leave Greg alone. As long as nobody finds him, he'll be safe." When neither Cisco nor Laurel moved, he opened the door and gestured toward it. "Go on. You don't want to hang around here."

He paused, then added, "*I* don't want to hang around here."

As they walked to the car, Cisco casually took in the neighborhood. Laurel couldn't see anything even remotely threatening, but Cisco's change in posture told her a different story. His shoulders were rigid, and his back straight.

"We're being watched."

"Where?" She glanced around.

"Don't do that. Act as if everything is perfectly normal. Just get into the car."

She slipped into the passenger's seat and breathed with relief as they got under way. "*Who* was watching us?"

"I don't know. But there was someone in the shadow of a juniper tree down at the end of the street. The person ducked around the corner of a house just as I looked in that direction, but he was there."

"A curious neighbor who doesn't want to be caught spying doesn't necessarily constitute a threat."

"No, but this is the same man I keep seeing. He's an outline playing out of sight, a flicker just out of the corner of my eye. He's there, and that's all the warning I need. Have you noticed anyone tailing you when I'm not around?"

"No, but if the person is really that skilled, I probably wouldn't."

He nodded slowly and glanced into his rearview mirror. "I can't see anyone back there right now, but it's easy to hide in these neighborhoods. The streets all curve and loop around. It'll be even easier to hide once we hit the traffic along Apache or Main Street."

"Are we going downtown?"

"I think we should go together to pay Sammie a visit. Having you there is going to give us an edge. A woman searching for her brother won't put him on the defensive as much as if I showed up asking questions."

"You know Sammie?"

"No. I just know *of* him, like every other cop in the area. Crooks and cops always seem to find one another in the long run," he added with a wry smile.

"Should I do most of the talking?"

"Yes. Pretend I'm your boyfriend, along for moral support. But don't be surprised if he suspects I'm a cop."

"From the television broadcasts?"

"That, perhaps, and instinct. If he has seen me on the news, then he'll know I'm wanted for questioning and on suspension. That'll work in our favor. He'll be more likely to talk freely in front of a rogue cop."

Ten minutes later, they arrived at Sammie's business, a few blocks west of where Behrend Avenue intersected Main Street. Laurel tried not to cringe. "Oh, it figures. A tobacco shop. Just what I need," she muttered.

"Will the odor bother you?"

"It does, sometimes. It all depends on how strong it is or if anyone's actually smoking at the time. A cigar will practically finish me off." She opened the car door. "Let's go give it a try. If I need to leave, you'll have to handle it."

As they approached, she saw that metal bars covered the windows, but the narrow brick storefront looked no different from any of the other retailers in the area. "Are you sure this is a . . . bookie joint?" she asked.

He smiled. "What did you expect?"

"I don't know. Something seedier, with men in pinstriped suits and overdressed blondes hanging on their arms, I suppose."

"You've seen too many movies. Sammie caters to a variety of customers, everyone from housewives to bankers, usually people who have money to gamble—that is, until Sammie separates them from it." He watched a clerk remove a display of briar pipes from the store window. "Let's go inside. Just remember, I'm right there with you to make sure nobody gives you a hard time. And if you need to leave, don't hesitate. I'll take it from there."

Laurel had no doubt she'd be safe with Cisco. She could feel the warmth of his body enveloping her as he stayed close. His hand was on the small of her back and remained there as if silently reassuring her. The problem was, his nearness and touch were making it hard for her to think.

"Should I just come right out and ask him about Greg?" she asked, struggling to stay focused.

"Yes. Don't try to play games with Sammie. He's played them all."

A chime sounded as they went through the front door, and the clerk taking down the front display looked up. A portly man with thinning black hair peered out from a door in the back. "I'm sorry, folks. We're closed."

"Remodeling or taking inventory?" she asked pleasantly, seeing the cigar boxes stacked on the counter by the cash register. At least the scent of tobacco was not heavy enough to bother her breathing.

The man from the back room came out and regarded her curiously. "I don't remember seeing you here before, ma'am. You're prettier than most of my customers." He smiled.

His insincerity somehow made her feel even more uncomfortable, but she forced herself to smile. "I'm trying to track down my brother. I understand he was one of your best customers. Will you help me?"

"I might if you tell me who your brother is," he answered.

"Greg Brewster."

His expression suddenly changed and became guarded. For the first time, he seemed to focus on Cisco's face, withdrawing his attention from Laurel. "I know you from someplace. You've got that cop look in your eyes, too."

Cisco remained silent, but met Sammie's stony gaze unflinchingly.

Sammie smiled. "Yeah, *now* I know. The bad-boy Navajo detective, Watch Man or something like that. You've been playing both sides of the street, so they say. Decide to do some taking instead of just watching, huh, Watch Man?'' He focused back on Laurel. ''Now, give it to me straight. Why are you really here? I would imagine I'd be the last person you'd want to see. You must know Brewster owes me a big hunk of change for certain debts I allowed him to incur.''

''I really am just looking for my brother. I have to find him. But before I try to convince him to come back, I want to make sure he's in no danger from you.''

''He owes me money, and I intend to get paid. But I do like my customers to remain in working order, so they can settle their accounts.''

''Do you know where Greg is?''

''No. My people aren't looking for him yet.'' His eyes narrowed pensively. ''But if you're serious about this search, I'm not the only person you should talk to. Greg has other people holding his markers, too.''

''Such as?''

''Jerry Hawkins.''

''Who is Jerry Hawkins?'' Laurel asked. ''I don't think Greg ever mentioned him to me.''

Sammie glanced at Cisco, then back to her. ''Your friend will tell you how to find Jerry. But watch your step. He's not a friendly type, not at all like me. But I do know that your brother mentioned working for Hawkins after a few episodes of bad luck at the tables and the track. You see, I insist on cash, but Hawkins has a service program. He gives certain people who owe him money a chance to pay off their debt.''

''Doing what?'' she asked.

Sammie shrugged. ''That would depend on the individual's talents or the business opportunities Hawkins sees they could bring.''

Laurel swallowed, but her throat was still as dry as sand. She knew what Sammie was implying, but there was no way she'd believe it. Her brother was an honest man. Maybe Sammie just wanted to get rid of them. What better way than sending them to someone who was "less friendly."

"Shall I tell Hawkins you sent us?"

Sammie blinked, then suddenly laughed. "Not unless you want to get on his bad side in a hurry. Our kind of fund-raising opportunities have a tendency to get rough. Business competitors are seldom drinking buddies in a small market like Farmington." Sammie gave Cisco a hard look, then turned and went into the back room.

"Wait," Laurel said, trying unsuccessfully to catch Sammie before he left.

Cisco placed one hand on her shoulder. "We have what we need. Let's go."

Seeing the warning look in Cisco's eyes, she walked back to the car. She didn't interrupt the silence between them until they had pulled out safely into the street.

"There's something creepy about that man," she said at last. "He's well dressed, and the shop isn't unpleasant, but he makes my skin crawl."

"He should. He's bad news."

"Are we going to go find Jerry Hawkins?"

"We're going to *try*. I know where he usually hangs out. But Sammie wasn't exaggerating. Hawkins is dangerous. He likes to play with people. He's been under arrest so many times, but witnesses against him never show up in court. Nobody's ever been able to pin a thing on him, and he spots vice sting operations a mile away."

"I can't believe my brother would work for someone like that."

"He may not have had a choice. Hawkins has a way of making people see things his way. And if your brother owed him money..."

"Well, Greg might have done some work for him, but he wouldn't have broken the law."

"You're missing a vital point. Dealing with bookies or playing poker for money *is* illegal in Farmington."

His voice was gentle, but the words inflicted painful wounds. "Okay, I never said Greg was a saint, but he never stole a dime from anyone in his entire life. Even though he's in trouble, he would never betray the trust his company and your tribe placed in him. Try to see it from his point of view. To him, gambling is something he does with his own money, and if he loses, well, that's his problem. Taking from someone else is an entirely different ball game."

As they drove across town, Laurel's gaze drifted to Cisco's hands. They were strong but capable of so much gentleness! And she needed his tenderness now. For one wild minute, she pictured Cisco's hands on her body, loving her, making her forget everything but him. Realizing the direction her thoughts had taken, she glanced away.

"What are you thinking about?"

Something in his smile told her he'd read her mind accurately. She felt the hot flush that rose to her cheeks. "About heat and summer," she replied vaguely, avoiding his gaze.

Cisco drove east to a new bowling alley in a heavily traveled area of town. When he parked, Laurel glanced at him in surprise. "This guy works from a bowling alley? You've got to be kidding."

"He manages the alley and works out of a storeroom in the back."

Laurel tried to brace herself. This world her brother had chosen was as frightening as it was confusing. Nothing was ever the way it looked. As they walked inside through a service door in the alley, Cisco moved in closer to her. "Here you'll have to follow my lead, okay? I've had a run-in with Hawkins before. No matter what happens, let it play out."

She tried to swallow back her fear, though she was suddenly far more afraid for Cisco than for herself. "Maybe I should go in alone."

"You won't get in. At least not to see Hawkins. Just trust me." He gave her a cocky grin and a wink.

The bitter taste of fear filled her mouth. She prayed neither of them would ever have reason to regret this move.

Chapter Eight

Cisco led the way through the bowling alley, then turned the corner and walked toward a door at the end of a long hall. As they approached, a tall Spanish man stepped out of a side room and blocked their way.

"Watchman," he acknowledged in a low, lethal voice, "you're not welcome here. Take the lady and get out. Mr. Hawkins told you last time that he never wanted to see your ugly face again."

"Really? I thought he was talking about you. Nobody considers *my* face ugly."

The man took one menacing step toward Cisco and crossed his brawny arms over his chest. "Don't push it. You don't have enough backup today." He stood in front of the closed door like a giant sentinel.

"Just be a good boy and go get your boss."

The end door was suddenly opened, and a tall brown-haired man stepped out into the hall. "I thought I heard your voice, Watchman," he said, his eyes shining with hostility. "You must be feeling suicidal if you came here. From what I've heard, you're not a cop anymore. We could dance on your face, and the police would probably send us a thank-you note."

"I'm here on behalf of my client," he said, gesturing to

Laurel. "She's looking for her brother. I have no intention of leaving until you answer some questions for her."

"Do you want me to remove him from the premises, Mr. Hawkins?" the guard asked quietly.

Cisco turned to look at him. "You could try. But then Hawkins would have to fetch his own coffee and answer the door himself while you spend the next few weeks in the hospital. If I'm not a cop, as you insist, then I don't have to restrain myself and worry about your rights anymore."

"Is this necessary?" Laurel stepped between the two men. The confrontation was getting out of hand too quickly, and she didn't like the odds. She forced herself to meet Hawkins's eyes with a direct, honest gaze. "Look, Mr. Hawkins, my brother, Greg, is a gambler and not a very good one, I'm afraid. Now he's disappeared, and I'd like to find him. Mr. Watchman is helping me, that's all. Without him, I wouldn't have been able to even find *you,* and I was hoping that you would help me."

"Why should I?"

"Because you have no reason not to," she answered softly. "If my brother owes you money, you'll want him back so he can pay off his debts. In the meantime, helping someone like me and earning goodwill can't possibly hurt you. You're a businessman—surely you recognize the value of what I'm proposing. You stand to gain, not lose, by providing me with a little information."

"How far will your goodwill get me?" he goaded.

She struggled to control her temper. The man was a sleaze, and the gleam in his eyes made her sick to her stomach. "You never know when you'll need a character witness. You've created a tough reputation for yourself, and it's one that's eminently useful to you. But there might come a time when you want the world to see another side of you. Why would you throw away a chance to garner some goodwill?"

Hawkins smiled slowly. "I'll help because I like you, lady. You're a straight shooter, though your choice of company stinks." He glared at Cisco and then focused back on her. "I do know your brother, but he doesn't owe me a dime. If he owes anyone, it's Sammie Ortega. Your brother was a gambler, but not an idiot. He steered clear of problems with me."

"Why should she believe you?" Cisco challenged.

Hawkins's glare was ice-cold. "Because, unlike you, I don't pretend to be something I'm not. I don't hide behind a badge while I'm lining my pocket with bribes. I am exactly what I seem to be." He shifted his gaze to Laurel. "You better take a long, hard look at my competitor, Sammie Ortega. Old Sam doesn't hurt people directly. He messes with their minds instead."

"What do you mean?"

"Maybe he pushed your brother too far. Or if he sent goons after him, your brother may have bolted just to stay alive."

"Thank you, Mr. Hawkins." Laurel took Cisco's arm. "Let's go."

Hawkins moved in front of Cisco. "How's it feel to know that the department is slowly barbecuing your butt? Who would have thought that under all that self-righteousness beat the heart of a thief?"

Cisco took a step back, shifting into a defensive posture, feet apart. "I think you better step aside."

Jerry's guard came to stand beside his boss, just as another burly man came down the hall.

"Walk away," Laurel said to Cisco, moving beside him and taking his arm. "We have work to do." His body thrummed beneath her hand as she steered him toward the exit. His outrage and frustration was palpable. Had she not been there, she was certain someone would have ended up in the hospital. Instinct told her that if it had been Cisco, he would have had a lot of company.

After they returned to the car, it was a long time before he spoke. "You shouldn't have interfered. Those types understand brutality. It's the law of the jungle out in the streets. Now, next time they challenge, it'll be more serious. They'll see what happened today as weakness."

"But that's not the real reason you would have fought them. It angered you that Ortega and Hawkins said you were becoming just like them."

Cisco nodded slowly. "I've been branded a thief and a traitor, but coming from the mouths of lowlifes like them, it's even worse," he admitted.

"There was a time you were very sure you would be cleared. Are you having doubts about that now?"

"I *will* be cleared eventually. But in the interim, I have to live with those accusations." He took a long, deep breath. "It gets tougher every time somebody like Hawkins gets in my face."

"Then maybe you should stop searching for the treaty and my brother and concentrate on your own problems."

Cisco shook his head slowly. "All the department has are unsubstantiated charges of bribery coming from some 'unnamed source.' No proof will be found against me, because none exists. The treaty, on the other hand, demands my immediate attention. I have to take an active part in the search-and-recovery effort. I have no choice." He glanced at her, then back at the road. "It's a matter of honoring a tradition that's as much a part of me as—" he struggled to find the right comparison "—my secret name," he added finally.

"Your what?"

He took a deep breath, then let it out slowly. "Navajos are given many names, but only one is secret. It's a very important part of our heritage. We guard that name because it is said to have special power."

"Will I ever know what it is?"

"Maybe someday."

She tried to mask her disappointment. It would have been wonderful to share such intimate knowledge with him. Yet it was unrealistic to expect such closeness between them, now or ever.

As Cisco drove past the tobacco shop and continued on, she glanced around. "Where are you going?"

"Sammie's tobacco shop is closed. The lights were off, and the doors shut. If you remember, Sammie was putting stuff in boxes and closing up well before his posted business hours. I'm going to play a hunch and go to his house."

"You know where it is?"

"Yeah. I was part of an undercover operation with the Farmington police a few months ago. It was a big waste of time, since someone tipped Sammie off. As it turned out, he'd skipped town for a few days."

Cisco arrived at a south-Farmington trailer park a short time later and went to the rear of the lot. A new-looking double wide had been placed next to a chain-link fence. Its front door was half-open. Someone seemed to be inside, though no cars were parked nearby.

As they walked up to the door, a young woman in her late twenties came out to greet them. "Are you coming in response to the ad? The property won't be ready to be shown until tomorrow at the earliest."

"So it is for sale?" Cisco asked, playing along.

"Yes, and it's very reasonably priced, too. It's under market value." The woman handed Cisco and Laurel business cards listing her name and that of a local realty office.

"We'd like to talk to the owner, Sammie Ortega," Cisco said. "Do you know where we can find him?"

"Mr. Ortega left with the last of his belongings less than an hour ago. We're taking care of liquidating all his properties. He's moving to Mexico, I believe."

"He's left town? Are you sure?" Laurel felt her heart sink. She'd had a feeling that Sammie had been trying to get rid of them. Now she could see that her suspicions had been right.

"He came into a large inheritance and has decided to retire," the woman explained pleasantly. "He'll be sending me his new address when he gets settled. If you'd like to contact him about the property, I can forward a message then."

Thanking her, Cisco walked with Laurel back to the car. "You can bet the address he sends her will be a post-office-box number. We need more to go on, but our sources are drying up. I wish there was some way for me to access the department's computer. That could really help us about now. I could use it to try and locate Lachuk and his pal, for instance."

"Do you have your own password?"

"Yes, but I can only go through the computer that's on my desk in the office. That's set up with all the right programs and whatever." He shrugged. "I'm not a computer type. All I know is which buttons to press."

"I have a laptop in my purse right now, if it still works after all the jostling we've been through. With a phone line to tap in to and the password, you should be able to get in from anywhere. But they could have changed *your* access code when you were suspended so you couldn't access your old files and change something. Or if they're extrasneaky, they could have set it up so that anyone using your password triggered a trace. We'd never know it, either."

He considered it. "There may be another way, depending on how knowledgeable you really are about computers."

Laurel smiled, almost reading his mind. "Breaking into computers is done all the time in movies, I grant you, but believe me, it's a very difficult thing to do without being detected. My health requires me to stay practically inert sometimes, so I play with computers a lot, but I'm no hacker. Trust me when I tell you that you can't just break into a system that's filled with safeguards without taking risks.''

"What if you have what they call a 'back door'?''

She looked up at him quickly. "You mean the password programmers use to bypass security when they need to access the main programs?''

Cisco nodded. "My cousin is in charge of maintaining the tribe's local-area networks. He has to be able to access all the systems regardless of the time of day, and fix problems. We were having a few beers once, and he told me the password he uses. It was so dumb I never forgot it.''

"What is it?''

"Me Tonto.''

"I can see why you didn't forget it.'' She laughed. "But let me warn you, even though you have a valid password, what you're suggesting is completely illegal. If we get caught or traced, we're going to be in even more trouble than we are now. The feds have passed some new laws, and they'll be all over our case.''

"What we're doing is in the cause of justice and we have no other choice. We have to gather more information to continue our investigation. We also desperately need to know what the Farmington police have by way of evidence. We can access that information through the tribal network, too.''

"All right. Let's go somewhere where I can hook up my modem to a phone line, and we'll see what I can get for us.'' She paused thoughtfully. "Problem is, where do we go? If we go to your place, we might get spotted or traced. Same with mine. I have a cellular phone in my car, but we should use a regular phone line to do this type of work, not a radio link.''

"There is one place we can go that I don't think the police will have staked out. But it's up to you.''

"Where?''

"Your brother's.''

Laurel nodded slowly. "You're right. With Greg on the run, and Kyle... gone, it's as private there as it can get."

They arrived at the small apartment complex a short while later, but before getting out, Cisco insisted on driving around the block a few times. Satisfied at last that no one was staking out the apartment, at least from a vehicle, they hurried inside. "We can't stay here very long. It won't be safe for more than a short time, since there are others, besides the police, who are after your brother."

"I'll work as fast as I can. What kind of information do you want me to target, and can you tell me which files they'd be in?"

After giving Laurel the necessary information and the phone number, he sat beside her. Soon she was into the tribal-police system, and information began appearing on her small screen.

Using the back door, she accessed the chief's files. All information on the bribery allegations against Cisco had come from an informant code-named Hosteen Doe.

"Is that a common name on the reservation?" she asked.

Cisco smiled. "It means Mr. Doe."

She continued searching, but there were no references at all to the theft of the treaty. She then pulled up all the information pertaining to Kyle's murder, taken from the Farmington-police homicide reports. Details were sketchy at best.

"I don't understand," Laurel said. "By now they should have more. Yet according to this, all they have is one partial print that is so indistinct and smudged it could have been left ages ago on that lug wrench."

"But they probably suspect that the wrench is mine," Cisco said. "And it is, because someone took it from my truck. The smudged print is undoubtedly mine, too. The killer must have been wearing gloves when he handled it, and that would account for the smudging. So as of right now, I'm the only link they've got to that murder. No wonder they'd like to haul me in for questioning. Cops can get a suspect into an interrogation room, imply that they have a strong case and then play all kinds of mind games to try and extract information.''

''Fortunately you know all about those games already,'' Laurel mumbled, still dreading the thought of Cisco being degraded by being given the third degree.

''Still, that can be an extremely tense situation, especially if the suspect is another cop. Officers always take it personally when one of their peers makes them look bad. And insisting you're innocent only makes it worse, believe me.''

''Then let's download what we need quickly, while we still have a connection. Tell me how to do a search on Lachuk.'' Laurel could feel Cisco's tension. He'd already been through the wringer with his own department. The thought of going through more of the same with the Farmington cops must have been like facing the prospect of a return visit to hell.

Cisco directed her through the system until they got information on Lachuk. ''According to this,'' he said, scanning the rap sheet, ''Victor Lachuk was dishonorably discharged from the Marines for going AWOL. He was an explosives expert. As of the time this was last updated, Lachuk was unemployed. He was recently booked for driving while intoxicated and resisting arrest. He served jail time because he didn't pay the fine.''

''Sounds like the guy we met.''

''I recognize that home address,'' Cisco said, reading the data. ''The place is a cheap motel at the eastern city limits. At least that's a start.'' He shrugged.

As Laurel tried to search for any cross-references on Lachuk to locate his friend, she caught a brief flicker on her screen. All the characters became dim, and a message appeared at the top: ''Please enter user code or transmission will be terminated.''

She reached for the switch immediately and shut the computer off.

"What happened?"

"I'm not sure, but I think they were trying to trace us. Something must have tipped them, or the sysop—the system operator—noticed we were accessing files from outside the system. There's always a chance of getting caught when you do this type of thing, you know. Maybe your cousin was in the system at the time and realized someone was using his code. Who knows? Breaking into a computer network is never foolproof, not even with a back door."

"Let's get out of here, then, just in case they traced the call."

They packed up Laurel's equipment quickly, but as they started out the door, Cisco caught a glimpse of chrome gleaming in the fading sun from behind a stand of piñons. Instantly he pulled Laurel back into the shadows.

"What?" she whispered, looking around.

"We're being watched." He gestured toward the spot where he'd seen the flicker, explaining.

"It could be just a parked car, or a couple parking," she argued.

"It wasn't there when we first pulled in. I was very careful. I'll bet it's the same shadow man I keep telling you about. He's good, very good."

"We can't stay here, so how do we duck him?"

"We'll go back to the rez and let him follow. I can lose anyone once we get there."

After strolling casually back to the car, Cisco drove back to the reservation. By then the sun had set, and night was closing in around them. Taking advantage of the twilight, he pulled off the highway and headed straight across an open area of desert, paralleling a series of ten-foot-deep arroyos.

"Are you sure you're making the right choice heading across here? This place is like a meteor-impact zone."

"It's our only hope of losing this tail." He switched off the lights and slowed down slightly. "I've always had an instinct about this land. I can't explain it in words, but trust me when I tell you I won't get bogged down out here."

"What makes you think we're still being followed? I don't see anyone, and in this light, neither can you."

"Keep your eyes on the rearview mirror. Every once in a while, you can see a light dusting of sand rising into the air. The moonlight catches hold, and the uplifted particles seem to glow for just a few seconds before settling. There's a vehicle back there. Bank on it."

Despite the lingering heat of the day, Laurel broke out in a cold sweat. Everywhere they turned, there was more danger awaiting them. "If he's that good, can you lose him?"

"We have to," he said, and gave her a slow, lazy smile. "I have plans for tonight that require privacy."

His gaze had held hers for only a second, but the jolt that traveled all through her left her body tingling with expectation. "What do you have in mind?" she managed to ask, a shiver coursing up her spine.

"I thought I'd spice up the night for you," he said in a rich masculine voice. "Gentleness and patience can accomplish much. Shall we give *breaking and entering* an entirely new meaning?"

Chapter Nine

Cisco drove slowly across the rocky flats, trying to avoid the deep ruts and sharpened rocks that could disable their vehicle. At least he'd managed to distract Laurel from her fears. Blood thundered through his veins as he recalled the way her cheeks had flushed and her mouth had parted when he'd flirted suggestively with her.

In the past few years, no one had gotten past the armor he'd encased himself in. Yet this woman stirred him in a way he'd never dreamed possible. Having her with him so much of the time was knotting up his insides. He wanted her with every part of his being. He needed to feel her against him, naked, skin against skin. He wanted to drink in her heat and hear her crying out his name as he took her here in this land that stood in defiance of convention and civilization. He groaned as his body tightened with an unbearable pressure in response to the thought. Damn, this wasn't the time. He had to evade whoever was after them and keep them both alive.

Sometime later, he stopped the car at the base of a low mesa. He glanced at Laurel. She hadn't said a word throughout the latter part of the drive, allowing him to concentrate solely on evading their pursuer.

"I'm going to climb to the top of the mesa," he said. "Wait here. I'll be back."

"No way. I'm going with you. I can climb. Not as fast as you, that's all."

"I know, but for this, time is critical, and you'll slow me down." He smiled at her gently. "Relax. We'll both be all right. But stay in the car. That way, you can move a bit without creating any additional footsteps that might mislead me."

Cisco slipped out of the car quickly. He didn't really want to leave her in the car unprotected, but if someone was after them, he would rather face the person alone. So far, her breathing had remained steady, but her condition was sporadic, and he didn't want to jeopardize her in any way. The woman had courage and she was coming to mean a great deal more to him than just an ally or even a friend.

Cisco stopped and listened as he reached high ground. His eyes were sharp, even in the night, a by-product of being raised where there were few streetlights, he supposed.

As a cold wind swept over him, he forced his body to grow still, trying to detect anything that would give his enemy away. Minutes ticked by. Nothing. The fetish rubbed against his skin, almost chafing him. He adjusted it, but the sensation persisted. He focused away from it, using his instincts. He was being watched. No—he was being stalked.

LAUREL SHIFTED nervously in the car. Something was wrong. Why was Cisco taking so long? After the problem at his home, she'd agreed not to go charging in anywhere, to be more patient. But at the moment, keeping that promise was turning out to be more difficult than she'd ever dreamed.

She moved the switch on the dome light so it wouldn't come on, then opened the car door slightly, telling herself it was a precaution. If someone was out there, it was conceivable she might have to make a run for it, so she better be ready.

Hearing a soft rustle somewhere behind her, she froze and listened. Adrenaline coursed through her, making her heart pump frantically. At least with that hormone in her bloodstream, she could count on not having an asthma attack.

Minutes ticked by, creating their own eternities. When she heard the rustling sound again, it was much closer. As she pushed the car door open all the way and started to step out, she saw the source of the sound. There on the ground just inches below her was a rattlesnake, coiled and ready to strike.

She froze, her foot suspended in midair. The reptile did not move, except for its tongue flitting about as it sensed her presence. The sound of rattles furiously shaking was the only noise that mattered all of a sudden. She frantically tried to think of a way of escaping. Perhaps yanking her foot back was best, but she had no idea how far the creature could strike. Trying to jump over the snake seemed more foolhardy, but she didn't want to leave her foot dangling there any longer, like bait.

"Don't move." Cisco's soft whisper was almost lost in the night breeze.

She did as he asked. Then, in the blink of an eye, he threw his jacket over the coiled snake. Laurel quickly ducked back into the car, closing the door, as Cisco pushed the reptile out of the way with a stick. Carefully he lifted his jacket off the angry reptile, standing back as it wiggled away into the brush.

Moments later, they were under way. Laurel's hands were still shaking. Cisco sat ramrod straight, his face stony. She suddenly realized how much that encounter had unnerved him. To appear that emotionless actually took a great deal of effort and self-control.

"Rattlers are most active at night," he said, finally interrupting the tense silence between them. "That's when they hunt. I have a feeling that for an asthmatic, a bite might be even more dangerous than for the rest of us. Why didn't you stay in the car?"

"I heard the snake moving, but I thought it was a person sneaking up on the car," she said quietly. "I will never repeat *that* mistake again."

"With computers, you are the expert. But this land is my home. It's no shame to lean on someone whose knowledge is greater than yours. Learn to rely on my judgment, not just my ability to fight, to keep you safe."

"Then give me more to go on. You could have warned me about rattlers. Asthmatics like me don't go camping a lot, especially during the pollen season. We tend to favor rooms with air purifiers."

"So it's *my* fault?"

"You make mistakes, too—you're not perfect. And if you really think you are, and this comes as a shock, that just proves how flawed you are."

"I *am* perfect in the ways that matter. You just haven't seen the best of me yet," he said, giving her a slow, sensual smile.

Her throat tightened, and her heart began to race. "Really? Just when will this startling revelation take place?" she countered, determined to sound casual and totally unconcerned.

"Probably the same day I tell you my secret name," he said, his tone serious.

"If you're planning something this bold, don't you think you better give me some advance warning?" She wouldn't let him see how his words affected her, though her body ached with desire. She'd taken his flirting too seriously before, when he'd obviously been teasing.

"When the time's right, we'll both know it." Cisco's voice was a fiery whisper in the darkness.

Something indefinable yet incredibly powerful made the air between them dance with electricity. As they crossed farther into a low, wide canyon, her mind reeled with images too deliciously erotic to brush aside.

As the car slowed, she struggled to banish the vivid mental pictures that made her pulse beat wildly. They were caught in a life-or-death situation. She couldn't afford to fail him and herself by giving in to these imaginings.

"We're not being tailed right now," Cisco said, interrupting her thoughts. "It's time to take the initiative before our shadow catches up to us again."

"What do you have in mind?"

"Breaking and entering, like I said a while back," he answered with a thin smile. "I'm going to head for the tribal government building."

"You want to break in *there?* You can't be serious! We'll get caught!"

"It's not as impossible as you might think, though we are going to have to be careful."

"What is it that you're hoping to find out?"

"Your brother was meeting with a member of the tribe. From what we've learned from the bookie and Greg's friend, we know it's someone high ranking enough to be in on the security details pertaining to the treaty. There are only three people I know who have that clout."

"Who?"

"Henderson Atcitty, the tribal president. The attorney, Wilfred Tso. And Police Chief Begay. Of course, they have subordinates and assistants who will follow their orders, but in this case, it may be easier to go from the top down."

"I still don't understand why we're breaking in. What exactly are you looking for?"

"Once we're inside the building, we'll go to their offices. Using the password my cousin gave me, we'll try to access their private files. We won't alert a trace if we're right there using their own terminals. While you're doing that, I'll also check their appointment calendars and see who they've met with in the last few weeks. We'll look for anything that could help us identify your brother's tribal contact.''

"Do you realize that, assuming we get inside, we could still trigger some other device, anything from a burglar alarm to an automated computer shutdown installed to stop pirating?''

"We won't get caught.''

"You're very sure of yourself.''

"Yes, I am.''

His confidence was unshakable, and she found herself trusting him. From what she'd seen of Cisco so far, he wasn't one to overestimate his capabilities.

The drive seemed to take forever, even after they reached the highway again. With only the low beam of the headlights to cut through the gloom, it was as if they were traveling through a giant black tunnel. As they arrived in Window Rock, their perspective suddenly changed. Here, among the lights of a thriving community, they were more exposed and vulnerable.

"Duck down. I'm going to the back of the tribal government's main parking lot. Staff and fleet cars are kept there, and we can hide your car among the others. We'll go through the loading dock in the rear of the building. Crime isn't a big thing on the reservation, so I don't think anybody's ever bothered to replace the old latch there. It'll be fairly easy to snap open.''

Cisco parked in a row of two-door sedans. "Stay in the shadows as we cut across, and if you hear or see anyone, duck down fast. If either of us gets spotted here at this hour, we're not going to be able to explain it away that easily.''

"The only people here now are security guards?''

"And anyone working late. Since elections are coming up, that's not the remote possibility it usually is.'' He hurried across the parking lot and led her to the loading dock.

Cisco snapped open the old lock with a hefty pull. Within seconds, they had rolled up the garage-type door enough to slip under and were inside the building. "There are cameras in here, so make sure you stay alert and avoid them. They're by the main entrance mostly," Cisco muttered.

As he led the way down the hall, everything was quiet. Only the vague hum of watercoolers and soft-drink machines marred the silence that dominated that section of the building.

Laurel felt her skin prickle. There was something threatening about the silence that encompassed them. It made it hard to hide even the most minute of sounds. Her heart pounded loudly in her own ears, and her breath sounded like a hurricane.

When Cisco stopped halfway down the hall and held up his hand, she heard faint footsteps. Yet in the silence of the building, it was hard to tell how real the threat was. As she listened, the footsteps faded away.

"The tribal attorney's office is straight ahead," Cisco whispered. "He's been known to work late from time to time, and even spend the night here, so be careful. Approach carefully."

"Count on it."

Cisco crept toward the closed door, listened, then finally tried the door handle. It opened easily. He smiled back at her. "Nobody locks doors much around here. If you did that, *then* people would wonder what you're trying to hide. Mercifully there aren't too many like us willing to take advantage of the general feeling of trust that prevails."

Laurel hated the comment, though she knew he'd only been teasing. She'd lived her life based upon honesty, and now, in order to serve justice, she had to betray the codes that had structured her life. Invading someone's privacy, breaking and entering and spying on others—all were actions abhorrent to her.

"I hate this," she muttered.

"Think about it later." The spotlights illuminating sections of the parking lot shone through the partially opened curtains, giving him a clear view of the room. Cisco pulled out the attorney's leather chair. "Sit. Make yourself at home," he whispered.

She scowled at him. "We're breaking the law. At least try to look remorseful."

"I have no regrets. Despite our actions, we're upholding the spirit of the law. No harm will come to the innocent because of what we're doing. We're on the side of justice, and for now we're fighting in the only way we can."

"I know that, too, but right now I wish I were anywhere else but here." Laurel sat down behind the computer and began working. Several files were encrypted in a way that meant it would have taken hours to access them without the password. Bypassing those, she used the back door the programmer had installed into the system to get into the operating and utility systems. From there, it was easy to access the other files. Information soon began to scroll down the computer screen.

Cisco looked through the desk calendar on Tso's desk while she worked. "There's nothing in here that mentions any meetings outside the rez," he said. "Yet I know for a fact that he was at a meeting last week with Farmington officials."

"He has a computer memo-pad utility in here. Let me check that."

Cisco rose and came to stand behind her. "Have you found anything in his notes?"

"Nothing useful. He's got a new bill he wants the state legislature to pass, and he's also working with two other tribes to ease the restrictions on gambling within the reservations. It's sensitive information, but not what we're after."

She accessed the daily planner. As dates and information began to appear, she studied the entries along with Cisco. "Wait a minute. 'S. Ortega' appears here several times."

"Ortega is a common name around these parts. We can't verify it's Sammie, particularly now that he's left town."

"Here's an entry that's interesting. I recognize one of these names he has scheduled for a lunch meeting at the Ranchers Club. Harmon's been in the papers a lot lately. He's one of the racing-commission officials named in the scandal about medications used on horses at the track. I don't remember the details, though."

Cisco continued looking over her shoulder. "Scroll down. Let's see who else is listed there."

"The only other name that appears repeatedly is Harmon's." She glanced up at him. "What do you make of it?"

"It may or may not have anything to do with what's happening on our case. All this *might* prove is that Tso may like to gamble. That, in and of itself, is not a crime. Lots of VIPs in the tribe gamble. Even Chief Begay, who's as straitlaced as they come, owns interest in a racehorse."

Hearing approaching footsteps, Cisco held up a finger to his lips and turned off the lights. Someone walked up and down the hall, as if looking for something, then stopped in front of the door to Tso's office. For a moment, Laurel didn't even breathe.

As the footsteps continued down the hall, she gulped in a lungful of air. "That was close!"

"Too close. I don't like this. Turn off the computer and let's get out of here. I'm getting a bad feeling."

A cold chill swept over Laurel. She wasn't sure—she'd never been in jail, but somehow she didn't think it would be a very good place for an asthmatic.

Laurel shut off the computer, then met him at the door. "Ready."

Cisco peered down the hall, then slipped out, cautioning her to be as quiet as possible. They were three-quarters down the empty hall, when the building suddenly seemed to fill with shouts and running footsteps. An alarm sounded, rising and filling the air with its deafeningly shrill scream.

Cisco took her hand and ran down the corridor. "Get your puffer handy, because we have to make a run for it *now!*"

Chapter Ten

They'd only made it down the first corridor when sirens began to wail outside the building.

"It sounds like they're surrounding the building! Did we trigger a burglar alarm of some kind?"

"Maybe. We won't know unless they catch us, and personally I'm not interested in that option." He stopped, ducking into a recess leading to the rest rooms. "We can't go out the same way we came in. The guards must have called for backup."

Cisco stepped over to a window and glanced out cautiously through the blinds. "There's an ambulance out there, and two police cars. And here comes a rescue unit."

"They want to make sure we have medical help after they arrest us?" she blurted, aghast. "They must be planning on violence."

Cisco smiled and shook his head. "I don't think they're after us. My guess is someone in the building has had a medical emergency. Several Navajo officials are quite old." He shook his head. "No, that doesn't feel right, either. There must be more to the situation than that. There are even more cops pulling up outside now, and they're getting organized. Something else is going on, and if we don't get the heck out of here, we're going to be swept up into the middle of it."

He started to lead her down to the right, but then they heard the sound of several people moving toward them. Loud thumps were followed by silence, then running footsteps. This sequence kept repeating, and with each event the sounds continued to come closer.

"We have to find another way out. They're doing a room-to-room search, heading this way," he said.

Ducking into an open office, Cisco pulled Laurel into the shadows with him. His arms were around her, and for a moment, she allowed herself to find comfort in the safety of his embrace. Her cheek was pressed against his hard chest. He was warm and muscular, all male power and strength. A thrill coursed up her spine, and she trembled.

"We're not finished yet," he whispered. "I have a plan, but first, we have to make sure we're not running straight into a trap."

"How?"

Before he could answer, Cisco heard the sound of a familiar voice nearby. "I don't care what it takes," the man said. "Find whoever did this. If he's still here, I want him."

"That's Wilfred Tso, the tribal attorney," he whispered. "But I don't know why he's calling the shots. He's no cop. There's something strange going on here." Cisco moved closer to the doorway. "Come on. We have to move fast. We'll take a shortcut to the rear entrance by cutting through some of the adjoining offices. We can beat the search team coming down the hall if we leave now."

They moved quickly, but when they reached the end of the hall, Cisco suddenly pulled her next to the watercooler. He held a finger to his lips and crouched down beside it, shielding her with his body.

Two men rushed up to where they'd been standing a second earlier, then a third arrived. "Sir, don't go into that section of the building. We haven't searched there yet. It's not secure."

"Then search my office now, and get on your way," Tso said. "I've got to make phone calls and concentrate on damage control. The Dineh will have to be told something about what happened here today, but it will have to be handled carefully. I don't want vigilante help. Our president had many friends, as well as enemies. I have to make sure neither group turns this situation against us by interfering with what needs to be done."

When the men walked off, Cisco turned to Laurel. "The man the attorney is talking to is my brother-in-law. But this isn't his beat," he whispered. "I don't know what he's doing here. I'm going to find out, though. They won't be coming down this way for a few minutes, and that's all the time I'll need."

Taking advantage of the reduced lighting used at night to conserve energy, Cisco moved down the hall openly. As he approached Tso's office, four uniformed men came rushing around the corner, heading directly his way.

Trapped, Cisco remained cool and hoped his bluff would work. Nodding to the men, he forced himself to continue walking at a moderate pace. His only chance was to brazen it out. They'd be looking for a suspect on the run, not one who looked totally at ease. He glanced at the men, relieved that no one he knew was among them.

"Hurry," Cisco snapped. "Someone took off around the corner."

The team rushed past him. As soon as they entered the attorney's office, Cisco turned back around. As he did, he saw Laurel peering out into the hall. "Head toward the lunchroom," he said in a harsh whisper. "It's farther down the hall on the left. I'll come back for you."

Blocking out the fear he saw etched on her face, he ducked around the corner. Just then, he saw another search team ahead. SWAT officers working their way down opposite sides of the hall would soon trap Laurel in the middle, unless he acted fast.

Knowing she'd hear them coming, he tried to anticipate her next move. Her only option would be to go down the main hall. But there were cameras there.

He glanced up at the air-conditioning vent. It was his only choice. Taking a trash pail from the corner by the snack machines, he turned it over and hoisted himself up. Just as he replaced the screen, he saw his brother-in-law approach and meet with the search team.

"Anything?" Phillip asked.

"No, of course not," the other man replied. "What exactly did you guys expect us to find? This has all the earmarks of an accident."

"We had to cover all the bases. When the tribal president is discovered on the floor with his neck probably broken, we can't make assumptions."

"So, we continue searching the building?"

"Yes, definitely. Finish what you started."

As the search team moved off, Phillip saw Tso. "Is the tribal president still alive?" he asked quietly.

Tso nodded. "He's in bad shape, though. The paramedics are still working on him downstairs. They need to stabilize him enough to transport, but it doesn't look good."

"He's still alive, so we'll hold to that," Phillip answered flatly. "I don't even want to think of what might have happened if Chief Begay hadn't scheduled that meeting with him. If he hadn't acted as quickly as he did, the president would be dead by now."

"Where's the chief now?" Tso asked. "I shouldn't be in charge of the building search. He should be."

"He's working out security details. The ambulance taking the president to the hospital will need an escort, just in case this was some kind of attack."

"I was told that the chief suspects the president was reaching for a book on the top shelf and just slipped off that chair."

"I know," Phillip said. "But we can't count on his theory being right, not at this stage anyway. The president could have been attacked."

As the two men moved on down the hall, Cisco wound his way through the vent passage. By now, Laurel must have seen the camera and either decided to wait for him by hiding in the janitorial supply closet near there, or was busy searching for another way out of the building.

As he reached the main hall, Cisco peered out of the vent and saw Laurel crouched next to the wall behind a silk ficus tree. She held the inhaler in her hand, and her face was as white as the walls themselves. She looked scared, but not in serious trouble with her breathing.

He pulled a wall vent loose and called to her. Laurel glanced up. "How... ?"

"There's no time. Take my hand." He started to pull her up into the crawl space. The instant her shoulders cleared the vent, she began to cough.

"I can't...breathe in here. It's too dusty and it smells like oil or something." She jumped back down to the floor quickly. "Go. No sense in both of us getting caught."

His gut knotted as he saw her glancing up and down the hall, fear etched on her face. No one had ever been willing to make such a sacrifice for him. He gazed at her with awe. Her loyalty to him touched him more than he would have ever been able to put into words. His chest tightened with unaccustomed emotions.

"I'm not leaving, woman. You don't have a chance of getting past these teams alone." Cisco lowered himself to the floor and replaced the vent.

Getting Laurel past the cameras was going to be tough. No way she'd ever pass for a Navajo woman, not with that auburn hair of hers. "If we go past the camera, we'll be recognized for sure. But if they catch us here, then they're going to frame us for what happened to the tribal president. Our chances of getting out of jail, even on bond, will be slim.''

"What's going on around here? Did you find out?" she asked, then shook her head. "No, tell me later. I'm scared enough already.''

He gazed ahead, his mind formulating a plan. "Okay, this is how we're going to get out of here. We'll have to go past that camera, but when we get within its range, I'm going to lean down and kiss you. That will block both of our faces and throw anyone watching the tape. Fugitives would run past the camera, not stroll by, kissing. Just don't try to pull away from me."

"Have I ever?" She smiled thinly.

He gave her a crooked smile. "Get ready."

Cisco placed his arm around her shoulders. As they turned the corner, he tilted her chin upward and took her mouth with his own.

He'd expected to keep the kiss businesslike and cold. They had major problems to worry about. Yet the second he tasted her lips, desire clawed at his gut. He wanted this woman who made him feel whole and brought out a side of him he'd pushed back and forgotten until now. With her, he could be gentle, tender—traits he never bothered with anymore, because they weren't in keeping with the image he wanted to project as a cop, an image that had become his life.

As his fingers wound through her hair, keeping her near, her lips parted. He deepened the kiss, his tongue mating with her in a way symbolic of his deepest needs. Fire sizzled down his body, battering his reason.

The second they cleared the viewing field of the camera, he released her. "Damn, woman, you tempt me far too much.''

"In that, we're even."

The words stoked the fires inside him, making them burn even hotter. She desired him. The knowledge filled him with pride and passion. He glanced away from her, forcing himself to stay focused. "At least our faces were hidden. They won't be able to make a positive ID." He took her hand and hurried toward the back door. "Yet all that's going to do is slow them down. Once they find the lock's been jimmied, they're going to put things together and come after us with everything they have."

Pulling the door open a crack, he glanced outside. "We'll have to move fast. And I mean *fast*. Are you up to it?"

"Do I have any choice?"

"Not really."

"Then let's go."

As they stepped outside, Cisco saw a team of medics near the front. They were loading the wheeled stretcher carrying the president into a waiting ambulance. No one was looking in their direction.

"It's now or never," he said. "We'll run as far as the trash Dumpsters, then duck down and hide. If we try to make it all the way to the car, they'll catch us for sure."

He sprinted across with Laurel, keeping her hand firmly in his, then ducked behind the Dumpsters. "We'll wait until the emergency vehicles leave, then head for the car."

"They'll see us the second we drive out of the parking lot!" she warned. "Some of those cops are going to stay behind."

"We won't head out in their direction. We're going to take one of the little dirt tracks across country and not go on to the highway until we're several miles from here."

As the vehicles sped out with a squeal of tires and the wail of sirens, Cisco led her out of cover. "Don't run now. We'll catch somebody's eye. Stay low and walk as silently as you can from this point on."

Cisco set the pace, glad to be able to slow down for her. He'd never felt as close to anyone as he did to the woman beside him now. No partner he'd ever had in the field, no friend, had ever shown more faith, courage and loyalty.

Alert for danger, he remained aware of everything around them, particularly Laurel's breathing. She seemed to be holding up just fine, but he was determined not to continue taxing her endurance. They were working as partners, and he would watch out for her, as she had for him.

It wasn't until they were well under way that he allowed himself to relax. He glanced at Laurel and saw her leaning back in her seat, her eyes closed. "Are you okay?"

"Yes. But let me tell you, I've never been so scared in my life."

"You handled it well."

"You were pretty cool yourself."

"Not after we kissed." The memory made him ache with the need to kiss her again.

She smiled as if reading his thoughts. "Good."

"But dangerous. We can't get distracted. The stakes are higher than ever now. And the worst is yet to come. My guess is that everything is going to hit the fan soon."

"What was happening back there?"

Cisco told her what he'd learned, adding, "It was no accident, I can tell you that, though I'm not at all sure of what happened."

"If you're not sure, then how can you make that judgment?"

"I've dealt with the tribal president many times before. I remember commenting once on all the leather-bound books he kept in the top shelves of his library-office. He started laughing and told me they were there to impress people. He'd never read any of them and didn't intend to. That's why he kept them so high up on the shelves. They looked impressive, were highly visible but still out of his way."

"Then you think someone tried to kill him and make it look like an accident?"

"Yes, and failed, hopefully. Which means they'll have to try again in order to tie up that loose end."

"We have to warn the authorities."

He shook his head. "It's not necessary, at least not at this moment. Nobody will be getting close to him. Chief Begay won't allow it. He's an old hand in law enforcement, and I'd bet his gut instincts are working overtime. He knows the president better than I do, and I have a feeling he won't buy the theory of an accidental fall." Cisco paused, lost in thought. "The thing that puzzles me is what my brother-in-law was doing there."

"He may have heard the call over the radio and come in response."

"It's more than that. I don't believe in coincidences, and his appearance back at the tribal building is one too many. You see, though I can't be sure, I think he was the man who shot out your tire at my uncle's. My brother-in-law is a pretty good shot, and the outline I saw in the dark matched him. I'm beginning to suspect that he's the person following us—or at least one of them."

"Is there anyone who could tell us what he's up to, or who may be in a position to find out?"

He took a deep breath and let it out slowly. "My wife had a very good friend. She was as close to us as family. My brother-in-law has also known her for years. This woman would know, if anyone does. We could pay her a visit. I don't think she'd turn me away if I ask for her help. Her husband has been away for a week visiting his sick brother near Teece Nos Pos. But I don't want to kid you, it's still a risky proposition. I haven't seen her in many, many months, and then only in passing."

"Do we have any alternative?"

"No, not at this time. Unless you want to go looking for those guys from the bar."

"Not really. I vote we take a risk with your wife's friend." She paused. "Is she traditionalist or modern?"

"She and her husband live on a small ranch that has all the amenities. Why do you ask?"

"If they have a phone, I want to try and use the laptop to break in to the tribal police's computer again. I think I know what to watch for now, and I'll be careful not to trigger a trace. I'll tap into the data base through the communications center. That's available to everyone. I doubt they'd have a trace on that."

"If you're wrong, it'll lead straight back to her."

"I can't make ironclad guarantees, but I'm confident I won't endanger anyone, including us." When he said nothing, Laurel continued the logic of her argument. "Look at it this way. We need to know if they've managed to place us at the tribal building. We have to know if we're going to be the focus of a manhunt."

"All right, but don't try to tap in until you're alone. It's better that way. It'll be safer for her, as well as for us."

THEY ARRIVED at the isolated ranch house as the first rays of light cleared the horizon. Of course, considering the fact that livestock needed vast areas for grazing, since vegetation was sparse in the desert, Laurel supposed that the ranch was no more isolated than any other around.

"Your friend may be asleep," Laurel said, and stretched. "I wish I was," she added.

"No, she's always been an early riser." He gestured to his right. "That's her now. She's finishing her prayers to the dawn."

Cisco stepped out of the car, but asked Laurel to remain seated. "Give me a chance to talk to her."

Laurel watched him approach the young woman. She was beautiful, with waist-long black hair that flowed away from her face in the morning breeze.

She watched them, but it was impossible to read anything from their expressions. Soon they began walking back to the car. Laurel stepped out to greet them.

"You are welcome here," the woman said, her voice gentle. "This man is no saint, despite what he tells you," she said, giving Cisco a quirky smile, "but he is honest. The day he's capable of doing what they accuse him of is the day that I can pass for the First Lady's twin. You may stay here until my husband, Leroy, gets back, which won't be until late tomorrow."

Laurel smiled at her, warmed by the reception they'd been given. "Thank you for helping us."

"My name is Lois," the Navajo woman said, leading the way inside the house. "Tell me what I can do for you. Would you like something to eat?"

Laurel gave her a weary smile. "What I need the most is some sleep."

Lois gave her a sympathetic smile. "No problem." She showed Laurel to a bedroom down a dark hallway. "This is our guest room. The bed is really comfortable."

The room was sparsely furnished, just a double bed and a freestanding closet, but at the moment, the room looked as inviting as the penthouse of a four-star hotel.

Laurel sat on the edge of the bed. The mattress gave slightly, just enough to tempt her with the promise of a comfortable sleep. "This is wonderful," she said, trying to stay alert enough to be polite to their hostess.

"Get some rest, then," Lois said, "and don't worry about anything."

As Lois left, Laurel lay back on the bed. Now that she was alone, she should have been searching for a phone outlet to plug into with her laptop. But she was too tired to even think. She shut her eyes, intending to close them only for a moment, but weariness conspired against her. She drifted off to sleep almost immediately.

She wasn't sure how much time had elapsed when the sound of a barking dog jolted her awake. She sat up, checking her watch. She'd slept six hours!

Feeling guilty, she stood up, trying to force herself to become quickly alert. Her thoughts still seemed encased in cobwebs. What she really needed was a shower.

Hearing a light knock on the door, she went to answer it. Lois stood there, holding a stack of neatly folded clothing. "I thought I heard you getting out of bed. I wondered if the old mutt woke you. Cisco is still sound asleep in the living room, but he stayed up later than you did. We had some catching up to do." She placed the clothes on the bed. "From what I've heard, you've been through a living nightmare."

"It's been rough. We're both very grateful to you for offering us your hospitality."

"You and I are almost the same size. Why don't you choose something from these that you feel comfortable in? I figured you'd want a shower and a clean change of clothing when you woke up."

"You read my mind. But you've already done so much! I hate to impose any more."

"It's not an imposition. This is my chance to settle a debt. Cisco's wife, Carol, was a good friend of mine. Years ago, when we were both still newlyweds, we made a pact. If anything ever happened to one of us, the other would look after the family left behind."

"You must have shared a wonderful friendship."

"We did. I miss her. Cisco does, too, I'm sure. Carol was special."

"I asked Cisco about her, but he didn't say much. Of course, we're not exactly friends, in the conventional sense. We were thrown into this partnership by circumstances."

"Even if you were a close friend, I doubt he would have told you much. It isn't his way. It was a painful time for him, not something he'd want to talk about and remember."

"His feelings run deeper than he likes to let others see. I know that much about him."

She nodded. "They had a good marriage. Carol was the only woman who was able to compete with his passion for police work—that is, until now."

"What do you mean?"

"I've seen the way he looks at you and how he wants to protect you," Lois said, her gaze as knowing as it was penetrating. "Surely you are aware of that, too."

"You don't understand," Laurel answered, explaining patiently. "We're on the run, and he's aware that I have a problem with asthma. It's not protectiveness you see as much as concern that my health might yet interfere with what we have to accomplish."

"It's more than that." Lois met Laurel's gaze and smiled. "Deep down, I think you know that, too." She went to the door but stopped before going out. "I'm driving to the grocery store to get a few things, but I'll be back soon. There are fresh towels in this bathroom. My room is down the hall. Feel free to help yourself to whatever you need, from perfume to makeup."

"Thanks so very much. I really appreciate that."

As Lois left, Laurel stepped into the bathroom and undressed, allowing her dusty clothing to fall to the tiled floor. It was heaven to be able to rest and then wake up to a shower and clean clothes!

She took a leisurely shower, enjoying the homemade soap and yucca-scented shampoo. The warm water felt wonderful against her skin. By the time she stepped out, she felt completely revitalized.

She'd just entered the bedroom when a light knock sounded at the door. Thinking Lois had returned, she smiled, glad to have the opportunity to thank her again for her kindness. Laurel held the towel around herself with one hand and opened the door. Her breath caught in her throat as she saw Cisco standing there alone.

His eyes glittered with dark intent as his gaze seared over her with a hunger that couldn't be disguised.

Her knuckles curled around the edges of the towel. "I thought it was Lois," she managed to say in a thin voice.

"Wrong." His gaze drifted over her like a gentle lover's caress. "You're beautiful," he said, his voice a husky murmur.

Everything feminine in her came alive. Cisco wanted her, and the knowledge sent a thrill coursing through her.

Her gaze drifted down him, imagining the masculine body beneath the chambray shirt and jeans. Her heart went wild as her body responded to his maleness, leaving her tingling in all sorts of places, though he had yet to touch her.

"Do you have any idea what you're doing to me right now?" His voice was a jagged whisper.

"Or you to me?"

He drew in a breath, reached for the edges of the towel, then stopped. Perspiration beaded on his forehead as he forced himself to withdraw his hand. "No. This isn't our time. We're in danger here. That's what I came to warn you about. Hurry. Get dressed. We have to leave."

"Turn around, then tell me what's going on."

When his back was to her, she dropped the towel. Her body trembled with awareness and need, and knowing he was so close only made things worse.

"What's wrong?" she asked, disciplining her thoughts.

"You have to try and tap into the computer at the department now. We don't have much time."

"Explain."

"I can't. It's just a feeling I'm getting, like having ants crawling over me. We can't stay here."

Once dressed, Laurel hurried to the living room and set up her laptop there. As she glanced at Cisco, her gaze fell on the fetish around his neck. It seemed to grow darker as she stared at it. A heartbeat later, she began to share in the restlessness that was gnawing at him.

Laurel quickly located and downloaded all the pertinent files she could find into her own computer's memory. Just as she closed the laptop, they heard the back door open and the sound of more than one person's footsteps.

A second later, Lois and a tall Navajo man holding a shotgun burst into the room. "Don't move," the man snapped.

"Leroy," Cisco acknowledged. "Your wife said you weren't coming home until tonight." Cisco looked at Lois, then back at her husband.

"I didn't turn you in," she said sadly.

"When I heard you were on the loose, I figured you'd come here." Leroy glared at Cisco. "That's why I came home early. I'm going to turn you over to the police. Our tribal president lies dying, and it's time for you to answer to the people you've betrayed."

"We had nothing to do with what happened to the tribal president," Laurel protested.

Leroy scarcely gave her a glance. "Explain it to Police Chief Begay. I called him from Shorty's Mart after I saw Lois buying extra food and supplies. The chief's wife is gone again for the summer, and he was in a sour mood until I told him you were here. Catching you is really going to help his standing around these parts."

"Let them go, husband," Lois said calmly. "This is not the way."

"They'll go, when the police get here." He moved to one side, ensuring Lois stayed behind him.

"Help me honor the debt that I owe my friend," Lois pleaded softly.

As Leroy's gaze shifted to his wife, Laurel threw the laptop she was clutching in her hand directly at him.

Leroy staggered back from the impact, and Cisco, reacting instantly, grabbed the shotgun barrel and used the leverage to swing Leroy over the sofa. He slammed against the wall, bumping his head and knocking the air from his lungs. With a glazed look, Leroy slid down the wall, the weapon falling out of his hands and clattering to the floor.

Lois quickly picked up the shotgun. When she broke it open, they could see it hadn't even been loaded. "I'll tend to my husband. Go, and take the sacks with supplies that are still in my truck. You'll need them.''

Laurel picked up her laptop from the top of the sofa where it had somehow landed. It didn't appear to have sustained any external damage. With a bit of luck, it would still work.

Cisco stood at the door, holding it open. ''Come on. Hurry. He'll get his bearings in another second or two.''

As they rushed out the door, Laurel gave Lois a worried glance. ''Will you be all right?''

She nodded. ''He will blame you two, not me. But you must go *now*. You have your own destiny to follow. Walk in beauty,'' she said, gently adding the Navajo blessing.

Cisco took the grocery sacks from the back of Lois's pickup and hurried to Laurel's car. In a few seconds, they were under way.

''Where are we going?'' she asked.

''Not far, apparently,'' he answered, pulling out onto the highway. ''There's a roadblock ahead.''

Chapter Eleven

Cisco slowed down and turned off the highway onto a dirt side road. His hands clenched and unclenched around the steering wheel, betraying his tension. "I don't think they spotted us. They're still too busy getting the roadblock set up. The good news is that your new, shiny little car looks just like any other well-used vehicle around the rez."

"Don't expect me to do handsprings about that," Laurel answered as Cisco drove down a bumpy, deeply rutted track that seemed to lead nowhere. "I know you've got to avoid the police, but do you know where you're going?"

He gave her a wry smile. "I'm going to do the last thing they expect."

He waited for her to ask, but she remained silent. Puzzled, Cisco glanced over at her. Comprehension dawned over him as he studied her expression. The woman was showing him that she trusted his judgment enough to put herself in his hands.

The knowledge made him feel soft and all crazy inside. He'd never felt that way about any woman, except his late wife. They were truly allies now, working together as one.

"If they decide to search along this road for us, it's going to be tough to hide. There's nothing around here," she commented matter-of-factly.

"There's a house just ahead. If I'm right, it'll be empty."

"Won't they check there, once they fail to intercept us at the roadblock?"

"No. Chief Begay's home is the last place they'll figure we'd go, particularly because he's got two Dobermans as watchdogs."

Her eyes widened. "How do you plan to get in there?"

"One of my relatives trained the chief's dogs. I used to visit the kennels once in a while and play with them. They aren't mean, at least not with me. They'll remember my scent."

"And if they don't?"

He shrugged. "I'll go in first, of course, but the dogs usually aren't a problem unless you're afraid of them. They'll sense that."

"I'm not generally calm around dogs who are trained to rip someone's throat out," she snapped.

"I'll take care of the dogs. Leave that to me."

"What makes you think the house will be empty?"

"You remember what Leroy said? The chief's wife has gone for the summer. She leaves every year to help her sister tend sheep up in the mountains. Since their kids moved off the rez to take classes in Albuquerque, nobody else will be there. The chief's married to his job, like a lot of cops."

They arrived at the house several minutes later. Two dogs stood behind the chain-link fence, staring at the car, but not making a sound.

"They don't look vicious," she said slowly. "That means they probably are."

Cisco reached into his pocket and took out a candy bar. "Good thing I raided Lois's stash. I have a feeling I'm going to need this now."

He stepped out of the car and walked to the gate, which wasn't locked. Obviously the chief didn't think it was necessary. As he unlatched the gate and stepped inside, the two dogs charged up to him, growling and showing inches of teeth.

Cisco pressed his back to the fence and froze. "Come on, guys, remember me?" He slowly eased to the ground, ending up on his knees.

The dogs, surprised by his action, backed up a step but kept growling. Continuing to speak softly, Cisco carefully offered each dog a piece of toffee, placing it on the ground before them. As the sticky candy clung to their teeth and gums, their animated chewing became the entire focus of their attention.

Cisco patted the one closest to him. "That's a good boy!" The dog wagged its bobbed tail.

Cisco finally stood up. "It's okay. They remember me now." He held the gate open for Laurel.

As Laurel stepped inside the gate, the female dog suddenly stopped chewing and trotted over to her. She froze, scarcely breathing.

"It's okay, girl," Cisco said, patting the dog.

The dog watched Laurel for several seconds, then started sniffing Cisco's hand curiously. He gave the dog another piece of candy.

"When they were pups, they had a real weakness for the same toffee bars I eat," he said with a grin. "I gambled that they'd remember the candy, and me by association."

"I thought you were a goner when they charged up to you."

"They looked impressive, I'll admit, but I knew I'd be okay. They're trained to defend but, like most dogs, they key on certain behavior patterns, like aggression and attempts at stealth. I'd learned from my cousin what not to do."

They walked up to the front door and went inside without any problems. The door had been left unlocked. Cisco glanced around. The place had a bachelor feel to it already. The chief's dinner still lay half-eaten on the coffee table.

"Summers must be hard on the chief. His wife never wanted to move from their old home. It was near her sister's and the rest of their family. She doesn't consider this place hers, though by Navajo custom, the house belongs to the woman. The chief, used to the station, likes modern conveniences, but his wife prefers the old ways, like cooking over a fire. Every summer she goes up to the mountains, using her sister as an excuse to get away for a few months.''

Cisco stood by the pile of law-enforcement magazines that littered the floor beside the couch. It had a familiar feel to him. ''I'm not sure why the chief doesn't just retire and go up with her. He spends most of his days at the station instead of home when she's not here. A home with one of the marriage partners missing feels emptier than anything else on earth.''

As if she could feel the pain behind his words, Laurel placed one hand on his arm. He covered it with his own. No words were necessary. With just one touch, she'd told him that the struggle wasn't his alone. Not anymore. Perhaps it had been nothing more than simple humanity. Yet by reaching out to him, she'd once again slipped inside his defenses, carving a spot for herself in his thoughts.

Cisco walked to the kitchen and took a loaf of bread and a package of cold cuts from the fridge. ''I can just see the chief's face when he finds out we were here, eating his food.'' He laughed as he fixed a sandwich for her and himself.

Laurel took a large bite, aware suddenly of how hungry she was. ''From the glimpses I got of the stuff I downloaded before Leroy interrupted us, I think the chief is in big trouble right now. My guess is he wants to make sure he can retire with his pension when the time comes. For that to happen, he's got to stay in charge while the heat is on him.''

''What are you talking about?'' Cisco asked.

''You're making news, both on and off the reservation, and making the chief look bad. The tribal council wants explanations from you and from the police department.

They hold the chief responsible for all the bad press the tribe's been getting. The chief, in turn, sent out a general memo to the entire department, saying you're to be brought in by any means necessary."

Cisco finished his sandwich, then glanced at the desktop computer on the small table in the living room. "Take a look at his terminal here. I doubt he'll encrypt his files at home, and we may find a few pieces of information that'll be useful to us."

Laurel went to the computer as Cisco sorted through a stack of mail on the chief's desk. "Did you learn anything about your brother-in-law from Lois?"

"Nothing new. Phillip's hated me for a long time, and he's determined to haul us in. I still don't know what he was doing at the tribal building, unless he's allied himself with Chief Begay and the tribal attorney, who both seem to be out for my blood."

He pulled a letter from an opened envelope that held the tribal seal, and read it. "The chief is under fire from a variety of sources, it seems. Some in the council are opposed to his continued term as police chief because of his ties to the gambling world with that racehorse he owns. The fact that I've managed to elude him is being used to support the claim that he's got too many conflicting interests, and he's no longer able to perform his duties adequately."

"Do you know if he's a serious gambler? If he does more than race that horse, he may be up to his neck in whatever is going on with my brother. And what better person for Greg to trust, than the chief of the Navajo tribal police."

"I've known this man for many years. We used to talk about our families over coffee before the shift started. He's dogmatic, stubborn and a pain in the neck at times, but I don't think he's capable of jeopardizing the treaty for personal gain."

Laurel retrieved the letter file. "Come read this memo he wrote to the tribal council," she said slowly.

Cisco noted her tone and felt the hairs at the back of his neck stand up. He looked over her shoulder, reading the screen.

Detective Watchman has been suspended, pending criminal investigation. There are recent reports that he's been engaging in activities detrimental to the interests of the tribe. Rest assured that I've assigned officers to locate Watchman and bring him into custody to avoid unfavorable publicity. I've informed the press of my actions.

"So he's using the ongoing search for us to divert attention from himself," Cisco said pensively.

"He's using the press, playing you up as a threat to the tribe. He's victimizing you to save his own skin."

Cisco read it over again, allowing the words to sink in. Even those in the tribe he'd always held in high regard were turning against him for reasons of their own. The knowledge stung.

"What he's doing is simply human nature," Cisco said, forcing his tone to remain casual. "He's trying to save his job and the status he's got here. A man has the right to protect himself."

"But not at the expense of an innocent person. You wouldn't have done that to him, had the positions been reversed."

Laurel was right about that. He would never have done that to anyone. He pushed back his anger, knowing it would only cloud his thinking. While Laurel browsed through the computer directory, searching for interesting files, he focused his attention on the rest of the mail.

"We're in more trouble than we thought," she said suddenly. "Someone recognized us from the security camera at the government building. I think you better take a look at this memo the chief was sending to the tribal council."

Laurel stood up and moved aside, allowing Cisco to take her chair.

He read the report, fighting the gut-wrenching feeling that the net was being tightened around them. Time would prove they were both completely innocent, but at the moment, he was beginning to doubt that they'd be able to stay alive until then.

"They've become convinced you and I are responsible for Kyle's murder and the assault on the tribal president," she stated in a shaky voice.

"And they'll do their best to find evidence to support that. Believe me, when cops want someone or something badly enough, they'll work around the clock until they succeed. All they can get against us is circumstantial evidence, but enough pieces strung together can be just as damning."

"It gets worse," she warned. "Read the very end of that report."

Cisco scrolled down. A large sum, almost the equivalent of a year's salary, had shown up in his bank account.

"Someone's sure doing their best to see I burn," he growled.

Laurel placed a hand on his shoulder. "You've known all along that you have enemies. This is just another attempt against you."

Cisco gazed at Laurel, searching her eyes for a seed of doubt or perhaps regret that she'd become part of the trouble he'd been in. Yet all he could see reflected there was compassion. She seemed to sense how the pain of betrayal was knifing at him.

What she didn't know, couldn't know, was that their desperate situation had all been part of a master plan, now gone dangerously awry. He wasn't guilty, but the ones who could have furnished proof of that now had agendas of their own.

"Feeling abandoned by the people you trusted is the worst feeling in the world," she said softly. "I felt that when my father turned away from Greg and me. But you're not alone in this. I'm with you all the way."

"But not by choice."

She smiled. "I never said I was perfect. But I do believe in you."

"Even after you saw this? Why?" Cisco held her gaze. She'd known the bitter taste of betrayal, yet instead of making her cynical, it had opened her heart to compassion. Her gentleness touched his battle-scarred heart. "Don't you wonder if it's true, if somehow there's more to this mess than what I've told you?"

"Oh, I'm certain there's more to this than you've said."

Her answer surprised him. Maybe she was staying with him out of necessity, and her faith in him was based on expediency.

"You've held things back," she continued, "but I have a feeling it's out of a higher sense of loyalty, rather than the desire to keep something from me. You're not a game-player. You're up-front about everything. That just isn't the trait of a crook."

"Maybe I'm a new breed of crook." Cisco narrowed the gap between them. "I wish you'd never become involved in this mess, but I am glad I found you." As he brushed her face with his palm, she leaned into him, kittenlike. A flash of heat wound through him. "You deserve so much more than days and nights on the run."

"I've found a friend. That's gift enough."

"We're more than friends, though less than lovers. For now," he added in a voice as rich and deep as distant thunder.

Hearing the sound of sirens out on the highway, he strode quickly to the window. "We can't stay here any longer. It's time to go. At least we have more information now."

"Where to, then?"

"We have to find the tribal attorney and get some answers from him. He's involved somehow, and we need to know what part he's playing in this."

After putting everything back the way they'd found it, they left the chief's home, closed the dogs inside the gate and headed out across the desert. This time, they followed a narrow pair of tire ruts in the opposite direction. "If we keep moving west, we'll connect with another junction in the highway several miles from the roadblock."

"What's your plan after we find the attorney?"

"I intend to confront him, face-to-face."

"Why? What can you possibly expect to prove by that? He'll just turn you in."

"No, I don't think so. He won't want the publicity that'll result from having the tribe's most publicized fugitive being arrested in his own home."

"So we'll invite ourselves into his house and try to get him to help us?"

"No, not 'we.' This must stay between him and me. That's the only chance I have of getting some straight answers. I have a feeling he'll know, or at least suspect, who's behind the money that appeared in my account out of nowhere. It's probably the person who's pushing the hardest to build a case against me. The attorney is also the one person who will know what, if any, progress has been made on recovering the treaty. After I have answers to those questions, I'll have a better idea of what we should do next."

They drove slowly across the desert. The heat beat down on the car as they traveled across land filled with low mesas and deep, water-carved arroyos. The sparse vegetation had come to life with the summer rains, and desert flowers bloomed.

"I'm starting to get really scared," Laurel said slowly, her thoughts returning to their precarious situation. "Instead of finding answers, all we're really doing is getting deeper and deeper into heaven knows what kind of trouble."

"Frustration and fear can undermine you faster than anything else. You have to fight that." Cisco reached for her hand. "We are making progress, though as it often is, it's slow going."

"Aren't you worried at all?"

"At the beginning, I was confident that I could get all the answers I needed quickly. But now I know that's not possible. People I trusted have betrayed me."

"Like Chief Begay?"

"Him, and others, too."

"Who?" she insisted. "We've been through a lot together. Don't you think it's time you stopped holding back on things? To survive this, we're going to have to show greater loyalty for each other than we are for anything or anyone else."

"Trust me and believe in me as you've done. You know the truth, what else is there?"

Cisco saw the disappointment on her face and felt as if he'd been kicked in the gut. This woman's company and her friendship had come to mean more to him than he had any right to claim. Yet what drew him to her was stronger than logic or intellect. He fought against an overwhelming sense of futility. Feelings like these only led to pain. They were born in dreams that soon turned to nightmares. He knew too much about himself and life to believe in happily-ever-afters. Men like him were not meant for love, because their love would destroy whatever it touched.

They arrived at Tso's hillside home forty minutes later. The neighborhood was quiet. Houses, larger than most on the reservation, were spaced on half-acre lots along a tall bluff overlooking the San Juan River below. He'd been here a dozen times before, but it had never been as risky as it was now.

"Keep an eye out for patrol cars," Cisco warned. "The department takes care of this area, since many of the tribal bigwigs live here." Cisco parked against the curb, just outside an empty driveway. It was the perfect spot if they ended up having to make a fast getaway. "If anyone comes by, duck down before they see you."

AS THE TEMPERATURE in the car rose, Laurel cracked open the door. Cisco had been gone for an eternity. Then again, maybe it was the heat that made it seem that way. She got out of the car and sat in the shade it cast. As she leaned back against the side of the car, she heard the sound of a vehicle driving up the road. A police cruiser was approaching.

She forced herself to remain very still and prayed she wouldn't be spotted on the curbside. The patrol car went by at a snail's pace but showed no discernible interest in her vehicle. After a minute, it turned the corner. She glanced up and down the street, searching for Cisco, but he was nowhere to be seen.

Fear turned her throat dry. What if something had gone wrong and cops had been waiting inside? All kinds of scenarios flashed in her mind. She had to get closer to the attorney's house and take a look. If Cisco was okay, then she'd come back to the car.

Staying low beside the stunted junipers and desert shrubs that made up the landscaping, she approached the side of the house. She squeezed in between the juniper hedge and the adobe wall and, trapped beside the cool mud bricks, she listened to the conversation going on inside.

"When the president approached me with his plan, I was glad for the opportunity to get involved," Cisco said. "Only the three of us were to know that the bribery allegations against me were part of the undercover operation. That tactic was effective at the beginning, but now, things have changed. I need my good name back in order to track down leads on the reservation. This case has taken a twist none of us expected. It's no longer a matter of pursuing thieves beyond our borders. The answers lie here on our own land."

Laurel smiled to herself. So it had been as she suspected. He was innocent. From what she'd just heard, he simply hadn't confided in her because of his tie to the department.

"You knew the risks when we set up this operation. Don't ask me to help you out now—I can't. My appointment as tribal attorney is dependent on the goodwill of certain people. Coming out with the truth now would be political suicide."

"It was agreed from the beginning that the truth would be revealed whenever I gave the word. Don't back out now."

"The agreement was that, in an emergency, you could divulge the truth to whomever you wished, and we would back you up. But circumstances have changed."

The attorney's words fell over her senses like a blanket of fire, the initial pain so intense, it soon numbed her. Her heart ached from Cisco's betrayal. Why hadn't he confided in her? Had he wanted to play on her sympathies so she'd help him find Greg? It hadn't been a matter of higher loyalties, as she'd thought. He'd been free to tell her, and others had known the truth all long.

Perhaps she'd only been kidding herself. To Cisco, she'd only been a means to an end. Laurel forced herself to concentrate and listen to the angry voices coming from inside the house. She had to know the whole story.

"At least tell Chief Begay," Cisco insisted. "He doesn't even know the treaty is missing or that you helped set me up."

The attorney laughed. "No way. He's got problems of his own. Keeping his people focused on tracking you down is all that keeps the heat off him. That's why he appointed Sergeant Aspass, your brother-in-law, to head the investigation against you."

"What?"

Tso chuckled. "That was a touch of genius on Begay's part, actually. No one wants your hide more than Phillip does. Did you know he's already put through the paperwork to access your bank and telephone records? The chief is really impressed. Let's face it, the more of a stir Aspass creates against you, the better off Begay will be. If Begay had to go on record now and tell everyone that the case against you is part of an unsuccessful investigation *he* didn't even know about, he might as well kiss his career goodbye. Of course, if you had *answers* for us, like the location of the treaty, then it would be a different matter."

"I'll *get* answers," Cisco said, his voice reverberating with anger. "But first, I want you to tell me who padded my bank account. A deposit was made right after the assault on the president's life."

"How did you know that?" Tso demanded.

"I know it. That's enough."

"Not for me. I want to know how you found out."

"Why? Were you responsible for that?"

"You were in the tribal government building with that security guard's sister and left your calling card on the surveillance video. I figured I'd just help your cover by implying you'd been bribed again. It seemed like a good idea at the time."

"Just so I'm clear on this," Cisco said, his voice low and deadly. "You're willing to let me go down so that everyone's political career will remain nice and safe?"

"All I'm asking is that you get me something to fight with," Tso countered. "Find the answers you promised to deliver when we began the operation. Be reasonable. If I went on the record and admitted that you've been working undercover for us, we'd lose any chance of recovering our treaty. The idea all along was to keep the theft a secret while you went after it. By the time the Dineh found out it had been stolen, we'd have the thieves in custody and the treaty back safe and sound. If you recall correctly, you did agree to do whatever was necessary to get the treaty back. In fact, you *insisted* it was a matter of personal and family honor."

"Don't try to tell me you're worried about my honor. You're just trying to save your own skin at my expense."

"Let's just say I'm a survivor. So do your job and get out of my way while I do mine. Don't even think of turning against me. It's the last thing you can afford."

"You're cutting your own throat in the long run. By refusing to clear me now, you're going against the president's own orders."

"It's my call now, under the circumstances. And should the president's health improve, he'll be free to countermand my decision. But if I were you, I wouldn't count on his help. He likes being tribal president, and right now, you're a political time bomb. Now get the hell out of here before someone sees you."

She heard some quick footsteps, then the attorney's voice rose in panic.

"You're a damn fool, Watchman. If you take one more step toward me, I'll shoot you myself."

"You don't have the skill or the guts to take me out, Tso. And I wouldn't dirty my hands with your blood. Stop being paranoid. I was only going to check outside before I leave."

Laurel hurried back to the car. Cisco's undercover operation had gone horribly wrong, and now they were both wanted by the authorities. No matter how she looked at it, she was trapped in an alliance with a man who was a friend to no one, including himself.

A DARK SILENCE DESCENDED over Cisco and Laurel as they drove back out into the desert on a little-used gravel road. The temperature inside the car was hot enough to bake bread. Cisco was glad the clouds were gathering overhead, knowing that they would eventually offer a respite from the unrelenting heat.

At first, he'd been too angry with Tso to think much about it, but as the miles stretched out, her silence began to get under his skin.

"You're too quiet. What's wrong?" he asked at last.

"I have nothing to say," she answered calmly.

He allowed the silence to stretch out longer. As the road circled farther south, the sky became like an inverted black bowl. Torrential rains would come soon. Already the air was stirring with a breeze. "We'll go to high ground and set up camp for the night," he said. "Nobody will be able to sneak up on us out here, and right now, we have to guard our backs."

"You're good at protecting yourself. I suppose I'll continue to get the benefit of that, so long as I'm with you."

The warmth he'd associated with Laurel—which was so much a part of her smile, of her touch—had disappeared. Someone distant and emotionless was in the place of the gentle woman he'd known.

Cisco said nothing for a moment, considering what was happening. "As usual, you didn't do as I asked," he concluded, comprehension finally dawning over him. "You left the car and overheard my conversation with the attorney." He had no doubt about it as he glanced at her stony expression. "You understood all along about my loyalty to the department."

"The secret *was* yours to share, Cisco. There were others, too, who knew the entire story. You used the secrecy of your undercover operation as an excuse to keep from taking me into your confidence, to keep me at arm's length. You don't let people close to you, that's why you're so alone. I thought you and I shared something special. But to you, my loyalty was simply another tool at your disposal to help you achieve your goal. You don't know the meaning of friendship, or of—" She clamped her mouth shut.

Laurel's pain speared through Cisco. As it had been in the past, he'd hurt the one person he'd wanted most to shield.

He deserved her anger, but feeling her pain was destroying him inside.

"What do you know about hope and how it betrays," Cisco demanded, his voice taut, "or about dreams that lure you like a siren song, then rip out pieces of your heart and leave you bleeding?"

Laurel looked at him in surprise. Her eyes, so filled with anger seconds before, were suddenly awash with compassion. "I know all about wishes that come from the heart, and how reality often shatters them. After enough hurt, it's tempting to stay on the sidelines of life, never truly getting involved in anything, shielding yourself at all costs. But I also know the price of decisions like that, which in their own way eventually become a death sentence."

He'd known life had been hard for her but, until that moment, Cisco hadn't realized the dear price she'd paid with her own tears. He'd known her background, but facts alone hadn't conveyed the depth of wounds life had inflicted on her. One parent dying, another who didn't care, her health—all spoke of strength forged in adversity. Her willingness to trust him, as she had at one time, despite the lessons life had given her, chipped away at the ice walls he'd fought so hard to keep in place. "Don't."

"Don't what? Don't care? It's too late. I hurt because I *do* care and because perhaps I thought you did, too. But now I see I was only looking at a mirage. You've forgotten how to reach out to someone and how to truly open your heart."

"I haven't forgotten," he said quietly.

Peals of thunder shook the car. The earth had lost all color, shrouded in the dark grays and blackness of the angry skies overhead. Cisco drove to an area of high, solid ground and parked. Aware of the lightning risk, he made sure they weren't the highest objects around. A small hill rose up farther ahead.

"Hear me out before you judge me any further," he said. "It's important that ... you understand."

"Important?"

"To me. Please." Cisco reached for her hand, but Laurel pulled away. Before he could stop her, she threw open the car door and ran out.

Chapter Twelve

Cisco hurried out, around and caught up to her easily. He stood with her next to the shelter of a piñon tree. The wind was picking up swirling around the hill and filling the air with the dusty scent of rain. "Come back to the car. It's going to pour soon."

"No. You'd better tell me here anyway."

"Just what you want to hear." Do you still have enough to do your job next time?"

"Just I mean, I can just tell something locked up here with you."

Without Cisco swallowed hard his feelings. He focused on trying to reach Laurel before he'd slipped so far away from him. I'd have me go back. He placed a gentle hand on her shoulder. "Let me show you just once more.

"You always find these for emotions without part of you."

"It's easy to make it easier for you to find my feelings."

He placed his palm on her pulse point is seen. Holding his fingers, he forced her to turn around and face him. You know what and you're not some scare to believe that you just held your life breath. All along I've done my best to protect you ... won't give up at all."

He could count who wants to be behind a past lover impulse stood away from him. "You could have told me. I have better I'd said.

Chapter Twelve

Cisco hurried after Laurel and caught up to her easily. He stood with her next to the shelter of a piñon tree. The wind was restless, swirling around the hill and filling the air with the damp scents of rain. "Come back to the car. It's going to pour soon."

"No. I can't breathe in there anymore."

Fear shot through him. "Do you still have enough of your medications?"

"It isn't asthma. It's just too stifling, locked in there with *you.*"

Aching, Cisco swallowed his own feelings. He focused on trying to reach Laurel before she slipped so far away from him he'd never get her back. He placed a gentle hand on her shoulder, but she drew away once more.

"Everything I mistook for emotion was just part of your strategy to make it easier for you to find my brother."

He placed his hands on her shoulders again. Holding her steady, he forced her to turn around and face him. "You know *me* and you know better than to believe what you just said. Think it through. All along, I've done my best to protect you—from me most of all."

"I'm not a child who needs to be looked after!" She stepped back away from him. "You could have told me. I heard what Tso said."

"Then remember *all* of that conversation. I was free to divulge the truth to someone else only in case of an emergency. There was no emergency. My keeping that secret did not place you in more danger than you already were. I wasn't prepared to break my word simply because it would have made things easier for me with you in the long run." He captured her gaze and held it. "Think it through. Would you want any part of a man who broke his word so easily?"

"With you, everything is always logical!" She hurled the words at him, tears stinging her eyes. "For once in your life, *stop thinking!* If you *feel* anything for me, then *show* me!"

In a heartbeat, Cisco pulled her to his chest. His kiss was hard and hungry. He wanted Laurel, and her goading had made his control snap. He thrust his tongue forward, tangling with hers, filling her mouth in the way he wanted to fill her softness.

She sighed, melting into him. He felt her surrender with every fiber of his being. Her own needs raged as hot as his own. She wanted to be conquered as much as he wanted to conquer her.

With a peal of thunder and a lightning flash that lit the desert in an unearthly glow, the skies suddenly opened up. Torrential rains cascaded down over them.

He held her firmly against him, and she made no move to pull away. "You want to know secrets," he growled in her ear. "But are you prepared to make them your own and risk the pain that may yet be waiting? Are you willing to open your heart and your body to me?"

"There's nothing I would deny you," Laurel managed to answer, trembling with desire.

The yearning he saw in her eyes matched the burning passion inside him. Oblivious to the cold rain pouring down, he stripped off his shirt, his arm still wound around her waist. As her hand caressed his rain-slicked skin, he groaned.

Cisco tried to pull her against him, but her hands moved downward, unsnapping his jeans. Her touch felt like firebrands on his skin.

Tenderness, this woman needed tenderness from him. He had to slow the pace down. The words swam in his head as he pulled off her blouse and tasted her rain-soaked flesh.

Laurel shuddered wildly as his lips found her breasts and sucked the tiny peaks into his mouth. "No more, please. It's too much and not enough."

"That's how it should be, until that moment when you feel me inside you," he whispered. Undressing her and kissing the areas he exposed, he dropped to his knees, leaving a hot trail down the length of her body with his tongue.

She writhed against Cisco, her hips thrusting instinctively toward him. Knowing her passion was at fever pitch, he gently pulled her downward until she knelt before him. Holding her close, he allowed her to feel his manhood pressing between her thighs. She whimpered softly, positioning herself to welcome him.

Lightning flashed jaggedly across the sky as he thrust into her, her softness encasing his flesh like a warm velvet glove.

She clung to his shoulders, weakened by desire, and he wrapped his arms around her tightly, supporting her as he thrust into her again and again.

Her soft cries incited him beyond reason. Then he felt her surrender. She came apart inside, her love engulfing him in warmth. With a cry of triumph, he exploded inside her.

Shuddering, he continued to hold her against him, nuzzling her neck and whispering of his love. The rain had gentled and now drifted down their bodies in soothing comfort. He kissed her eyes, her cheeks and then her mouth.

"I'm no longer a man of secrets, not with you," he said. "Our people say there are no secrets between a man and a woman who have made love."

She nuzzled the hollow of his neck. "But I still don't know your secret name."

He chuckled softly. The clouds parted, revealing a starry twilight sky as he stood, lifted her to her feet, then picked her up in his arms. "It is Naabaahii," he answered, carrying her back to the car. "It means 'Raider.' Today, for the first time in years, I think I lived up to it."

"No. A raider takes what isn't his and perhaps shouldn't be. You took what was freely given and gave a gift of equal value."

He stretched out in the rear seat of the car, gently drawing her body over his and wrapping his arms around her. "Sleep now. Desert nights can be cold, but tonight, I will keep you warm."

WHEN LAUREL OPENED her eyes, it was already morning. She was nestled in a corner of the rear seat, a blanket she'd kept in the trunk draped over her. Cisco wasn't in sight. She sat up, holding the blanket against her, and saw her clothes draped over the front seat, dry.

Hearing the crackle of a fire outside, she turned her head toward the sound. Cisco was standing bare chested near a roaring fire. His mahogany skin gleamed smooth, all muscle and masculine beauty.

"Come have breakfast," he invited. "Lois packed quite a bit for us. How about orange drink, and bread and chili?"

"Sounds fine. I'm famished!"

Laurel ate her food greedily, wondering if it was the outdoors or making love that had made her ravenous. Even her asthma had improved out here, away from the city's exhaust fumes.

Cisco seemed unusually quiet as he ate breakfast. His gaze was focused on the Chuska Mountains to the west, and his thoughts seemed far away.

As his silence stretched out, sorrow washed over her. He was retreating from her again. Their lovemaking had brought them closer, but that closeness was fading now in the light of day, and there seemed to be no way she could stop it.

"We need an edge to get out of the hole others have dug for us," Cisco said pensively, "but I can't think of what that could be." He stood and began to pace. "I wish I could change the way things have turned out, for your sake more than my own."

"My having overheard your argument with the tribal attorney could work on our behalf now. You need to prove you are still, and always have been, a good cop. I could swear to what I overheard—that it was all part of an undercover operation."

"We'd need more proof. We've spent too much time together for you to be a credible witness."

"Who else knows the truth about your involvement?"

"The attorney's administrative assistant was just outside the office the day we concocted this plan. It's possible she knows what's going on."

"How can we find her? And do you think she'd turn you in?"

"No, quite the opposite. In fact, I think she'd do her best to protect us. She's known my uncle for many years, and they're friends. Even if she doesn't know the truth and didn't overhear the conversation that day, I don't think she'd call the police, out of deference to my uncle."

"Then let's go pay her a visit. It's still early, too soon for her to have gone in to work."

It took them forty minutes to arrive at a wood-and-stucco house near the old high school, now an oversize elementary facility. An old pickup with a dented fender was parked near the front. Soon an energetic woman in her late fifties came to the door and waved an invitation inside. As Cisco and Laurel walked up to the entrance, the aroma of coffee tempted them.

"Evelyn Jim is never at ease around strangers, so we'll have to tread carefully," Cisco explained to Laurel.

As they entered the home, the woman smiled at Cisco, then gave Laurel a look filled with curiosity.

"She's a friend," Cisco said. "We came because we need your help and we have no place else to turn."

Evelyn waved them toward the kitchen table. "Sit. Now tell me what I can do for you." Evelyn sat across the table from Cisco and Laurel. "I hope you know that you've put me in a very difficult situation by coming here."

"I truly regret that. We'll leave as soon as possible," Cisco assured her. "But we need some information from you. Do you remember the day I went in for my last meeting with the attorney and the tribal president?"

Evelyn nodded but said nothing.

"You were close by when some sensitive issues were discussed."

"I was at my desk, working," she replied cautiously. "I wasn't asked to leave."

Cisco regarded her for a long time. "You know the truth, don't you?"

Evelyn glanced at Laurel, then back at Cisco. "Is this something that should be discussed in front of an outsider?"

"Normally, no, but the situation is far from normal. Surely you know what's been happening."

"Yes, but I don't understand any of it," she said. "They're saying that the man who supposedly bribed you also paid you again after the president's accident—or attack." Evelyn shook her head. "Maybe you changed your mind about what you were supposed to do and it all ended up becoming real."

"You know it was all set up from the beginning. I was handpicked by the president himself."

"And now he's in the hospital, under guard." Evelyn pursed her lips thoughtfully. "I don't know who is guilty and who isn't. But it's not for me to judge. I go in, do my

work and bring home my paycheck. You came to me for
answers, but I have none to give."

One question burned in Laurel's mind. She hadn't meant
to speak, hadn't wanted to risk making the woman even
more ill at ease than she already was. But before she knew
it, the words slipped out.

"Who is the man who supposedly bribed him?" she
asked, gesturing toward Cisco. "If you could tell us that
much, it would help."

The woman looked at her coldly. Distrust for a stranger
clearly showed on her features. "They say it was a *bilagáana,* a white man, by the name of Harmon."

Cisco stood and walked to the door. "I won't forget your
help."

The woman smiled. "I won't let you."

As the early-morning sun rose over the horizon, Cisco
drove out of the reservation toward Farmington, taking the
back roads through Fruitland and Kirtland to avoid en-
countering police patrols. Cisco never spoke, though his
face was lined in concentration.

"Don't do this," Laurel said softly.

He gave her a startled glance. "What?"

"You're shutting me out and drawing away from me, but
I don't know why."

His hands opened and closed around the steering wheel
in a familiar gesture that betrayed his troubled state of mind.
"I don't want to hurt you, but I may not be able to prevent
it."

Laurel felt her lungs tighten, but she forced herself not to
reach for her inhaler. She didn't want his sympathy; she only
wanted the truth. "I don't understand."

"Your feelings for me have led you into more danger than
you might have faced on your own. Eventually they could
end up destroying you. I'm tired of hurting the ones I want
most to protect. I won't go through that again. You were
right about me, after all. I am not capable of giving my

heart to anyone. Self-preservation has become too in-grained in me.''

"The ability to love is not something you can lose. It can be buried under negative emotions like fear, distrust or anger, but given half a chance, it will surface again."

"That's just it. I'm not sure I'm capable of lowering my guard and allowing it to happen. Not anymore."

Pain flickered across Cisco's face like shadows from a distant fire. Was he thinking of his wife or the pain her death had caused him? Or was it more? Did he now resent her because she'd brought him face-to-face with emotions he'd wanted to close out of his life forever? To reach for the future, he had to settle the past. But she wouldn't ask for his trust. Whether or not to confide in her would have to be his choice. She wouldn't beg for what he wasn't ready to give.

"This is something you will have to work out," she said sadly. "But I will tell you this. I have experienced enough of life to know how fragile it is. You have to be ready to reach out whenever it brings something good your way. Otherwise, the best of everything will pass you by."

As they left the farming community of Kirtland behind them, sorrow filled her. Last night, for one brief moment in time, she'd had it all. But now it had slipped through her fingers. She suddenly felt weary, of trying, of hoping and even of love.

Shaking the feeling, she forced herself to think of the answers they had yet to find. Her brother's safe return, and even Cisco's and her futures, depended on their success now. As she glanced at Cisco, she saw him check his rear-view mirror. "Are we being tailed?"

"Not that I can see. But I'm getting that feeling again."

Laurel glanced at the fetish around his neck. Once again she could have sworn it had darkened. "What now?"

"We forget about a tail we can't see and run down that address we found for Lachuk. Just because we haven't seen that pair in a while doesn't mean they're out of the picture.

We need to find out why they really wanted to find your brother." Cisco took the truck bypass and headed east.

"Do you suppose Greg owes them money like they claimed, or could it be possible that Tso or someone else hired them to track down Greg?" Laurel remembered their last encounter at the bar and hoped they could avoid violence this time.

"My guess is someone other than Tso hired them to go after your brother. Considering Lachuk's military background, I'll bet they were in on that shoot-out at the cabin and the bomb." Cisco pulled into the crumbling asphalt parking lot of the Prickly Pear Lodge. "I don't see any sign of that black 4x4 truck. Let's try to get some answers from the manager."

They went inside the fading green cinder-block building marked Office by a old neon sign. A redheaded woman in her fifties sat behind a counter.

"What can I do you for?" the woman asked, leering at Cisco and giving Laurel a wink.

Laurel felt her cheeks grow hot and knew she'd probably turned the color of the manager's hair.

"Do you have a guest by the name of Lachuk?" Cisco smiled, clasping a twenty-dollar bill in his hand as he scratched his chin. "I need to see him about a job."

"I did have, sweetie, until yesterday. Are you that Indian he and his partner are working for?" The lady reached over and tugged at her bra strap, never taking her eyes off the twenty in Cisco's hand.

"That's right, ma'am. Any idea where he went?" Cisco leaned on the counter and gave her a sexy grin. The woman immediately started smoothing out her already too-tight blouse and readjusted her bra strap again.

"Maybe I could steer you in the right direction. Victor Lachuk's no friend of mine. He stole one of the road maps I sell to the tourists and stiffed me for forty dollars in rent."

She glanced at Laurel and gave her a toothy grin. "Isn't that just like a man, honey?"

Cisco laid the twenty on the counter. "That's all I've got on me."

"I have another ten, I think," Laurel said, reaching into her wallet and extracting all the bills there. "We really do need to find Victor. But we can only cover thirty dollars of his bill. Will you help us?"

"Keep your ten, honey. I'm not used to dealing with honest folks like you two. Truth is, he only owed me fifteen for two nights and three bucks for the map." The manager grabbed Cisco's twenty. "Now that we're square on his bill, I'll be glad to help you find him. He and his pal got drunk and busted up a bar pretty bad. When the cops showed up, they resisted arrest, and last I heard, they're going to be in jail for a while. Neither can afford bail."

"Thanks for your help, ma'am."

"You two come back again when you can stay the night, okay?"

"Oh, sure," Laurel mumbled as Cisco led her out the door. Laurel didn't speak again until they were halfway to the car.

"Have you noticed that lots of people we want to talk to are suddenly out of our reach? Well, at least these two are safely out of our way."

"We still have leads. We're going to go to Harmon's home next. I drove Chief Begay there once for some kind of meeting, but I never met the man. I think it's time to change that."

"If the police think you're in league with him, won't they be watching his house?"

"I doubt it. They'd be far more likely to think I'd avoid Harmon like the plague right now. But don't worry. Just in case, I intend to be extracautious."

They traversed the streets of Farmington to a housing district on the north side, near the big golf course. At least one acre separated each of the homes, which were well hidden among the natural vegetation and strategically placed trees and bushes.

Cisco parked next to a cluster of piñons. Beyond was a stone house constructed beside a small canyon. A German luxury car was parked in the long brick driveway. "We'll walk from here. I don't remember Harmon's home having any remote security cameras, but just in case, try to act like we belong here."

Cisco led the way across the lawn and through the tastefully planned wooded area to the back of the house, checking the access road for surveillance vehicles as he approached. Convinced no one was around, he stepped up to the back porch. He peered inside the window, but the house stood silent and empty. As he went around the side, a flicker of light from the top of an adjacent mesa caught his attention.

He quickly stepped back into the shadows, pulling Laurel in with him.

"What's going on?" she whispered.

"We're being watched. Look just above the pines to your left."

After a second or two, she caught a barely perceptible glimmer of light that seemed to be shining off metal or perhaps a glass surface. "What is it?"

"Either a rifle scope or a pair of binoculars. We have to go back to the car, but we'll take a roundabout way there, using the house to screen us from view. We want to avoid making ourselves a target."

Remaining out of sight from their watcher, they headed back toward the road.

"Do you think it's the same person you've suspected was tailing us all along?" she asked.

"Yes, but in this case, I really think that the person already knew where we were heading. To follow us here, through city streets, would have taken a closer tail, and no-

body was back there. I was careful about that. My guess is
that Evelyn Jim must have spoken to someone.''

''But you were sure she wouldn't betray you.''

''I don't think she did. If I'm right and she did mention
it to another person, then it must have been someone she felt
could ultimately help us.''

''If she goofed and it turns out to be the same person who
shot out my tire, I hope we can avoid him altogether.''

''I'm going to try to do the opposite, so brace yourself.
When we get to the car, I'll get in and duck out the door
while you slip into the driver's seat after me. Then stay low,
so he can only see the top of one head. He'll wonder what
we're doing, but he won't be able to tell for sure. While he's
trying to figure it out, I'll circle around and go up the mesa
after him. It's time I met our shadow.'' He studied the mesa
with the sharp gaze of a hunter.

''You're going to have to table your plans,'' she said
abruptly. ''We can't return to the car right now.''

As Cisco glanced back, a patrol car suddenly pulled up
next to the driveway across the street from them, and two
officers got out.

Chapter Thirteen

Cisco waited, hidden by a cluster of tall shrubs, Laurel at his side. Her breathing was steady, but she was in no condition for a run uphill onto the mesa with cops close behind them. The prospect of evading the police and forcing a confrontation with their shadow held an undeniable attraction to him, but at the moment, he needed to come up with a more viable plan.

"They're looking around as if they know we're here," she whispered. "Maybe a neighbor saw us and called them."

"Or our watcher," Cisco answered, then held a finger to his lips.

Cisco kept his eyes on the older, more experienced officer. The man had loosened the holster strap that secured his weapon. Whatever they were doing here, they meant business, and that didn't bode well. On his own, he was sure he could have escaped without any difficulty, but under the circumstances, he was as trapped as the woman with him.

Glancing around, he spotted a small cottage or office about twenty yards away, hidden in a cluster of blue-green spruces. The older officer must have seen it at the same time Cisco did. The cop walked over and tried the door. Finding it locked, he peered through a window.

"This is clear," he called out.

As both officers turned and headed to Harmon's house, Cisco led her wordlessly to the cottage. He had noticed that the window, though small, was open about an inch at the bottom. It opened farther with barely a sound, and with Cisco's help, Laurel managed to climb through.

His plan wasn't to follow her in, but rather to work his way to the car and then lead the officers away on a wild-goose chase. But before he could carry it through, he heard the two cops returning from the house. Something had alerted them. Without hesitating, Cisco forced his shoulders through, skin scraping against the sides, and landed hard beside her.

As the officers drew near, Cisco lowered the window back down to where it had been before, then searched for a hiding place. The cottage was nothing more than a one-room artist's studio that was being renovated. Seeing Laurel crouched by a section of wall under repair, he picked up a piece of paneling already cut to fit for the wall.

"Step behind the paneling with me and get in the corner, then help me hold it in place," he whispered. "With luck, they'll overlook us altogether."

Although narrow, the space was wide enough to hide them. Cisco heard the officers slide a key into the lock and open the door. He pressed back against the outside wall, pulling in the paneling with his fingernails for a smooth, tight fit. Hopefully the panel would not slip out of their tenuous grip and fall forward.

Trying to squeeze back a little farther, Cisco turned to one side and felt the rawhide thong holding the fetish catch on a nail. The fetish dug into his throat.

Laurel scarcely moved, but from the raspy sound of her breathing, Cisco could tell that she'd had about all she could take. Dust and the turpentine smell of the unsealed wood was getting to her, and fast.

As he shifted, trying to get the thong free, it tightened even more, threatening his own air supply. He forced a finger between his neck and the thong, giving himself some breathing space. The leather dug farther into the back of his neck. Then suddenly the thong snapped, and the fetish landed with a hard clunk onto the two-by-six at his feet.

He had to act fast. They'd figure out where the sound had come from soon. "Stay hidden. When you can, meet me at the base of the mesa behind the house," Cisco whispered quickly.

Swinging his end of the paneling out just enough, Cisco slipped into view and dashed across the room. Catching the startled cops by surprise, he shouldered the younger officer out of his way, knocking him into his partner. As he leapt out the door, Cisco hoped he was half as good a runner as he'd been in high school. If he wasn't, this would be one hell of a short dash.

LAUREL HELD THE PANEL upright somehow and remained in the corner. She heard the officers curse as they scrambled out after Cisco, then the cottage grew quiet. When she finally moved the panel aside, she saw the fetish still on the floor. Leaning over, she picked it up. The small stone figure pulsed warm in her hand. As she clutched it, she felt her fear dissipate.

She was alone and not in any immediate danger, provided she acted quickly. She walked to the door and peeked out. Nobody was in sight. Instinctively she started to reach for her inhaler, but found her breathing had become easier on its own. She stared at the fetish in her hand and felt a sense of peace.

Laurel began to move quietly through the ground cover toward the mesa where she was supposed to meet Cisco. It wouldn't be an easy walk, but she'd make it, as long as she took it slow. Hoping and praying Cisco would be okay, too, she concentrated on staying out of sight.

Twenty minutes later, she arrived at the base of the mesa and located Cisco resting in the shade of a boulder. His face looked slightly flushed, but he seemed no worse for the experience.

"What happened?"

"I gave the two cops a workout. I used to be the best mile runner the Shiprock High Chieftains had. I guess I still have some of that conditioning. I led them around in circles for a while, then I saw a teenager coming up an arroyo on his dirt bike. I jumped down in there behind him. The cops were so far behind, it was easy to fool them into thinking it was me, particularly because the kid was wearing a blue shirt like mine. They ran back to their police cruiser and drove off after him. They'll never catch that kid, either, not off the road, but they'll stay busy trying," he added with a grin.

"Here." She handed him the fetish. "You forgot to take it when you made your getaway."

"I didn't forget it. I just had other things to occupy me at the time." He took it reluctantly.

"I'm not sure I understand how it works, but I've got to tell you, it helped me make it up here." She explained how she'd felt it pulsing in her hand and how it had helped her relax.

"I don't see it in the same light. Back in that little house, I almost strangled myself when the leather cord got caught on a nail. If it hadn't fallen off my neck and made so much noise, I wouldn't have had to make a run for it, either."

"But it does work for you. Whenever we were in trouble, I'd see it grow dark as it hung around your neck, and invariably you'd mention sensing danger. Remember that feeling of ants crawling on your skin?"

He hesitated, then finally shrugged. "I don't like relying on things like this, and I'm not quite as willing to attribute to it powers I can't prove," he admitted.

"I've judged it on results. Why are you so closed to it?"

"I'll explain some other time." He glanced around. "Since you believe it brings you good fortune, consider the fetish my gift to you. Unlike anything else I can offer, it will remain with you, close to your heart, for as long as you wish it to be."

His words filled her with an empty, lonely feeling. He spoke of endings far more easily than beginnings. Accepting what was beyond her control for now, Laurel fell into step beside him.

As they headed back to the car, she noted that Cisco's gaze kept darting everywhere. "Are we still being followed?" she asked.

"I don't know for sure, but if I had to guess, I'd say he's still out there."

"I'm so tired of running! I wish we could go somewhere and sit down in a real chair, have a decent meal and just relax."

He gave her a sympathetic smile. "I know a truck stop not too far from here," he said slowly. "The food is good, and nobody asks questions as long as the bill is paid."

"Then let's go. We deserve it. And if there's trouble, we'll cut and run. It wouldn't be any worse for us than it is now."

Cisco took them across town to the truck stop. Four large diesel bays surrounded a large service station, café and a small motel with a gift shop. Two long rows of eighteen-wheelers attested to the popularity of the truckers' oasis.

At first glance, the place looked like a biker's bar. Rough-looking denim-clad men and an occasional matching woman sat noisily at the wooden benches, wolfing down burgers, fries and homemade pie with strong coffee.

As they walked past the crowd, searching for an open table, faces turned their way. The looks were not hostile, just curious in a tired sort of way. Everyone seemed to give Cisco and her plenty of room, stepping aside or moving their chairs automatically as they passed.

Cisco's arm stayed securely around her waist, letting the unattached men know that she was his. In any other setting, she might have resented that, but in here, it made her feel protected, and she was grateful for it.

They sat down in a corner table and ordered the house special—green chili burgers and jumbo fries with the skins left on. It was such a simple thing to do, yet the ordinariness of it filled her with hope. For the first time in days, she felt a burst of optimism. "We *will* find the answers we're looking for soon. I just know it."

Cisco nodded slowly. "Yes, but it's also possible that neither of us will like those answers."

"You've always questioned Greg's innocence, but there's more than that on your mind now. Is it the person shadowing us that bothers you?"

He nodded. "He's so good, I'm almost convinced he's got to be a cop. That would also explain why Evelyn Jim trusted him without question. What bothers me most, though, is the possibility that there are traitors within the department itself. That means that if we do get arrested, our chances of making it to jail alive will be slim. Dead fugitives are a lot easier to deal with than those who raise disturbing questions in people's minds."

As the impact of his words sank in, Laurel began to feel restless and uneasy. The feeling grew stronger with each passing minute, and she started looking around the room for potential danger. The tired faces of ordinary working people that had watched them come in earlier now held the possibility of betrayal.

"Relax," Cisco said. "Nobody's given us anything more than a curious once-over. I've been keeping track."

"I don't think we should stay here." She swallowed the last bite of her hamburger, wrapped up the remaining fries in a napkin and grabbed the pickle. "Let's go."

As they left the café and walked toward the car, Laurel stayed close to Cisco, her eyes darting everywhere.

"I hate to point this out," he said, "but your odd behavior has been calling attention to us. Ease up." He took her hand in his.

Normally his touch would have distracted her, filling her thoughts with delicious images, but the sense of danger was too overpowering right now. As they passed an old station wagon, she felt the fetish around her neck, tingling.

Cisco slowed down and then suddenly pulled her hard to one side, taking cover behind a Jeep.

"What—" she began, just as the sound of a car window shattering drowned out her words. Cubed glass showered down, tangling in her hair and falling onto her shoulders and blouse.

"That *phhhttt* sound, like an air gun, didn't you hear it?"

"I thought it was a bee flying by," she answered.

Cisco shook his head, his gaze directed toward the motel across from the diner. "It's a silenced weapon. Stay down." He looked back at the shattered window. "He's some marksman. That round went directly between us. By the time we heard it, it was too late. Had he wanted to take one of us out, we would have been dead."

Laurel shuddered violently and stared at her fries and pickles, now scattered on the ground.

"Let's go." He took her hand and dashed to the car. Within seconds, they were on their way.

As Laurel brushed the cubed glass from her hair, some of it fell inside the open collar of her shirt. "Ouch! As soon as you can, park somewhere. I've got to get this stuff off me."

"Okay, but first I've got to go around the block. The way I figure, the shooter was on the roof of the motel or the attached gift shop. I want to check it out."

"Cops are going to arrive here any minute. Don't you think we should be somewhere else when that happens?"

"Time's not that critical. No one besides us even heard the noise. When he comes out, the owner of the vehicle will see the broken windshield and assume it was vandalism. It's possible the cops won't even be called in, but even if they are, it'll be a while before a unit shows up on a low-priority call. We've got some time, and I intend to use it."

Cisco drove up the alley behind the motel building and got out. Shaking the glass out of her shirt, Laurel followed.

Suddenly he broke into a run. "He's still here." Cisco sprinted to the ladder propped against the side of the building, and scrambled up onto the pueblo-style roof.

Laurel caught a glimpse of a long-haired man wearing a floppy cowboy hat. He was running along the roof of the adjacent motel, racing toward the end. When he reached the corner, he climbed down a vine-covered trellis and disappeared around the side of the building.

By the time Cisco reached the trellis, the man had crossed the highway and disappeared into a trailer court. Laurel had followed as quickly as she could on the ground, but they were both hopelessly outdistanced.

Cisco gauged the strength of the wooden trellis, now weakened by one climber, then came down off the roof quickly, judging correctly that it would withstand his weight. "I won't be able to catch him now," he said, watching Laurel, who was breathing hard but apparently not in distress. "Be careful where you walk. There'll be tracks in the soft ground, and we need as much information about him as we can get."

Crouching down next to some boot tracks imprinted in the soil, he measured the size, gauging them against his palm. "It's a new boot, around a size nine. That fits a lot of our suspects."

Laurel held up a shell casing she'd picked up on the sidewalk near the ladder and showed it to Cisco. "What do you make of this?"

He rolled it in his palm. "It came from a .22 semiauto pistol. There are ejection marks on the case. He must have searched and found it, then dropped it again in his haste to get away." He studied it pensively. "There aren't many people who could have made an expert shot like that one. A silencer cuts down on the effective range of a weapon, and with a pistol, it would have been even more difficult."

"He may not be an expert at all. Maybe we just got lucky. How do you know who or what he was aiming at? Fact is, maybe he's a lousy shot."

Cisco shook his head. "I have a feeling this is the same guy who shot out your tire with the hunting rifle. He's skilled, and that means he *deliberately* placed that shot directly between us to let us know he was there. It was a close call meant to get our attention without alerting the police at the same time."

She began trembling again, but this time, she couldn't quite will herself to stop.

He placed his hand over her shoulder. "We've been through worse," he said quietly.

"The warnings are getting deadlier."

"Yes, but with every attempt, we learn more about him. Silencers are illegal. You can't just go buy one, like you can buy a rifle or pistol. It takes the right connections or the acquired skill to produce your own." He walked to the curb where the sniper had paused before escaping across the street. On the ground was a cheap black cowboy hat, and a long-haired wig that seemed almost glued into it. "So much for that part of the physical description." He picked up the evidence and brought it with him as they walked back to the car.

"Why bring that stuff along? Can you learn something from it?"

"Not while we're on the run. I can't get this analyzed now, because my connections are gone. But it may come in useful yet."

"You know, your theory that a cop is behind all this seems to make more sense by the minute. His disguise, his expertise, all tell me we've got a very dangerous enemy."

"Yes, but who is it?" he asked, his tone speculative. "My brother-in-law has the marksmanship skills, but his knowledge is broad based. I can't see him fashioning a silencer, or even using a .22. He'd be far more likely to use a .44 Magnum so the whole world would hear it coming.''

"Who, then?"

He hesitated. "I can think of only one person, Chief Begay. He was a marksman during his stint in the Marines before he became a cop. He has kept up his training, too. He goes out to the range four or five times a week."

"If your boss is the person after us, he's got every resource and advantage right at his fingertips."

"Yes, and we have precious little in our favor." Cisco remained quiet for several long moments. "When this whole operation started, I did something totally unauthorized. I'm still not sure what compelled me to do it, but I taped the meeting where Tso and I discussed the plans in detail."

"Then you *can* prove your innocence."

"The tape isn't admissible in court but, at this moment, it's the only thing I have that substantiates my claims."

"Let's go get it."

"It's not that simple. It's at my home, and I'd be willing to bet there's a stakeout team in that immediate area just waiting for me to show up."

"Can we get around it?"

"Maybe. Let me think." He smiled. What he loved most about Laurel was her fighting spirit. He gazed appreciatively at her for a moment. Actually a lot could be said for her other attributes, too. He liked the way the soft shirt and jeans clung to her, accentuating her womanly shape. A vivid image flashed in his mind as he remembered how he'd known and loved her.

The woman had become a part of him forever, and although it would come close to breaking him, he also knew that someday he would have to walk away from her. She was not his and never could be. She deserved more than he had to offer. Aching from the pain he knew he'd cause her by staying and the heartache that would come from leaving, he avoided her eyes, hiding the darkness within him.

"I can get in and out of the house, but only with your help," he said at last, forcing his mind back on the case. "You'll have to create a diversion for me and give me a window of time to operate in."

"Fine. Just keep in mind that running isn't what I do best."

"You won't need to run." He headed back into the reservation. "We're going to make one stop. Charley Curley loves fireworks. He stockpiles all kinds and he's often hired to put on unofficial firework shows. We're going to borrow some of his cache, the ones that have more gunpowder than is allowed around here for individuals. They'll be perfect for our use."

After a half hour of driving down dirt roads between corn and melon fields, they saw a gray stucco farmhouse nestled against the side of a low hill. "That's it," Cisco said.

He parked farther down the road, out of sight behind an orchard, then led the way around the hill to an outcropping of rocks overlooking the home. Cisco gestured to the small wooden building next to the main house. "Can you see him through the window? Charley's probably working on some jewelry. He takes it in to Gallup to sell. He'll be absorbed in his work, so that'll make it easier for us to do what we have to do."

"Where does he keep the fireworks?"

"In that little building that looks like a detached garage."

"Where that old pickup is parked?"

"Yeah, he keeps it there for show. Inside, it's wall-to-wall rockets, firecrackers, cherry bombs and so on."

"How do you know this?"

"It's common knowledge. We raid him every once in a while, but he pays his fine and then makes a trip east to restock."

"But if everyone knows, kids could come by and steal him blind. Fireworks and teenagers are a bad combination."

He shrugged. "Charley has made sure that everyone knows he'll use his shotgun on anyone he catches near the shed. The threat is effective, since he's home most of the time, working."

"So how the heck are *we* going to get in there?"

"Not we. Me. I'm going to break in through the side window that faces away from where he's working. If I recall, it's just a screen propped up that's easy to snap off. I'll go in, grab a can of black powder, a length of safety fuse, some M-80s and get out."

"What's an M-80?"

"They pack almost as much punch as a quarter stick of dynamite."

"No wonder they're illegal. But what if Charley Curley hears you?"

"He won't. I can be fast and silent when I need to be. Don't worry. I'll be back before you know it."

She doubted it. He was still here, and she was already worried. Her chest began to tighten again as he darted toward the garage. Reaching in her purse for her medication, she swallowed back a pill and used her inhaler. If she could only relax a bit, she'd be fine.

Just then, her skin began to prickle. She reached for the fetish around her neck and held it in her palm. This time, instead of helping her relax, it was doing precisely the opposite. Something was wrong. She could feel it with every beat of her heart.

She focused back on the house below. As she watched, she saw Charley come out of his home, shotgun in hand.

Laurel left cover and made her way slowly toward the storage building. Her breathing still sounded wheezy. Cursing the way asthma cropped up at the worst possible times, she forced herself to keep moving.

As she reached the back of the storage building, she saw Cisco coming out. Before she could warn him, Charley Curley intercepted him at gunpoint.

Cisco froze in his tracks.

Laurel glanced around her, searching desperately for a weapon, and saw what she needed in a stack of firewood. Picking up a sturdy branch, she moved closer, intending to hit Charley over the head.

"Stop, lady," Charley Curley said. "Unless you want me to shoot him, come out where I can see you, and do it very slowly."

Chapter Fourteen

Charley was about Cisco's age, but he was out of shape, with a laid-back look about him. Even holding a shotgun, he appeared more curious than deadly.

Charley gave Laurel a long look, then smiled at Cisco. "You've got good taste in women." He gave Laurel a wink, then lowered his weapon. "Now, why didn't you just come to the door if you needed something?"

Cisco gave him a crooked smile. "Hey, Stumps. How you been doing?"

Laurel stared at the two men in stunned silence, trying to figure out what was going on. Her breathing, aided no doubt by an adrenaline burst of fear, had returned to normal.

As she studied Charley's relaxed expression, she felt the tension leaving her body. At one time, she'd believed Cisco didn't have any friends at all, but that obviously wasn't so. The truth was, he didn't have many, but the friends he did have seemed very loyal. She gazed at him pensively. That shouldn't have surprised her. He did have that effect on the people who knew him well, including her.

"I didn't want to get you involved," Cisco explained. "I'm sorry you caught us."

"You *are* hotter than a burger on a grill right now, that's for sure."

"You two *are* friends, right?" Laurel interrupted.

Charley grinned. "You might say that. We've known each other since the third grade or so. We both have our own lives nowadays, but the old days still count for something. I figure I owe you one, too," he added, looking back at Cisco.

When Cisco shook his head, Laurel considered strangling him. She didn't care what was making Curley so cooperative, but if he thought he owed Cisco, this definitely was not the time to argue with him.

"You helped my kid brother," Charley said. "He was heading down the wrong path and wouldn't listen to anyone. You took time out for him, talked to him, played basketball with him. You helped him turn things around. Now he's got a good job over in Albuquerque." He studied the bundle Cisco held in his arms. "What did you get?"

"A half-dozen M-80s, twenty-five feet of safety fuse and a pound of black powder. I left an IOU for twenty-five bucks on top of the black-powder crate. Is that enough?"

"Close enough. What else do you need? Matches? You're on the run. You got food?"

"Not a lot. And yes, I need matches." Cisco grinned.

"Come to the house. You can take whatever I got. I can buy more later."

Before long, Cisco had parked the car next to the main house and loaded it up with food and supplies, including a pair of Charley's binoculars.

Charley stood by Cisco's door. "Go in beauty," he said according to custom.

Cisco started the car. "You, too, old friend."

As they began the journey to Cisco's home, Laurel's mind was filled with questions. "How did you happen to get involved with Charley's little brother?"

"He was getting busted for shoplifting and misdemeanor crimes all the time." Cisco shrugged. "The kid needed someone, and as a cop, I just happened to be there at the right time."

"Do you get involved with kids like that often?"

He shrugged again. "If the opportunity happens to come my way."

"That's not an answer."

He gave her a quick glance and shifted uncomfortably. "I think you're reading too much into this and seeing too much in me, as well. It wasn't a big deal, okay?"

"Don't worry. I don't think you're a saint and I won't ask for your blessing," she teased. "Does that satisfy you?"

"For now," he answered, a tiny smile playing at the corners of his mouth.

THEY STOPPED more than a mile away from Cisco's home. Laurel took a quick swallow of the last of the orange drink, washing down the bitter taste of her inhaler. The medications were getting a field test like never before.

She fingered the fetish, drawing strength from the small carving. It was primitive, filled with history and beliefs that had sustained the tribe through incredible hardships. It was impossible for her not to be affected by its power. Though she still wasn't certain exactly how it worked, it was enough for her to know that it did.

She gave Cisco a long, furtive look. Maybe there was more to his desire to distance himself from Navajo traditions than he'd said. The death of his wife might have turned him away from the beliefs his people had held to for centuries. People often reacted that way to tragedy and the pain it left behind. They simply lost faith.

"If I'm not back in twenty minutes, take the car and go somewhere you think is safe. I'll do my best to keep them busy so you'll have time to get away."

She thought of arguing with him, then decided against it. If he did get arrested, she would have to avoid capture. He'd need her to continue working on his behalf more than ever then. Yet the thought of abandoning Cisco left her feeling sick.

As he moved away, she tried to fight the despair that was growing within her. They continued to risk everything, but the gains were minimal. She wasn't sure how much more she could take.

After an eternity of waiting, Cisco finally returned. "Guess who's part of the team watching the house?" He didn't wait for her answer. "Chief Begay."

"Does he usually go in for this type of duty?"

"I've never heard of him doing stakeout duty before in all the years I've been on the force. It's usually long, boring work, and anyone with clout gets out of it. He must have figured I'd come back here sooner or later and wanted to be part of the collar."

"Then we should forget about retrieving the tape. It's possible they already have it."

"No. Even if they knew about that cassette, I doubt they'd find it without tearing the house apart first. But they'll do that sooner or later if they get frustrated enough."

"Where did you put it?"

"Behind a phony electrical panel I built into the wall. It looks like the real thing, with bare wires and switches. An electrician could find out it was phony by testing for current, but cops and burglars would most likely leave it alone."

"Good hiding place," she acknowledged. Laurel glanced around, studying the terrain. "I vote that we set up the fireworks inside the arroyo. It's far enough not to injure anyone, but close enough to get their attention."

"That'll work. But we're not really setting off fireworks. I'm going to use the black powder to create a small explosion." Cisco brought out the cardboard canister of black powder, slit open the side carefully with his knife, then buried the M-80s inside with their fuses outside the slit. Taking the safety fuse, he connected each M-80, then sealed the canister back up with masking tape. The long, remaining safety fuse extended from the end of the bomb.

"It looks like an enormous rat." Laurel said. "What do I do, light the tail and run as fast as I'm able?"

"That's about it," Cisco confirmed as he wound the fuse around the cylinder, then taped it lightly in place. "Make sure the tail is relatively straight, light the end and get away as quickly as you're able to without being discovered or getting an asthma attack. The fuse burns at about two feet per minute, and it's twenty feet long. The M-80s will go off in ten minutes, acting as detonators and providing some extra punch. Just make sure you're well away by that time. Some of the M-80s may fly off before they explode, and with that black powder, there's going to be a big cloud of smoke."

Laurel felt her heart begin to hammer. She hadn't anticipated that part. Smoke, in any form, was an asthmatic's adversary. She automatically reached inside her purse and touched her inhaler. "If something goes wrong and the cops catch me, don't give yourself up to help me. This is an equal partnership. The same rules that applied to me also apply to you. If I get caught, you'll be the only real chance my brother and I have. You'll have to leave me behind."

He took a long, deep breath. "Jail can be difficult even without a physical disability."

"I'll handle it. I can do anything I set my mind to."

He nodded slowly, handing Laurel a book of matches. "If I have to leave you behind, know that I *will* be back for you, with the answers you need."

"I *know* that! Why do you think I can afford to be so brave?" She was glad when her reply coaxed a grin from him.

Bomb in hand, Laurel crept away toward the hillside, her heart pounding. Though she'd tried to sound confident, she was terrified of the possibility of landing in jail. Would she be given her inhaler or would she have to ask for it each time she needed a puff? She'd read in the newspaper of cases where inmates had died because their medications hadn't been made available to them.

Fear kept Laurel moving forward, her breathing steady, her movements silent. Terror heightened her senses. When she finally reached the right spot, she set up the charge, lit it according to Cisco's directions and hurried back toward the car.

She was more than halfway there when she heard a big thump, followed a few seconds later by two loud but lesser blasts. The sounds echoed for miles, shattering the stillness. A dense black cloud rose high into the air, but none of the noxious smoke reached her. There was barely a breeze at all, but it was blowing in the other direction.

She'd just reached the car when she heard shouting behind her. She turned around and saw Cisco being pursued by two officers who seemed as fleet-footed as he was. He was ahead by a good two hundred yards, but she'd have to act fast to help him.

Laurel rushed to the car, started the ignition, then stomped on the accelerator. She headed straight for where Cisco was, then screeched to a stop beside him. Sand and dust rose in the air as the car spun halfway around. "Hurry! Get in!"

As he scrambled into the vehicle, one of the officers in pursuit stopped and fired his shotgun. The range was extreme, and only a few of the pellets bounced off the top of the car, rattling like hail.

"Keep going!" Cisco said, taking a pistol out of his boot and firing a shot back.

"Stop! You could hit one of them!"

"No way. I shot way over their heads. But it had the desired effect. They've taken cover. Head for the highway, then back to Farmington."

Moments later, as they reached the asphalt, she increased her speed. "Are they chasing us?"

"No, their cars were on the far side of the house. They have to go back for them or hope the chief brings a vehicle around."

"What happened?"

"My brother-in-law spotted me on the way back, as I crossed a neighbor's yard. He alerted his partner, and they both came after me. The chief didn't follow. He went to call for backup, I guess." He drew in a jagged breath.

"That was close," Laurel said with a sigh.

"Yeah, too close." Cisco patted the cassette tape, which was buttoned into his shirt pocket, then turned around, studying the cloud of dust and dark gray smoke. "The surrounding brush must have caught fire from the blast. That means they're going to have their hands full. They can't allow that to spread to any houses, since it might be an hour before the fire department arrives. We don't have any stations nearby. Those officers are duty-bound to stay and fight the blaze, so it looks like luck's with us."

"Won't someone follow us, like maybe the chief?"

"Probably, but my guess is that he'll be the only unit right away. It's no big deal. We've got a great head start, and he has no idea where we're going."

Laurel tried to take a deep breath, but her chest felt as if it were weighted down by bricks. "I hate to tell you this, but I've been pushing myself too hard. I need time to take another pill and allow the medications to work. Otherwise, I'm going to end up in the hospital."

Cisco muttered a curse. "Pull over, I'll drive. If you need the hospital, I'll take you there right now."

"No. It's not that bad yet. I just have to relax." She reached inside her purse, popped another pill into her mouth, then used her inhaler. Her breathing still sounded like bagpipes, which, of course, beat no raspy sounds at all. It was a small consolation, though. This was the last thing she needed right now.

She pulled to the side of the road and slid over to the passenger's seat. As Cisco took the wheel, she turned on the radio. "Music will help keep my mind off my breathing."

As they headed down the road, the music was suddenly cut off with a Navajo-language broadcast. Cisco glanced at her. "The brush did catch on fire. They aren't giving any explanations of how the fire started, but they expect to get it under control before it reaches any homes." He glanced at the sky. "And it looks like we're going to have rain this afternoon, too. They'll be okay. What about you?"

"Don't fuss over me," she said quietly. "I'll be fine."

She glanced up at the storm clouds and saw a flash of jagged lightning split the dark sky with a bright horizontal line. It was that peculiar type of lightning she'd never seen outside New Mexico. Somehow, just seeing nature's power made her feel better. It was good to know that some things didn't change, even if her own world was coming apart at the seams.

As thunder rolled across the horizon, Cisco glanced over at her. "Maybe the storm is a good omen, not just because the rain that'll follow will put out the fire, either," he added, saving her the need to talk. "My people say that thunder has the power to find things. Yellow Thunder knew the clouds so well that he was sent to look for Holy Boy when he disappeared. Would you like to hear the story?"

She nodded, absently fingering the fetish around her neck. Tradition sustained him even now, whether he knew it or not. She sat back, glad that he was willing to let her see into his world and, in that way, into himself.

"Holy Boy was a visionary. His brothers went to the Thunder People, who dwelled above the clouds, and asked for their help finding Holy Boy after he fell into the water and Fish carried him away. When the Thunder People located him, they told the gods where to find him by means of lightning." Cisco glanced at her and smiled. "Who knows? Maybe they're using lightning to guide us now."

Laurel took a deep breath and realized that the air no longer felt heavy and she could actually breathe without difficulty. She released her grip on the fetish, feeling more relaxed again. "I see lightning over by Farmington. Who do you think they want us to find there?"

"How about Harmon? Somehow, we need to track him down. But to get answers from him now, I think we're going to need subterfuge. He'll know who we are and clam up otherwise."

"He doesn't know *me,*" Laurel reminded him.

"Remember that you had a break-in at your home. Any of the suspects could have had a hand in that, and Harmon's high up on our list. The person was undoubtedly searching for your brother, but he may have seen a photo of you there, or even you in person while casing the place. We can't risk it. It's just too bad we can't recruit a third party to help us now, but that would be too dangerous for them and us."

"I have an idea. Why don't you let me try some hair rinse and then some makeup. It can do wonders. Do you like blondes?" She smiled.

Cisco laughed. "Can you take the stench of those dyes?"

"I was thinking more of a shampoo rinse, something nontoxic to small mammals and asthmatics."

"I'm game if you are, but for you to meet Harmon and set up the sting I have in mind, you're going to have to look very different than you do now."

"Leave that to me. Tell me your plan."

"I want to take him as much cash as I can withdraw and tell him it's a down payment for his next job, but he has to get the details from his boss. Then we'll hang back and see who he contacts. But first, I'm going to have to get some cash. I have an account outside the rez, and hopefully those funds haven't been frozen. We'll try the automated teller in a few minutes. And while I'm thinking about it, we need to get some stamps and a padded envelope. I want to mail the cassette to my brother in Montana.''

Cisco stopped at a chain pharmacy along their way, and Laurel went inside. She came out a short time later. ''I got your stamps and envelope. I also found an herbal dye that takes a minimum of time and has no strong chemicals. I decided to try black hair. Going from auburn won't be that giant a leap, but with the makeup and a new hairstyle, I think it'll work.''

He went to the automated bank machine next and withdrew the maximum amount possible without creating a problem, placing it in one of the bank's deposit envelopes. ''Obviously no one knows about this account yet. The downside is that it only has the paycheck I put into it. It would have been real nice if someone had padded it. We could have used the extra cash.''

''Hey, at least you were able to get the money.'' As they returned to the car, she glanced at the paper sack with the purchases from the pharmacy. ''We're going to need to rent a motel room. I need somewhere to do my make-over. And don't go to the same place Lachuk and his pal stayed. That desk manager will remember us for sure.''

''I know a place.'' Cisco drove to a run-down motel at the western edge of town. The building was nothing more than ten rooms all in a row. ''They won't ask questions here. They rent by the day or week to people who can't afford an apartment.'' He handed her some cash. ''Rent it for a day. I'll wait here. An Anglo woman alone will raise fewer questions than if we go in together.''

Laurel felt awkward going into the motel's office. The proprietor eyed her in a way that made her skin crawl, but she tried hard to act casual. Payment in cash, thankfully, ended the skepticism in his voice when she signed as Lisa Smith on the desk register. Moments later, Laurel and Cisco were in a small, shabby room one down from the north end of the row.

Laurel walked to the bathroom and glanced in the shower. "Lovely accommodations," she quipped, trying to lighten the somber mood between them. It would be only too easy to give in to depression right now, and that's the last thing either of them needed. "Make sure that you feed the cockroaches. Otherwise, they might get mean and declare war on us."

"There are no cockroaches here."

"Really? Then there's a creature trapped in the shower stall that's going to have an identity crisis real soon."

Cisco nodded absently as he peered out the side of the curtained window. Once again, Laurel felt him pulling away from her. She was doing her best, but he seemed determined to draw back into himself. She decided not to let it pass, not this time.

"What is it with you?" she asked quietly. "At times, I think we're closer than any two human beings ever have been. But then, out of the blue, I feel you backing away. You start acting as if our relationship is nothing more than an inconvenience, something to be discarded as soon as possible."

It took Cisco a while to reply. "It would be better for you if that's precisely what I did."

"Don't tell *me* what's best for me. Stop evading, and talk to me. I deserve some honest answers from you."

Taking one last glance outside, he moved away from the window and turned to face Laurel. He leaned against the wall, watching her speculatively. "You ask difficult questions, woman."

"Start with this one—is it my asthma you find distasteful? You said it wasn't before, but you seem to pull back each time I have a problem."

"I don't like to see you having difficulty breathing. I wouldn't wish that on anyone. But it hasn't pushed me away. My real problem is just the opposite."

"What do you mean?" she asked, completely confused.

"I'm in love with you," he said gently. "But that's not what either of us needs."

At first, her heart had leapt for joy, but seeing the sorrow on his face now, it began to ache. "Love is a gift, something to be cherished. You're treating it as if it were a curse."

"It can be, believe me." He sat down wearily and regarded her. Pain clouded his eyes. "You know I was married before and that my wife died. What you don't know are the circumstances. It's time you did."

Laurel saw the slight tremble in his hand as his gaze grew distant. She fought the urge to wrap her arms around him, knowing that her sympathy was the last thing he wanted right now.

"It was our second wedding anniversary. Carol planned for us to meet on top of one of the mesas for a picnic at sunset. I was going to come up after work. It was a beautiful day, so she took her mare and rode up early. But there was this accident...." His voice shook with emotion. "I was late. I'd been working on a case and, as always, I lost track of time. Hell, I lost track of what day it was! By the time I remembered where she was and rode up, it was too late."

He stood up and went to the window, and stared outside for a moment. "I found her right where the horse had thrown her, on top of some rocks. Maybe if I'd ridden up with her, I could have helped. Or if I'd just been on time... She didn't die right away. That much I know."

"But it wasn't your fault!"

Cisco held up his hand and continued. "My brother-in-law never forgave me, and I'm not sure he should. She died alone on that mesa. I wasn't there when she really needed me."

"How long are you going to blame yourself for that?" she asked gently.

"It's not a matter of blame. I've accepted what happened. But now you've come into my life. I can't risk you, too."

"I don't understand." Cisco's pain was unbearable to her. She struggled to see into the man and ease the burden he shouldered alone.

He sat on the edge of the bed and met her gaze. "Your health makes you vulnerable. You may need me to be around when you're in trouble someday. I won't risk failing you also."

His anguish cut her like a knife. She walked across the room, threw her arms around Cisco and kissed him. He held her tightly, pressing her against him with the desperation of a man who'd known the pain of irretrievable loss.

When he eased his hold, Laurel reluctantly moved away. "This is something you have to work out, but hear me out. Asthma *can* incapacitate me at times, and it's also true that I can't predict when it's going to affect me. Had you told me that you couldn't deal with my illness and the uncertainty of it, I wouldn't have tried to dissuade you. But that's not the case. What's making you pull away is just a false sense of responsibility. Tell me this—when you look at me, what do you see?"

"A strong woman who is sometimes frail and needs to be protected."

"But at times, we're all frail and in need of protection. I grant you that asthma can be life threatening—it's nothing to trivialize or ignore—but I've lived with it all my life. I know my limits. I may never be able to become a long-distance runner, but so what? There are so many things that I *can* do! And there is so much of life I can enjoy!"

"But like you said, it can be life threatening, and you may need help when no one is around."

"I carry a cellular with me so I can call 911, and I try my best to have the medications on hand that I may need." She moved away from him, struggling to keep her thoughts clear. He needed logic now, not more of emotions he was already having problems accepting. "Human beings all have a very fragile link to life. It can be taken from us at any time. That's why it's so important to really live to the fullest. You have to embrace life—otherwise, it just slips away."

Cisco gazed at her for what seemed an eternity. Laurel could sense the struggle going on inside him. Although she'd given him something to think about, the pain he'd kept hidden under layers of armor remained with him. He still hadn't truly let her in, so the battle would be one he'd have to face alone.

She turned away. "I'm going to get ready."

Cisco nodded. "I'll get the cassette ready to mail to my brother."

The make-over process took a long time. She kept the bathroom door closed as the transformation took place. Finally, with a new short hairstyle, black hair, bold red lipstick and heavier makeup than she ever used, she stepped back into the room.

Cisco blinked and then very slowly smiled. "Wow."

"So, how do you like me with black hair?" She brushed the straight bangs toward her face, as well as the wispy curls that now framed her face.

"I had my doubts, but not now. You're just as beautiful, yet you look totally different."

"Then let's get going. We've got a job to do."

As they left the motel, Laurel kept hoping he'd talk about their relationship or give her some sign that he'd understood what she'd tried to tell him. As the minutes stretched out, she reluctantly came to the conclusion he would not broach the subject. Cisco was a man who dealt with facts far better than he dealt with feelings. It was going to take him a while to consider what she'd said.

"You better fill me in on the details of your plan," she said at last.

"I've got three hundred in this envelope," he said, reaching into his pocket and handing the packet of twenties to her. "We're going to go to the racetrack where Harmon spends his time. When we get there, I'll point him out to you. I want you to go up to him and hand him the envelope. Tell him you were asked to deliver it, then walk away. We'll follow him after that and see what he does."

"I have a better idea. I'll tell him it's a bonus for setting you up and for the work he'll be doing against you in the future. Then we'll hang back and see what his next move is."

"I like that," Cisco said. "It's more direct and to the point, like you," he added with a tiny grin. "Just remember, if he gives you any trouble, bail out. I'll take care of it."

"I'm counting on that, partner."

Moments later, he pulled into the racetrack parking lot and took the binoculars from the back seat. "If he's here, he'll be by the paddock with the trainers. I'll point him out, but after that, it's your show."

Laurel went inside first and stood by the bleachers watching the horses being taken for timed runs. Cisco remained high up in the seats, searching the area with his binoculars. For the longest time, nothing happened, and she began to think that they'd wasted their time.

Suddenly Cisco came down and walked quickly past her. "Tan cowboy hat, tall," he whispered, "by the trainer clocking the horse on the track now."

Laurel spotted Harmon, then without looking back, went outside to meet him.

Chapter Fifteen

Laurel walked up to the metal fence that lined the track, leaned against it and waited. When Harmon glanced at her, she gave him her best smile.

He strolled up to her casually. "You like playing the ponies?"

"Yes, but that's not why I'm here," she replied in a low voice. "I was sent here to find you." She glanced up at him, reached into her purse and took out the bank envelope. "It's a bonus for that business with the black-sheep cop."

Harmon's eyes narrowed, and he held her gaze for longer than was necessary. "Who *are* you?" he said without reaching for the envelope.

"I'm just a messenger, that's all. Neither one of us have names, do we?" She continued to hold out the envelope.

"I've never seen you before."

Laurel shrugged. "Look, if you don't want the money, that's okay by me. I've got other things to do today."

Harmon stepped in her path, blocking her way. "I changed my mind. Let's have it."

Laurel handed him the envelope. "Now that it's in your hands, I'm out of here. Throw away the envelope and forget you ever saw me."

Harmon tore the envelope open and quickly counted the bills. "What's this, a joke? I've never been paid less than four figures. This isn't a payment, it's an insult."

"Then take it up with you-know-who, not with me. I'm just the messenger." She started to walk away, but he grabbed her arm.

"Let go of my arm," Laurel snapped firmly. "You want me to yell for security?"

"Chill, okay? I just wanted to know if there was an explanation for this."

"I was told it was a bonus, and a down payment for future work on that same matter. That's all I know, and that's all I wanted to know." She walked around him. "Now, like I said, I've got things to do."

Laurel forced herself to walk casually toward the side exit, across the parking lot and to the car. Cisco was nowhere to be seen.

She slipped behind the wheel and sat there with the window down, waiting. Soon she heard the passenger's door click open, and Cisco slid inside, staying low. "Nicely done. Now let's leave. I don't think we're being watched, but you never know."

"I think it went well." Laurel repeated what she'd told Harmon.

"I watched him through the binoculars after you left and saw him go to the phones and dial a very interesting number, one I recognized. I wasn't far away and fortunately I got close enough to hear the last few words. They're going to meet at the other person's house."

"Who's the other person? Who did Harmon call?"

"Wilfred Tso, the tribal attorney."

"Then Harmon *is* connected to whatever is going on."

"But to what extent? All we really do know is that you made a reference to me, and he called the attorney."

"So what now?"

"Following Harmon or tracking down Tso would be too risky. If they're going to meet and it's not strictly on the up-and-up, they'll be watching for a tail. Our best bet is to pre-empt both of them and go directly to the attorney's home. We'll be there first and in position. Are you game? It may not pan out at all, but if it does, we'll be right in the thick of things again."

Laurel pulled off to the side of the road. "You drive. You're better trained for following and evading people, and you know the reservation." Laurel slid over to the passenger's side, while Cisco took the wheel.

They drove in tense silence. Laurel tried to push aside the premonition that something was going to go wrong. The fetish felt warm as her fingers curled around it, but what was absent was the sense of urgency that had practically overwhelmed her at other times when they'd been in mortal danger.

"We have to stay alert," she warned, and explained as best she could about the fetish.

He said nothing, weighing what she'd said.

"You think I'm crazy or imagining things," Laurel concluded.

"No. I just don't want you to rely on the fetish too heavily. Life has taught me that relying on anything outside yourself just leaves you open to disappointment."

"Do you believe the fetish works?"

"I believe you've tapped into something useful," Cisco answered carefully. "But nothing in the universe is all-powerful or wholly good. That is also part of Navajo beliefs."

"So you're saying that the fetish has a dark side?"

"Not of itself. But if you forfeit your intuition so that the fetish becomes your master instead of the other way around, that reliance can only lead to more trouble. There must be balance before harmony can appear."

"It sounds like you're holding on to more of your beliefs than you thought."

He nodded slowly. "It appears so," he answered, a touch of surprise in his voice.

They were a few miles from Tso's home when Cisco veered off onto a dirt track leading in the right direction. "I'll take the car as close in as I can, in case we have to make a fast getaway."

Cisco maneuvered up the canyon behind Tso's home, then parked just below high ground near a rock outcropping. "Just in time," he muttered. Tso drove into his driveway in a new pickup, looked up and down the street, then went inside. "Now we wait. This is the hardest part of any surveillance. No matter how long it takes, we have to stay alert."

It was hot again, but the steady thrum of cicadas in the trees ahead had a calming effect on Laurel's jangled nerves. It was reassuring to know that nature continued thriving, despite the odds it faced out here in the desert.

"Do you think Harmon will show up soon?" she asked.

"Yes. He may be a little late, just to annoy Tso, but he'll be here. This is the perfect place for them to meet. It's away from where either of them work, so nobody is likely to think anything about seeing them together."

Laurel wiped the perspiration from her brow. At least the giant boulder behind them shaded their vehicle.

"It looks like Tso is about to get a visitor." Cisco handed her the binoculars. "I think it's Harmon, but with that hat over his eyes and those sunglasses, I can't be sure."

The man stepped out of the German luxury car and glanced around quickly before going inside the house.

"I think I recognize the car, but I'm going to go in closer," Cisco said. "Now that they're both inside, I need to hear their conversation."

"I should go, too, so that you'll have someone who can corroborate whatever you hear."

He shook his head. "No, two people will run a greater chance of being seen. Besides, if anything happens to me, I'm going to need you around to help." Cisco reached into his boot and brought out a small pistol. "Here. Keep it. If you get into trouble, use it."

"I don't know if I can," she said, keeping her hands on her lap.

"You don't have to shoot to kill, but it will give you a way to defend yourself if it's necessary."

Laurel stared at the weapon. She had no desire to take it, but it would be a show of force their enemies might respect. If nothing else, she could wave it in their direction and force them to back away. "All right."

"All you have to do is point it and squeeze the trigger," he said, leaving the car.

"Wait a minute. What about you? You can't move in without your weapon." She joined him out in the brush.

"I have one." He reached into his other boot and brought out a knife much bigger than the pocketknife she'd seen before. It had a serrated edge that looked particularly deadly. "In this kind of situation, I prefer a knife. It's quieter and more accurate in the right hands." He glanced at the house, then gave her one last look.

He gave her a smile that stole her heart. "Good luck and be careful," she said quietly.

"I will be. Don't worry."

Laurel watched Cisco make his way toward the house. Finally losing sight of him, she used the binoculars to scan the area. No one was around. For now, they were safe.

After several minutes, she saw him come out of cover and move to another hiding spot near the side window, just inches from where she'd hidden the last time she'd been here. Minutes passed, then suddenly the front door crashed open and Harmon hurried out.

For a second, Laurel thought Cisco was about to be caught, but he ducked down, and Harmon continued to his car. Before getting in, he waved one arm as if dismissing Tso, who stood near the back door. As Harmon sped off, Tso disappeared back inside.

Before she had time to speculate on what she'd seen, Cisco came up silently and joined her. Frustration was clearly etched on his face. "I heard enough to pique my curiosity, but nothing else. More than anything else, they seemed worried about turning the situation with the treaty and murder to their advantage." He made a visual search of the area around them. "Right now, we've got another problem." He nodded toward a mesa about two hundred yards away. "Our shadow's back."

"Why isn't he shooting at us like before?"

"I get the feeling he's toying with us. He wants to keep us on the edge. Then, when he's good and ready, he'll blow our brains out all over the desert floor. Hot lunch for the coyotes."

"You have such a way with words!" she said with a grimace.

Cisco gave Laurel a sheepish smile as he walked with her to the car. "Sorry about that. I was thinking out loud, and you've been with me for so long now, it's hard to think of you as someone outside law enforcement."

A wonderful, warm glow spread over her as she realized the full meaning of his words. Law enforcement was Cisco's entire world, one he hadn't shared with anyone before. "Maybe after this, I'll apply for a job. You think they'll overlook a little wheezing now and then?" she teased.

"You could try to persuade them. You can be very convincing when you want to be," he said with a tiny grin.

She gave him a startled look. Did that mean he had begun to see her point, that he was blameless for the death of his wife and that he would never be responsible for whatever happened to her healthwise? Before she could ask him more, she saw him staring at her, concern clearly etched on his features.

"Speaking of wheezing, how are you doing?"

She gave him a long, pensive glance as they got under way. "Please don't start doing this to me now."

"What?"

"Friends who care sometimes think they're being supportive by trying to second-guess when an attack is going to come. They start looking at me funny, searching for signs of trouble. But it doesn't work that way," she said with a shrug.

"Okay," Cisco admitted, "maybe I am worried about you. I've seen how serious asthma can be. How else do you expect me to react? I care about you."

"Then accept the things that are beyond your control, and mine, and know that I'm already doing all I can."

"Worrying about someone is part of caring. You can't ask me to do otherwise."

"If you truly care, then you have to trust me and accept the uncertainty that has always been a part of my life."

He nodded but said nothing, allowing the subject to drop.

Cisco drove to the main road, but then took another nearby dirt track, staying in the same area of Tso's home.

"What are you doing?" she asked. "You think our shadow won't attack if we're close to Tso?"

"That's a thought, but not what I had mind." He picked up the receiver. "I have a plan I'd like to try. I know Tso has a cellular phone much like yours. The tribe pays the bills, so he uses it all the time. With a bit of adapting and channel surfing, I might be able to find the frequency he's using. Then we'll be able to listen in on his conversations."

"I gather you've got a lengthy stakeout in mind. But what about the person watching us?"

"He hasn't come any closer, and he had his opportunity back in the canyon. My gut instinct tells me that he's trying to make up his mind about something. There's nothing we can do about him at the moment, so I say we get to work on something else."

They drove up a deserted street with only two houses, and immediately Cisco spotted an open back gate. From the tire tracks on the ground, it was clear that the owner of the property often drove along that path as a shortcut to the highway.

"What if someone's home?"

"There's no vehicle there, just tracks. For now, it's a good bet."

Laurel watched Cisco pop the telephone open with his pocketknife, then inspect the electronic components. He worked for several minutes with the knife tip, then finally glanced up.

"Okay," he said at last. Taking the padded envelope with the tape of his conversation with Tso—his only proof of the operation at the moment—he wedged it between the cushions in the back seat. "It'll be safer here than with us," he explained quickly.

"We should have mailed it before now."

"I wanted to drop it at a post office. We've had a tail on and off, and I didn't want to risk its safety." He glanced around. "Come on. Let's go. We'll use the coyote fencing that lines his property as cover while we listen."

Laurel followed him, staying low and in the shadows just in case Tso looked out. Finally they sat, backs against the fence. Cisco held the phone in one hand and brought out the fine tip of his pocketknife again.

"Now we wait," he said.

An hour passed with agonizing slowness. She stared absently at her phone. "Do you think it'll work?"

He nodded. "It'll work. My cousin taught me how to do this and he knows electronics. We just have to wait for a call."

She wiped the perspiration from her brow and edged closer to the fence, trying to make the most out of the meager shade. Everything was quiet. It was as if the desert were cowering from the merciless sun. If the person tailing them had any sense at all, he was holed up someplace cool. As if to answer her musings, she heard Tso open the back door so that air could flow through the screen unimpeded.

Cisco shifted, trying to find a comfortable position on the hard ground. "Stakeouts are always like this. Long periods of nothing, then when you're bored into paralysis and have given up hope, something finally happens."

Sleepy, she felt her eyes closing. The heat and the inactivity were conspiring against her. Fighting against it, she shifted, trying to remain alert. Suddenly the phone inside the house rang.

Cisco positioned the phone between them, turning something inside it with the knife point. There was static, then suddenly a voice came clearly from the speaker. Harmon didn't identify himself, but they both recognized his voice.

"That jockey we first bet on is still a thorn in our sides," Harmon said. "It's clear now that he got cold feet about the big race. You wasted a good bottle of Scotch on him."

Laurel gave Cisco a puzzled look, but he shook his head and shrugged.

"You should have disqualified him when you had the opportunity. Now he's long gone," Tso answered. "But what the hell. The race is over, and we've got the winning ticket. That's enough."

"Where is the ticket?" Harmon asked.

Tso laughed. "It's in a safe place again. But first things first. That jockey has to be located and disciplined. He's liable to disqualify all of us unless we take care of that problem."

"I'm on that now," Harmon said. "Along with your hired help."

"Last time, you made a mistake, and that brought us too much attention. You think you can get it right this time?"

"Yeah," Harmon replied sourly. "What about the owner? He's pulled up lame, and there's no telling which way that'll go."

"We've got to help him along, that's all. I've got some nice lilies in my yard. Maybe it's time to put his worries to rest. A visit from a friend or two is all he really needs."

"That sounds good to me, too. This evening?"

"Yes. Around nine would be the best time," Tso answered.

Hearing the dial tone, Cisco pursed his lips, lost in thought.

"That double-talk was more than two people putting each other on," Laurel whispered. "My guess is that it was some sort of code. I'd be willing to bet that the tribal official who kept pressuring my brother is Tso."

"Maybe. But all we know is that he's careful on the phone."

She glared at him. "But with a little creative interpretation, his conversation suggests he's guilty."

"Go on."

"The jockey who got cold feet, likes to drink Scotch, the one who needed to be disciplined—that's got to be Greg."

He nodded slowly. "How do you read the rest?"

"'Last time, you made a mistake'—that must be a reference to Kyle's death."

"So far, I agree, but what's that reference to the owner pulling up lame?"

"I have no idea," Laurel answered wearily. "Maybe it's a reference to the man shadowing us. He could have hurt his leg getting away at the truck stop."

Cisco started to reply when the phone rang again. This time, the caller identified himself. It was Chief Begay.

"We need to bring Cisco Watchman in. One of my officers has a plan to draw him out. I think it'll work, but it may get messy. I doubt Watchman's going to be cooperative. You'll have to be there when we book him."

"You need me to come up with charges against him that'll stick, something more than bribery allegations?"

"Right. See if we have enough to charge him with misconduct, or anything else that will allow us to bury him in internal affairs. They'll find a way to keep him locked up and keep the details from the press. Right now, he's out there making the rounds to every lowlife in the county, skirting the law and slowly but surely getting a murder case built up against him. He's like a grenade without the pin. None of us know when he'll bury us all in an explosion."

Laurel glanced at Cisco and saw him staring intently at her car. Following his gaze, she caught a glimpse of a darkened figure moving in a crouch near the trunk.

Chapter Sixteen

Cisco placed one finger to his lips, his eyes on the shadowy outline near her car. "Stay here," he whispered.

He felt Laurel's fear and wished there was more time to reassure her, but at the moment, he had another priority. He spurted toward the hedge, moving laterally. The perp was now beside the back door on the passenger's side. In another second, he'd be inside. He couldn't allow that. The vehicle was their key to survival, and that tape between the cushions could be his only salvation.

Cisco gauged the distance between him and the car. He'd have to cross ten yards of open ground, and to do that and remain in one piece, he'd need all the speed he possessed. As the perp opened the car door, Cisco darted at full speed across the street.

As if warned by a sixth sense, his opponent jumped back out of the car and crouched behind cover.

Operating on instinct, Cisco zigzagged to one side and dived onto a lawn, rolling just as two rapid shots were fired. All hell would break loose now. That was no silenced weapon. Cisco turned to look for Laurel and saw she'd taken cover. Glancing past her, he caught a flicker of movement at Tso's house as a curtain moved back. No doubt, the attorney would call in the troops now.

The gunman's thoughts must have paralleled his own, because Cisco saw him sprint toward the canyon, running with amazing speed.

Cisco knew there was no time for a chase now. The best he could do was to get Laurel and himself out of the area before the cops arrived. He darted forward and jumped behind the wheel, grateful that he still had Laurel's keys.

Seconds later, he reached the spot where she was hiding. Her face was as white as chalk as she scrambled into the car.

"Are you okay?" he asked quickly, putting the car in gear again.

She nodded, and that assurance was enough for him. He slammed down on the accelerator, leaving a trail of dust in their wake.

Cisco concentrated on his driving. It would take at least another fifteen minutes for a unit to respond unless there was a police cruiser in the area already. The long distances cops had to travel here would work to their advantage now.

Avoiding the main highway, he stayed on side roads worn into the landscape. He was careful to travel at a speed that wouldn't engulf the car in dust and sand. Laurel seemed okay, but he didn't want to increase the chance of another asthma attack.

"What happened back there?" she asked.

"Our shadow decided to take a look inside the car. I'm not sure why. Had he wanted to disable our transportation, he could have done that with a pocketknife or one well-placed shot."

"So what's your theory?"

"Maybe he was another cop, investigating us. Or perhaps he wanted to put a homing device on the car." He paused, then glanced around. "Start looking around, particularly in the back seat, for anything that doesn't belong. It could be as small as a pack of gum."

Laurel turned around and leaned over the headrest, looking over at the rear seat and the floorboards. "I can't tell for sure from here. He might have slipped it under the front seats, for all I know. You're going to have to park somewhere and help me look.''

Cisco considered it. Finding someplace safe now seemed an impossibility. But she was right. A homing device could be anywhere, from under the fender to inside the rear cushion with his precious audiotape. As he weighed their options, an idea came to him. "I know one place on the rez no Navajo would ever willingly go. It'll provide us with shelter, and we'll have as much privacy as we need.''

"Where is this place? Why haven't we used it before?''

"It's a hogan, an old one, with a hole punched through its side,'' he said, his voice taut. "Do you know the tradition?''

"Air-conditioning?''

"Not quite. When there's a death in a house, the custom is to make a hole in the north side, the direction of evil, carry the body out that way and abandon the dwelling to the *chindi*.''

"The *chindi* is a person's ghost, right?''

"Yes and no. Our way says that at death, the good in a man merges with universal harmony. The evil in a man can't, so it stays earthbound and creates problems for the living. The *chindi* is said to cause illness and bad fortune. We are taught from our earliest days to avoid anything contaminated by it.''

"I gather you don't believe in that, and that's why you're suggesting we go there?''

"I made the suggestion because I'm not sure we have another choice right now. To be honest, I would avoid a place like that just like Anglos would stay away from a cemetery after dark. But that's exactly why it can be a safe spot for us—at least in terms of getting arrested. If there's a homing device in or on this car, going there will buy us time to find it. No one will be around that hogan, believe me. They'll search the entire area before drawing close to it. They'd work under the assumption I'd be as eager to avoid it as they are."

"If that's your recommendation, I have no objections."

Cisco drove up a dirt road for a full hour before the hogan came into view. He parked near the southern end, as far away from the hole as possible, and tried to push back the revulsion he felt. Doing his best not to even look at it, he retrieved the padded envelope, placed it inside his shirt, then concentrated on going over the car completely, searching for a homing device.

It took forty minutes before they were satisfied that the car was clean. "So we still don't know why he was breaking into the car," Laurel said.

Cisco nodded. "Too bad I didn't get a good look at the guy. I know most of the Navajo cops."

"Maybe he meant to plant a device but didn't have the time."

"Could be." Cisco studied the cloud-dotted horizon as the sun began to descend behind the Chuskas to the west. The skies were bathed in oranges and reds as vivid as any paintings he'd ever seen.

"It's going to take a while for the temperature to cool tonight unless we get some rain. It feels like it's still in the nineties. Too bad there's no shade around here."

"You want to stay here for a while?" Laurel asked.

Cisco took a deep breath and let it out slowly. "Yeah. We need to stay low for now, and this place is less likely to get visitors." He glanced at the hogan. "Let's go in there. It'll at least give us some shelter from the sun."

"Are you sure you want to do that?"

He paused before speaking. "No, but I'll do it anyway. It'll accomplish nothing to stand out here baking in the heat." Disgust filled him, but he forced himself to go inside the hogan. His skin prickled as he sat down on the dirt floor. "Let's discuss our progress," he said, determined to stay focused on the case.

"I've been thinking about that," Laurel said, sitting across from him. "Police Chief Begay wants to bring you in. That'll get him some good publicity, which he sorely needs. What we don't know is to what extent, if any, he's involved with the theft of the treaty."

"Tso knows I'm looking for the treaty, so he's not going to want me behind bars. But if it does happen, he won't lift a finger to help me." He stared at the sunbaked desert outside the open doorway. "I wish that gunshot had never been fired back there. Was anything else said in that phone conversation after I took off after our shadow?"

"No. That was pretty much it."

Laurel leaned back against the cool log wall of the hogan. Cisco quickly took her hand and pulled her forward. "Don't touch anything you don't have to."

She nodded, understanding in her eyes. "One thing worries me about that conversation," Laurel said, sparing him having to elaborate. "If I'm right, the tribal president is in immediate danger. The more I think about it, the more I'm convinced he's got to be the 'owner' they referred to. President Atcitty is the only person we know about who's sick or injured. You bring flowers to someone in the hospital."

"I agree. I'd pretty much reached the same conclusion. The lilies, agreeing to 'put his worries to rest' tonight, all spells out the same thing. The question is, what can we do about it? I will admit that if we do show up at the hospital and get caught, we'd attract more officers to the scene. That might deter the president's enemies, but once we're out of the way for good, they'd have a clear field."

"If we do nothing, and we're reading their conversation right, they'll kill him. It would be easy for a man in the tribal attorney's position to sidetrack security long enough for an assassin to get into the president's room."

"This is true—assuming we're interpreting the conversation right. If we're not, we're jeopardizing our chances of clearing ourselves and your brother, and of locating the treaty, for nothing more than the double-talk of a couple of lowlifes."

He shifted carefully, avoiding contact with the personal possessions of the deceased that remained against the wall. It was one thing to force himself to enter the hogan, but another to touch objects that had belonged to the dead, particularly when it wasn't in the line of duty.

"Before we decide to go to the hospital," he continued, "I want you to know that if they catch us there, they're likely to assume we're there to kill the president. They'll shoot first and ask questions later."

"I'm aware of that," Laurel answered simply.

Cisco looked into her eyes. She wanted to go, to do her best to protect the president from attack. But that was his job. There was no sense in endangering her also.

"I'll go alone," he said firmly.

"When pigs fly, you will. We stand a better chance if we go in covering each other's back. Besides, I don't look like a threat to anyone. You do!"

Thunder rolled in the distance. The approaching storm winds were building slowly, bringing the smell and feel of moist air with them.

Cisco stood at the doorway, enjoying the coolness the wind brought. "Wind is said to bring news and to have supporting power. The problem is, wind doesn't discriminate between good news and bad. It leaves the interpretation to the listener. That's the situation we're facing now. We're compelled to act, though we have no idea if our actions will bring positive results or our own downfall."

"We'll discover that soon enough." Laurel stood and brushed the dirt from her jeans. "We might as well go. Once the rain begins, we could get stuck here in a sea of sand and mud."

"All right. With your new hair color and the makeup, we won't have to worry about you being easily recognized, not at the hospital anyway. We have several Anglo women working there.''

''What about you?''

''I'm going to wear the long-haired wig and the old hat we found. Remember the sniper's present to us? We might as well use it now.''

Cisco avoided all the main highway junctions where he thought roadblocks might still be in place. Taking the detours would mean a longer trip but a safer one.

They arrived at the hospital over an hour later. Laurel tugged at her bangs and brushed her hair in a style that framed her face in uneven curls. ''When I look down, are most of my features hidden despite my short hair?'' She glanced at the floor of the car.

''Yes. What do you have in mind?''

She gestured toward the side of the building, where a utility closet was open. Beside an electric lawn mower was a cart filled with cleaning supplies. ''See that mop and bucket in the cart? I'm going to borrow them. Most people don't give the janitorial staff a second look.''

''Good plan. I've got to find myself a tool belt. I think I know where, too.'' He gestured to a van with an electrician's logo on the side. ''I won't even have to break in. The window's open.''

He met her by the side entrance moments later, tool belt in place. Laurel had her keys attached to her belt and held the mop in one hand and the pail in the other.

''Once we're inside, the first thing we have to do is find out what room he's in,'' she said. ''Any suggestions?''

''It should be near the intensive care unit. I don't think it'll be hard to locate. Just keep your ears open.'' He headed toward the lobby.

They split up and walked past the front desk. Cisco paused just long enough to place the stamped envelope containing the cassette into the hospital's mail slot. It was critical getting the tape mailed to his brother before something happened to it. The hospital's mailbag was probably more secure behind the counter than chancing an outside mailbox, especially when their tail could be watching.

He walked purposefully down the hall, his eyes on electrical fixtures as if searching for a problem. Laurel began mopping the floor near the nurses' station, hoping to overhear any casual conversation that would reveal what she needed to know.

Soon Cisco was at the end of a long corridor, pretending to fix a wall outlet. Laurel concentrated on keeping her face down, though no one seemed to be paying attention to her.

As two doctors walked past her, she overheard their conversation. The president's condition was still listed as serious, but they now believed he would be regaining consciousness soon, and eventually recover completely.

Laurel glanced at the clock on the wall. It was almost eight forty-five, and posted visiting hours ended at nine. If Tso was really going to make an attempt on the president's life, he would do it soon. Cisco and she would have to move fast.

Taking a flower arrangement from the nightstand beside an empty bed, Laurel went up to the nurses' station. "Flowers for President Atcitty," she muttered, peering at them from behind several tall gladioli.

"Third floor, room 312, but you'll have to leave the flowers outside. No one except those on a list of authorized visitors are allowed in the patient's room."

Laurel walked down the hall, then ducked into an empty room and left the flowers on a table. Motioning to Cisco, she picked up the mop and pail and went directly to the elevator.

Cisco followed and, when the doors closed, glanced at her. "Where to?"

"Third floor, room 312. But I don't think we'll be able to get close to Atcitty's room. From what the nurse said, only those on a list are allowed in there. That means they must have a guard posted to check his visitors.''

"A lot of good that'll do against the attorney. I'll bet he's on the list," Cisco said.

"But surely he wouldn't make an attempt on the man when they know everybody who steps in there!"

"No, their move would be more subtle. They only have to create a diversion to distract the guard, then strike. That is, *if* they strike at all, and this isn't just a waste of time."

"Or maybe someone else will show up instead to do the killing. We know there is at least one more person involved in this mess. Our shadow, for instance."

"Just stay sharp," he advised. "That's all we can do."

Minutes ticked by. Cisco kept checking on Laurel, but as she'd predicted, no one paid any attention to someone cleaning the floor.

He crouched before an outlet, unscrewed the cover and pretended to inspect the wiring inside. He was only fifty feet away from the president's door, but so far, only one nurse had gone into the room, and she'd come out fairly quickly. It was now nine-fifteen. Maybe this had all been a waste of time and effort.

Just then, out of the corner of his eye, Cisco saw a man step out of the elevator. It was Tso, carrying a vase of flowers. He stopped in front of the president's room and showed the flowers to the guard, who nodded absently.

Cisco glanced at Laurel. She was searching the hall for Harmon; he was sure of it. Her instincts were good. She wasn't being taken in by Tso, but rather looking for trouble from another direction.

Before he could formulate a plan of action, a three-tone signal and the announcement of a "code blue" came over the speakers. The nurses left their central station, rushing down the next corridor. He caught snippets of conversation as a medical team with an emergency-response cart hurried by. A patient's equipment had been disconnected somehow, and now he was in cardiac arrest. Cisco had no doubt it was a diversion created by Harmon.

Tso, who'd been talking to the security man, glanced around. He said something to the guard and pointed toward the stairs.

Unsure of what direction the threat to the president would come, Cisco moved forward to the next outlet, still keeping his head down.

The security officer hesitated, and Tso spoke again, raising his voice in anger so Cisco could hear clearly this time. "I'm telling you, I'll cover the door. But if you wait until the killers arrive instead of stopping them on the stairs, they'll get us both. The president's life is our responsibility now."

"Uh, you're right, sir. I'll cover the stairs." The guard's face was flushed as he strode off quickly toward the opposite end of the long corridor. His hand was on the butt of his revolver.

Tso waited until the guard was out of sight, then quickly ducked inside the room. Cisco followed. He had to do something fast, even if it meant confronting Tso face-to-face. Slipping into the president's room, Cisco found himself staring at a pistol aimed directly at his chest.

"Come to watch me finish him off? What's happened to your cop skills, Watchman? I noticed it was you in that ridiculous disguise halfway down the hall."

Cisco stared at Tso for a moment, then decided to try his best poker bluff. "Others on the force know you're involved in all this, and Greg Brewster is speaking to the Farmington police right now. Put the gun away and give it up while you can still hope to outlast a prison sentence."

"You have no evidence and therefore no case. Now, watch your alibi go right to hell," Tso snapped. He grabbed a pillow from the bed and jammed the pistol into the middle, aiming toward the unconscious president.

Just then, Laurel swung open the door, catching Tso in the back of the head with the heavy wooden edge. The gun went off with a muffled thump.

Cisco yanked the weapon from the stunned attorney's hand, then sent Tso crumpling to the floor with a kick to his solar plexus.

"Great entrance, partner," Cisco said, checking to see if President Atcitty had been struck by the errant bullet. Fortunately the round had struck the wall a good foot above the man's chest. "Help me get this scumbag away from Atcitty. We've got to run. Tso ordered the guard to the stairs, but he may be back any second." He glanced at the weapon in his hand. "This is *my* service weapon. Tso must have somehow gotten it out of the chief's office—probably making it look like I stole it—and was about to frame me again, this time for murder."

Cisco and Laurel pushed the unconscious attorney into a hall closet and wedged the door shut with a screwdriver from the electrician's belt.

Cisco slipped the pistol into his pocket as they ran to the service elevator. "No one will harm the president now," he said, punching the button for the second floor. Just before the door closed, he could see the security guard going back down the hall toward the president's room. "He'll see evidence of the fight and the gunshot. Then they'll have guards everywhere. But if they catch us here, the attorney will claim *we* made an attempt on the president's life, and we'll never beat that rap."

They walked as casually as possible out of the elevator, then strolled to the second-floor stairwell. As the door closed behind them, he increased the pace again. Laurel tried to keep up with him as they went down the stairs, but her breathing was labored.

"Are you going to make it?" he asked, slowing down.

"I can handle going down a lot better than racing up the stairs." She pushed Cisco to increase his speed again by increasing hers. "Can't talk and run though, even heading down."

"Then don't worry about it," he answered quickly.

As they came out of the stairwell on the ground floor, Cisco noticed two uniformed cops standing by the front door. One was using his hand-held radio. Keeping her hand in his, he led her down the side corridor and headed for the service elevator again. "We're going down to the basement."

"Why? We'll be trapped there!"

"By now, they'll have all the exits closed off. We've got to find another way out."

As soon as they reached the basement, Cisco ran across the room and began to move aside the tower of paper that covered the north wall. "I know there's a window behind this stuff. I used to come to this hospital a lot the summer my youngest cousin got sick. His brother and I would hide out here with a friend and sneak cigarettes."

"Which is why I knew I'd find you here," a voice said flatly.

Cisco turned, leading Laurel around behind him to protect her. "Hey, Tubbs. Er... *Captain* Tubbs," Cisco called to the bear of a man aiming a .45 at his chest. "You've got me *and* the president's real assailant. I just locked Tso, the tribe's attorney, in a hall closet upstairs. So let her go, okay?"

"Not so fast. I happen to be in charge of protecting Atcitty, and one of my men reported that someone took a shot at him. Has that pistol in your pocket just been fired?"

"Yes, but Tso did the shooting and he missed. My partner here ruined his aim by whacking him with the door. Do you really think I'd try to assassinate our tribe's leader?"

"I think you decided to do something on your own, forgetting that you're not the only cop in the department. By the time you realized you'd taken on more than you could handle, it was too late. Tso's secretary told me about your frame-up plan and the missing treaty."

"Then you have to believe that if you arrest me, I'll never be able to recover the treaty or prove that I'm innocent. Tso will claim *he* stopped me, and it would be his word against mine. Plus he's not working alone. The others involved might have powerful positions within the tribe."

"You've got almost the entire department out for your blood, too. I've got to tell you, buddy boy, only *you* could piss off so many people."

"It's my charm. So what'll it be? The next move's yours. You and I go back a long ways. Do you think I could ever commit murder, let alone betray my oath as a cop?"

"Nope," Captain Tubbs said slowly, holstering his pistol. "Being a cop is all you've got."

Cisco nodded thoughtfully. At one time, that had certainly been true. But it was no longer that way for him. He thought of the woman behind him. The thought of living his life without Laurel left him feeling hollow. She'd taught him to value each and every day as no one ever had. Through her, he'd found himself. At the moment, he would have gladly and willingly traded his life for hers.

"So what do you have on the tribal attorney? Any real evidence that we can use in court? He's a slippery weasel."

"We think he put the squeeze on Greg Brewster, maybe through some Farmington gamblers, and got the treaty switched for a fake. But without Brewster's testimony and the treaty itself, we have zip," Cisco admitted.

"Then you've got your work cut out for you, huh, Detective? Now, get outa here before I change my mind!" Tubbs said finally. "I sent some officers to cover the president, but now I've got to check on him myself."

Cisco hurried Laurel to the window and gave her a lift up. "I owe you, Captain."

"Damn straight, Detective."

"Let me give you something else you may be able to use. Tso is in this up to his ears, but I'm not sure of the other players. To be safe, don't let him, Chief Begay, Kelliwood or Blackhorse near the president alone. And watch out for an Anglo named Harmon. He and Tso are working together for sure."

"Anyone *not* on the list of suspects?"

"You're not. And get this. I think Tso was the one who put the president in the hospital, and paid Harmon to kill Kyle Harris."

The captain gave Cisco a quick nod. "I'm in charge of the president's security. I'll make sure he's not threatened again. Count on it."

Cisco followed Laurel outside, leaving the window open. "Walk normally to the car." Tossing his long-haired wig into the bed of a pickup they passed, Cisco stayed by Laurel. "Look at that," he said, glancing back. "The building's got cops at every entrance. Nobody's getting in or out."

"Then let's not stick around until someone spots us." Laurel reached for her inhaler, then let it drop back into her purse, unused. "You know what? With the amount of adrenaline coursing through me right now, I can probably avoid an asthma attack for years. Who'd have thought sheer terror could be such great therapy?"

They were miles down the highway when Laurel finally leaned back in her seat and relaxed. "From the looks of it, I'd say you've got more friends than you remember."

He shrugged. "Childhood friendships, though respected, don't normally play a part in everyday adult life. It's that way for everyone."

"It's even more so for those who forget to look around them and see what's there."

Cisco smiled ruefully. "Now you're a philosopher?" He turned on the radio, and they listened for fifteen minutes or so to country-western music. During a commercial break, just as Cisco was about to change the station, a special news broadcast cut in.

As Cisco heard the Navajo announcer speaking in their native tongue and the words sank into his consciousness, his gut clenched. Sudden anger shook him.

"What's happened?" Laurel asked quickly.

"The tribal president just died."

Chapter Seventeen

Cisco pulled over to the side of the road, picked up her cellular and began to restore it to its original configuration. "I'm going to call the captain. I know it's taking a big risk, but I've got to find out what happened."

"Won't he still be at the hospital, if he was responsible for the president's security? How will you reach him without tipping off everyone else?"

"I'll say I'm his cousin and we've got a family emergency. That'll work. They'll patch me through." Moments later, he heard Tubbs's voice as he identified himself.

Cisco began speaking, knowing Tubbs would recognize who was calling. "I warned our uncle to be careful," Cisco said, "but I heard he was in an another accident."

"Not at all. As a matter of fact, I've already booked a vacation for him so he can get away for a while. There's no problem. Our family's going with him."

"So the reunion we had planned hasn't been canceled?"

"Not at all."

"Thanks, cuz."

"Stay in touch."

"I'll try." Cisco cut the connection. "Tubbs apparently decided that the only way to keep the president safe was to have him moved and leak a phony report of his death. I think he's right, too. If I understood correctly, he'll have his own family protecting the president."

"Well, even if we didn't gain any solid evidence, we succeeded in preventing another murder," she said. "And we know Tso is the one out to kill the tribal president."

"We *have* made progress. We've got a very narrow list of possibilities for Tso's partners now."

"But which of the others besides Tso are guilty, or could it be that all of them are? And who stole the treaty?" Laurel asked.

Cisco rubbed the back of his neck with one hand. "The attorney is on my list for every crime. I bet he hired Lachuk and his big pal to attack your brother at the cabin and to set that bomb. Harmon, I think, must have killed Kyle, if you recall the conversation we overheard."

"But don't forget Chief Begay or the other two cops," she said. "Or even Phillip Aspass."

"Kelliwood and Blackhorse are soldiers. They wouldn't have initiated anything, if they're even involved. My brother-in-law is more likely telling them what to do."

"But would he be working with the bad guys just to punish you?" Laurel was skeptical.

Cisco shook his head. "I don't really know, but I doubt it. Our best bet is to concentrate on Tso. He'll lead us to the answers, one way or another."

"But what was Tso's motive for starting all this? He's already got power, and the tribe must pay him a bundle."

"We know he's the one who initiated the attack on the president, so the man's recovery would be a threat to him." He paused. "Let's put together a scenario and see if it works. The president never goes to the high shelves for a book, so maybe he was reaching for something up there that looked out of place to him. Whatever it was must have bothered him enough for him to actually climb up onto his chair," Cisco said. "Tso walked in about then, panicked and clobbered the president."

"Do you think that Tso took the treaty, then hid it in the president's own office?" she added quickly. "I guess that would be a safe place, all right. If it was discovered by accident, the only person who would be blamed, or at least embarrassed, would be President Atcitty. But why would Tso want the treaty in the first place?"

"There's only one reason I can think of. Once the theft was made public, he could have played the hero, finding it and restoring it to the tribe himself. The president, who loaned it out in the first place, would have been in a very bad position politically. The attorney could have then used that to gain even more power. Tso is an ambitious man, very un-Navajo, according to our elders. He probably has sights on the president's office, or maybe a congressional seat."

"Sounds logical." She considered it. "Admittedly those shelves in the president's office would have been an excellent hiding place. Imagine it there, not ten feet away, when you were putting your career and life on the line in a plan to recover it. But even if all this is true, he surely wouldn't have still left it there after attacking the president. He would have assumed the police investigators would take a close look around that office. Tso is not stupid."

"I agree. Now, think back to the night the president was attacked in his office. Everything went crazy. Cops and investigators were everywhere. No way the attorney would have tried smuggling the stolen treaty out of that building. He wouldn't have wanted to risk having someone find it on his person. His only option would have been to take it down from the shelf and hide it again—fast. If you recall, they found the president almost immediately afterward."

"But where could he have taken it? As you said, he couldn't have had much time."

He considered it for a moment. "Why not his own office?" He shrugged. "It's right next door."

Laurel weighed his suggestion. "I think it's worth looking into. But that'll entail breaking in there again."

"I know, but we've got to go for it. The net's closing in around us, and eventually we'll get caught. Our only hope is to recover the treaty and connect it to the tribal attorney."

"After what happened at the tribal offices, the staff is bound to have increased their security."

"You're right, so we'll wait until the predawn hours, when the guards will be tired. Then we'll go back and search that office from top to bottom."

As Cisco glanced in the rearview mirror, he spotted a gleam in the road behind them, like moonlight playing off chrome. "We have a tail."

She turned around, but the road seemed empty. "Where? I can't see anything."

"Not directly behind. Look to one side, running a parallel course. It's a clear enough night. Even though the vehicle's lights are off, you can see some dust in the distance. If you catch it just right, you'll see chrome gleam as the vehicle hits a bump."

She stared into the distance. After a few minutes, she caught a glimpse of the dust trail. "If he's tailing us, why from such a distance?"

"I wish I knew. But we know one thing for sure. It's not Chief Begay. Right now, he's got his hands full."

"Someone he sent, maybe? Remember how he mentioned knowing how to draw you in?"

He nodded slowly. "Good point."

"Or it may be someone we know nothing about."

"Do you have a person in mind?"

"I can't get Greg out of my thoughts. He would have tried to contact me again somehow. But if he saw you with me, he would hang back until he was sure it was safe to approach."

"But he wouldn't have shot at us, nor risked close calls," Cisco said. "And I don't think he'd be trained in car pursuits. I don't believe he's the one back there."

"You're right about all that. He wouldn't have endangered me in any way." Lost in thought, she lowered her head, staring at her feet, and a curl of black hair fell down into her eyes. She brushed it away impatiently.

"Greg wouldn't have risked sending me a letter at home," she continued. "That could have been too easily intercepted. But he knows I have a post-office box for business clients. Is it safe to check that?"

"There are no guarantees for us anymore, but that's the least risky of all the things we could do now. The lobby stays open until late on weekdays. We can go now if you want."

She nodded. "If we don't manage to find the answers we're searching for, and we end up getting arrested, the tape recording you sent your brother won't be enough. We'll need Greg to help us. He'll be the only person who can verify what we say is true."

"As a witness, he's not going to be very credible," Cisco warned.

"Because he ran or because he's my brother?"

"Both, and because of his background—involvement in the case, his debts and the murder of his roommate. They'll just arrest him, as well."

"I'd still like to check the post office. Maybe he's given me some way of contacting him. Who knows what he's managed to learn? We might find it useful, especially if it can lead to evidence against Tso and whoever is working with him."

They returned to Farmington, and as they traveled through mostly residential streets, Cisco kept his eye on the rearview mirror. "Our shadow's back there, I can feel him."

She placed her hand on the fetish. It felt cold. "But we're not in danger. You know, I'm beginning to think he's waiting for us to lead him someplace. If you look at it from that point of view, even the shots he took at us make sense. It's like he's trying to spook us into taking action. But what?"

"We won't know that until he catches us or we get him. At the moment, we can't afford to have either happen. Things are hot enough already."

They drove past the post office twenty minutes later, looking for signs of activity, then circled the block. Coming around again, Cisco parked and cautioned her to wait as he made a methodical visual search. "See if you can spot anyone who looks like they're killing time or seems to be watching the others."

The area was nearly empty. There were only two people coming out of the lobby, and they seemed focused on their own mail. "It looks safe enough," she said.

"Okay. Let's get our business here done quickly." He stepped out of the car, his gaze darting everywhere as he accompanied her inside.

Cisco waited near the entrance, keeping a casual watch while Laurel went directly to the postal box. Sorting through the envelopes and advertising fliers moments later, she walked with him back to the car. Most of the letters were from clients and prospective customers. Then, toward the bottom of the pile, she saw Greg's familiar scrawl on an envelope. "Here we go." She glanced at the postmark. "This is dated only a few days ago. He must have been on the move all this time."

Laurel ripped the envelope open as she slipped into the passenger's seat. A lump the size of an egg formed at her throat as she read the letter. "He's trying to explain why he ran," she said, her voice taut. "He says that Tso kept bothering him about treaty security until he knew all the details. Then sometime when Greg's attention was diverted, he switched a duplicate storage box and treaty for the real ones. When Greg confronted him, Tso claimed it was to protect the treaty. Greg didn't buy that, and that's when Tso offered him money to pay off his gambling debts. Tso assured him that unless Greg took the money, he'd make sure Greg lost his job and he'd have to face his creditors empty-handed.

"Greg went into hiding at the cabin, trying to figure out a way to recover the treaty. Then one night some men in a black pickup ambushed him while he was sleeping, and he barely managed to escape. He continued driving until he reached Mexico. He didn't have the clout or the money to fight the tribal lawyer. Greg's given me a number where I can reach him."

"We should try to find out what else he knows, even if all we get is a description of the other men he dealt with," Cisco said. "You have to call him."

"I can try, but I've never made an international call on the cellular. I don't know how clean it'll be, or even if it's possible."

"Then let's find another phone. We'll need someplace private, where we won't be interrupted or taken by surprise." He considered it for a minute. "Your brother's apartment is a possibility."

"Someone almost caught us there before."

"But it wasn't the police. They don't have the manpower to maintain surveillance there just in case we happen to show up."

"Tso and the others who are after my brother are more dangerous."

"That's true. But can you think of anyplace safer for us right now?"

She shook her head.

"We'll park in the area and come in through the back."

"My key doesn't open the back door. Do you think you can pick the lock? My brother did the few times he got himself locked out."

"What kind of lock?"

"One of those that you push a button on the inside knob to lock it."

"Yeah, I can usually get past those with a pocketknife."

As they headed for Greg's, Cisco continued to search the rearview mirror. "I don't see our shadow back there now, but he's tenacious."

"If you can't spot him, then try not to think about it."

Cisco nodded, unconvinced. He had an almost uncanny instinct for survival. It's what had kept him alive the past few years when he'd purposely chosen every dangerous assignment that had come along. But right now, his instincts were confused. They'd become a jumble of mixed signals that gave him no clear answers or direction.

He parked about half a block down in an empty driveway, then followed Laurel's lead, cutting through backyards and climbing over a low fence. A few minutes later, they stopped near the back door and listened. The only sound was shrill barking from somewhere nearby.

"Mrs. Mendoza's poodle," she whispered. "He's about the size of your hand. Don't worry about him."

Getting the lock to open was easy, and soon they were inside. Cisco waited near the window, peering out. "Call, and then let's get out of here. We shouldn't stay here one second longer than absolutely necessary."

He waited as Laurel dialed again and again. Finally she whispered, "It's ringing." She stood there for what seemed like forever, waiting and looking at Cisco. "He's not picking up the phone."

Cisco reluctantly moved away from the window and gestured to her, asking to take the phone. "Or he's just not there. He may have thought it unwise to sit around waiting for your call. We can try again later at night or early in the morning."

She tossed him the receiver, disgusted. "Just when I thought I might hear his voice again and know he's safe."

Cisco listened to the ringing for several cycles, when suddenly he heard a telltale click.

He hung up quickly. "We've got to get out of here *now*," he said, taking her hand. He hurried out the back with Laurel. "Stay low."

They had almost reached the car when he saw two men down the street running toward them. "Quick! Get into the car."

She dived inside, and by the time her seat belt was fastened, they were already two blocks away.

It took another twenty minutes of dodging into narrow streets and cruising through residential alleys, but Cisco managed to elude the pursuit vehicle.

"That was too close," he said at last. "But now we can't afford to go directly back to the rez. If those two were Farmington cops, and I think they were, they'll radio the county sheriff for backup and they'll have tribal officers watching for us near the main roads." He clenched his jaw, his thoughts racing. "We have Greg's letter telling how Tso switched the fake treaty for the real one, but we still don't know who besides he and Harmon are involved, and we're out of time. We have to go for broke, as they say. We have to go back to—"

Laurel shifted in her seat to face him. Suddenly, as if something had caught her eye, she turned around and saw someone rising from the back floorboards. As a hand snaked out toward her, she grabbed the cellular phone and started bashing the intruder, first on the hand, then over his head.

Cisco swerved into the parking lot of a convenience store, screeched to a stop, then jumped out.

As Laurel continued her barrage, Cisco threw open the back door, grabbed the man by the shirt and yanked him out onto the pavement. Before their intruder could react, Cisco slammed the heel of his hand into the man's neck, flattening him.

"It's my brother-in-law," he said, stepping back. "He'll be okay in a few minutes and be able to get help inside. Let's go."

As Cisco stepped toward the car, Aspass grabbed for his leg. Cisco kicked back, breaking free just as a clerk appeared in the doorway of the store, holding a shotgun.

"Hurry!" Laurel shouted.

Cisco dived back into the car and raced out of the parking lot. Laurel turned around in her seat and watched the clerk running after them, yelling and waving the weapon in the air. Luckily he didn't stop to fire a shot.

"He was trying to use you to get me to cooperate, but he underestimated you." As they escaped back down the highway, Cisco glanced in the rearview mirror and shook his head wearily. "We have no choice where to go next, even if Phillip overheard enough to piece it together." He saw the naked fear that flashed in Laurel's eyes, and his gut clenched. He would have traded anything he possessed to have been able to wipe all her worries away and give her some lasting peace of mind.

"I wish I could spare you what's yet to come," he added, his voice taut. "Your life and mine are on the line now, more so than ever. But if it comes to this, I want you to know that I'll gladly give up my freedom and my life for yours."

"This isn't about self-sacrifice or about dying. This is about helping each other stay alive and getting back our reputations and our lives," Laurel said gently.

He nodded slowly. "You know, I never spent much time worrying about staying alive, but since I met you, all my priorities have shifted. I want to get through this. We both have an entire lifetime filled with possibilities ahead of us."

"Yes, we do," she answered.

Her smile was gentle, and it filled him with a primitive feeling he wasn't sure he could name. It was an awareness that she was his and was more precious to him than anything else in his life. No matter what lay ahead for them, she was in his heart to stay. Even physical separation would never take her from him. She was a part of him forever.

A DEEP INDIGO BLANKET rested above the pale desert as the moon slipped behind a large thundercloud. Cisco found himself grateful for the cover it provided, instead of focusing on the limited visibility.

"Do you think you can disable any new alarms they may have added since we were there last?" Laurel asked, her voice taut as a bowstring.

"I can disable almost anything, but I'll have to be careful. Security devices have their own pluses and minuses, but it's possible to work around them, providing you have enough time."

"At least the time of night will work for us."

Silence descended between them as they neared the community of Window Rock. Cisco turned off the headlights, then continued down a gravel road behind a baseball field. "We'll be within viewing range of the building shortly, but we've got a long walk ahead of us. Is your breathing okay?" Seeing Laurel nod, he continued, "We can't afford to park anywhere near the building or the parking lot. They're going to be looking for vehicles that don't belong. If we walk over, we'll have a marginal edge since by now you can bet they know about your asthma. They won't be expecting us to attempt approaching on foot, so they won't be on the lookout for us."

She reached into their bag of dwindling foodstuffs for something to drink, then quickly took two pills. "I'll handle it," she assured him.

Cisco parked behind a red sandstone boulder as large as a house. Then, in the dark, he led the way over familiar ground to the tribal headquarters building. He knew Laurel could barely see to follow him, but she matched his pace, staying directly behind him and moving as noiselessly as he did.

By the time they reached the parking lot, Cisco's tension was palpable. His gaze pierced the darkness, searching for a way inside. Thankfully the only outside lights were attached to the building itself. "Stay here. I'm going to approach the front entrance on my belly from behind those shrubs on the side, then hide where those big planters are. There's plenty of cover there. I want to observe the guards and find out what's going on before we make a move."

"Good luck," she whispered.

He left her side, moving forward with speed and agility. He stayed low, crawling along the ground from shadow to shadow like a phantom. As he approached the building, his thoughts drifted back to Laurel. He could almost see her clutching the fetish. He wondered absently what it would tell her.

Cisco reached a spot next to an open lunchroom window and crouched in the darkness. His back pressed against the wall, he listened to two guards posted just down the hall at the security-camera monitors. Along with the breeze from the cooling system came their low conversation.

"The new safeguards are a pain in the butt," one said. "Every time I go into the VIP hall, I have to code in my ID number or my handgun will set off all the bells and whistles. One of the council members set it off this morning with his big belt buckle. Whose brainchild was it to install those things?"

"I guess the powers that be wanted to make sure they had the latest technology. The attack on the tribal president has made all of them jumpy."

"Yeah, yeah," the first guard muttered. "Whoever it was didn't need a weapon to push him off that chair and hit him in the neck, did they?"

"Enough of this talk of the dead. Even the radio hasn't said anything more about the president. Let it drop before you call his *chindi*. I'm going to get myself a sandwich from the lunchroom. You want anything?"

"No, thanks. I'm going to turn on the television and watch something light. The building's empty, and we've already made our rounds."

"Notice how everyone stopped working late around here?"

The guard switched on the TV, and the sounds of a sitcom's canned laughter filled the room. "Hey, at least they've got a good excuse."

"Which they're going to exploit to the fullest," the second guard replied, and moved off.

Cisco heard footsteps fading. Carefully he slipped out of cover and jogged down the side of the building to where Laurel was waiting. "I'm going to have to leave my gun and knives out here in some bushes," he said, filling her in. "I don't like the idea of going in without them, but I have no choice."

After ensuring that neither of them had any other large metal objects that would trip the sensors, Cisco led the way across the parking lot. The side door was securely locked and bolted. He moved down, but all the exits had been locked. As they moved closer to the front of the building, he realized that the only way in was the open window he'd been hiding beside before. "That's our only shot," he said, gesturing ahead, "but it's the lunchroom. A guard may be there now, and their post is only a short distance down the hall."

"Then we better check it out before we climb through the window," she said.

He moved forward, then after a few moments, waved at her to approach. "It's clear. The guards are probably watching TV. We'll have the noise from that to give us cover."

Cisco hid his weapons inside a bush, unhooked the screen, then pushed the window open just enough to squeeze through. He lowered himself into a crouch and immediately looked around. The room was empty. He could hear the television blaring farther down the hall. "Come on. Now's our chance."

Chapter Eighteen

Cisco opened the door and glanced down the corridor. One of the security guards was leaning back in his chair, busy watching television. The other one was nowhere in sight.

"Come on," he said after listening a moment.

They were halfway down the corridor, safely past a newly installed metal detector, when Cisco heard footsteps behind them. The other security guard was heading in their direction. Cisco ducked into the recessed area where the water fountain was located, pulling Laurel in beside him, and waited.

They heard the man stop at a vending machine, buy a soda, open it and take a drink, then walk back down the hall. Cisco breathed a sigh of relief. "Our luck's changing. We're okay, and the hall's clear."

They walked silently through the building, avoiding the few cameras, and a few minutes later arrived at the attorney's office. This time, the door was securely locked. Cisco retrieved a tiny piece of wire from his back pocket and tried to pick the mechanism. At first, nothing happened, but after a minute, the lock finally clicked open.

He turned the knob, pushed the door open an inch but didn't make any move to go inside. "There are no security devices that I can see." He searched around the doorjamb and edges for magnetic tape or switches. "We'll have to take our chances that there are no motion detectors inside."

"Couldn't we just move real slow?" Laurel suggested.

"No. They only work that way in the movies. We'll just have to risk it." He swung the door open, looking up at the ceiling. "Seems okay. It would be up high and would look a lot like a smoke detector," he said, stepping through the doorway.

"Then what were those things spaced along the ceiling in the halls?" Laurel muttered.

"Those were real smoke detectors. Motion detectors are placed in hallway corners and at junctions," Cisco whispered.

"What now?" She followed him in, closed the door behind them, hearing it lock, then turned on the room light.

"I know he's got a safe here. He mentioned it to me once. But I don't know where."

Laurel looked behind paintings hung on the wall, while Cisco searched the floor. Finally she discovered the built-in unit behind the wood-carved tribal seal. "It's here. And what better place. Right behind Tso's desk."

Cisco studied the mechanism. "This is not a discount-store wall safe. It's going to be impossible for me to pick. Start checking around his desk. See if you can find anything with a number sequence that looks like the combination. Most people write it down somewhere, like in an address book or under the desk pad, just in case they forget it."

In vain, she searched the places he suggested. "It could be in one of his computer files," she said. "Let me switch it on."

As she flicked the switch under the desk, they heard footsteps and faint voices coming down the corridor.

Laurel glanced at Cisco. "That's Tso."

"They'll be here in a minute or two. Hide!" he said, and handed her a small brass letter opener from the desktop. "Take it. It's the only weapon around."

"No. It'll do more good in your hands."

"Probably, but I have other skills."

She took the four-inch blade, then slipped the fetish off and placed it around his neck. "If the fetish works as I believe it does, then protecting you is the most important thing it can do for me now."

Cisco accepted it, giving her a smile of encouragement. "We'll be okay." Assured she'd found a safe place between the file cabinet and the bookshelf, he scrambled onto the desk and loosened the fluorescent tubes, plunging the room into blackness.

He felt his way down, then grabbed the metal fountain pen he'd located earlier on the desk. Moving fast, he ducked behind the leather sofa, pushing it out slightly from the wall.

The attorney said goodbye to the guard, who'd apparently escorted him, then used his key to open the door. Standing in the half-light of the doorway, Tso flicked the wall switch on and off several times.

Cisco waited, forcing himself to remain still. If his luck held, Tso would turn around and go searching for the circuit breakers or some replacement lights.

Tso remained in the doorway, not moving or calling for the guard. Finally he came in and closed the door behind himself, enveloping them in darkness again.

"You two just made a fatal mistake," he snarled.

As a police officer, Cisco had played these cat-and-mouse games before, so he remained motionless, listening and waiting for his night vision to sharpen. Then, just beneath the silence, he heard the faint sound of someone breathing. A chill ran all through him. Laurel was having problems with her asthma. If he could hear it, Tso could, too.

Cisco heard the attorney moving toward the file cabinet where she was hiding. She only had one chance now. He had to intercept Tso and take him by surprise.

His eyes now adjusted to the dark, Cisco could see Tso's outline less than ten feet away. As he heard the telltale click of the safety being thumbed off a gun, he knew there was no time to lose.

Cisco stepped around the couch, wielding the metal fountain pen like a dagger, when suddenly his boot bumped the front leg of the couch.

As Tso fired toward the sound, Cisco dived across the room, rolling across the carpet and beneath the desk. Tso stood silently, not moving. Cisco knew it was a game to draw him out. Tso didn't want Laurel as badly as he wanted him. Then, in the silence that surrounded them, one sound seemed to grow even louder. Laurel's breathing was more pronounced, the wheeze rising and dropping in a frenzied tempo.

Cisco suddenly realized she had left cover, trying to reach Tso before he decided to shoot again. He rose, ready to tackle Tso.

Suddenly the office door burst open, and light flooded into the darkened room. Phillip was standing there, pistol in hand. "Don't anyone move."

Tso spun around and fired, and Cisco saw his brother-in-law fall backward into the hall from the impact of the bullet.

Laurel cried out, and Tso turned back toward her. As he brought his weapon to bear, Cisco leapt into the line of fire.

He felt a flash of pain as the force of the bullet knocked him to the floor. He rolled to a sitting position, clutching his chest, but felt no wound or blood.

With a cry of rage, Laurel flew past Cisco, letter opener in hand, and drove the dull blade into Tso's arm.

He howled in pain, dropping the pistol. Trying to escape, he ran into the desk, knocking the keyboard off, and stumbled to the floor.

Phillip staggered to the office entrance, bleeding from the shoulder, kicked Tso flat, then tossed a pair of handcuffs over to Cisco. "Finish it. He's your collar."

"I'm wounded," Tso wailed.

"You'll live," Cisco growled. "She just got the side of your arm. It's nothing more than a messy cut."

The second Tso was handcuffed facedown on the carpet, Laurel ran to Cisco. She ran her hands over his shoulders, laughing and crying at the same time. "How...?"

"I don't know. And your breathing?"

"It's okay now. I tried not to use my inhaler because it would make even more noise than my wheezing. But he heard me anyway."

With his arm securely wrapped around Laurel's waist, Cisco glanced at Phillip. "I'll call for help," he said, moving to the phone.

Just then, the two security guards came rushing down the hall. "We've got you all covered, and backup is on the way. Drop any weapons you have right now!"

Phillip, who had sat down on the carpet with his back to the wall, clutching his wounded shoulder, held up his badge in one bloody hand. "I'm Sergeant Aspass. Arrest Wilfred Tso. Chief Begay told me this other officer is part of an undercover operation."

"I'm going to call for a rescue unit," Cisco said as Laurel helped Phillip.

A few minutes later, Cisco knelt by his brother-in-law. Laurel had ripped some fabric from the curtain, helping Phillip stem the flow of blood. Cisco pointedly ignored the attorney, who was demanding immediate medical help.

Phillip met Cisco's gaze and forced a thin smile. "You're a tough man to catch up to," he said.

"Do you understand what happened here?" Cisco asked.

Phillip nodded slowly. "At first, I wanted to believe you were a crooked cop. I followed you and tried to goad you into making mistakes that would give me the evidence to convict you. I figured all I needed was to give you a little push. I even threw a couple of bullets your way, intending to miss, of course.

"But the more I followed you," Phillip continued, "the more I knew that things weren't as simple as I'd thought. After a while, I realized that you were working so hard to prove your innocence, you probably weren't guilty. I had to rethink my plans then. I'd intended to help you two out when I sneaked into the car," Phillip said, and smiled at Laurel. "But you and your telephone never let me get a word in."

"Sorry about that," Laurel said, her face turning red.

"Anyway, once I realized that you were after hard evidence and would come here, I figured you'd need help. Tubbs and Chief Begay told me what was going on."

"How did Tubbs convince Chief Begay?"

Phillip shrugged, then groaned from his wound. "I called the Farmington police and asked them to pick up Harmon, then I waited outside until Tso appeared. When he came into the building, I followed him. I couldn't arrest him. I knew we didn't have anything solid enough to get a conviction at that point. We needed something more than our word against his. I had to let him play it out."

As the team of paramedics arrived to help Phillip and bandage Tso's bloody arm, Cisco stepped back, giving them room to work.

One of the guards came over to question Cisco. After a few minutes, he left to help his partner turn Tso over to the police officers who were just arriving.

Cisco led Laurel to Tso's computer. "You were about to check for the combination of the safe," he reminded her.

Laurel reached down to pick the keyboard off the carpet, and noticed the numbers *3-18-4* written on the underside. "I think we just found it."

With the combination, Cisco opened the safe just as Chief Begay joined them. "The treaty," he said, pointing to the contents.

"Good work, Watchman. The president just told me all about you," Begay said. "He regained consciousness earlier tonight, and Captain Tubbs brought me to where he was being hidden. Tubbs also told the president and me about Tso's activities. I was instructed to give you any cooperation you might need." Begay glanced at Laurel. "I've been on the phone to your brother in Mexico. I think you know we tapped his line.''

Laurel nodded. "How is Greg?" she asked anxiously.

"Fine, I guess." Begay shrugged. "He fingered Tso and is going to meet the state police in Las Cruces. They'll bring him back here as a material witness.''

"He's no thief, Tso switched the treaty. I hope you know that!" Laurel insisted.

"I'm sure everything will be sorted out in a few days. Tso is already singing like a canary about who did what, blaming Harmon and somebody named Lachuk for the dirty work. He couldn't shut up once he saw me. Wants to make a deal. You know lawyers." Begay laughed.

"We learned that Lachuk and his partner are in the Farmington jail on other charges, but what about Harmon?" Cisco asked.

"I sent Kelliwood and Blackhorse to assist the Farmington police in picking him up. Seems Sergeant Aspass told them he was a suspect in Harris's murder to get them moving fast. Now, if you'll excuse me for a moment, I've got to check in on their progress." Begay picked up his hand-held radio.

As officers swarmed inside the office, Cisco took Laurel into the hall, then drew her into his arms. He held her against him as if he'd never let her go.

"I really don't understand how you could still be alive," she whispered, snuggling into him. "He fired at practically point-blank range!"

She unbuttoned his shirt, which had a button-size hole right in the center, and ran her hand over him in a gentle caress, searching for any sign of a wound. There was an odd-shaped, nasty-looking welt on his chest, and that was all.

Cisco brushed her lips with a kiss. "You're making me crazy. You better stop doing that."

Before she could answer, she felt the fetish work its way into her palm. She drew in a breath.

Cisco smiled. "You, too? Good."

"No, it's not that." Laurel laughed, seeing the disappointment on his face. "Look!" She held the fetish out so he could see it. "That's what happened to the bullet. It struck the fetish and was flattened. It saved your life!"

"Remind me to thank you properly later for loaning it back to me." He rained kisses on her face, not easing his hold. "I need you, my beautiful woman. I've fallen in love with you, and I can't imagine a future without you," he said roughly.

"If that's a proposal, then the answer is yes, my Raider," she said softly.

Laurel's tiny sigh of contentment filled his spirit. Their hearts had joined and now beat as one. Nothing would ever threaten them again.

With the woman he loved in his arms, Cisco knew he'd found peace at last.

HARLEQUIN®

INTRIGUE®

COMING NEXT MONTH

#381 RULE BREAKER by Cassie Miles
Lawman

Aviator Joe Rivers was hell-bent on discovering the real cause for his wife's fiery death in a plane crash. But he didn't expect to find himself falling in love again—and with a prime suspect. After all, it was sexy Bailey Fielding who helped pilot the craft in which Joe's wife was killed....

#382 SEE ME IN YOUR DREAMS by Patricia Rosemoor
The McKenna Legacy

Keelin McKenna dreamed through other people's eyes...victims' eyes. And when Keelin came to America in the hope of reuniting the McKenna clan, the dreams intensified. This time she couldn't ignore them—because somewhere out there was a father whose teenage daughter was missing. Tyler Leighton would come to rely on Keelin much more than she ever dreamed possible.

#383 EDEN'S BABY by Adrianne Lee

In the past, a woman had killed for Dr. David Coulter's love. Now the lovely Eden Prescott has pledged her love to David. But when she discovers her pregnancy, should Eden turn to the father of her baby...or will that make them all—her, David and the coming child—mere pawns in the game of a jealous stalker?

#384 MAN OF THE MIDNIGHT SUN by Jean Barrett
Mail Order Brides

Married to a stranger.... They're mail-order mates, and neither one is who they claim to be. Cold Alaskan nights roused a man's lust for a warm woman—and Cathryn matched Ben's every desire. He would enjoy sweet-talking her into divulging her deepest secrets...for she had slipped right into the ready-made role he had planned for her. And right into the trap he'd set....

AVAILABLE THIS MONTH:

Look for us on-line at: http://www.romance.net

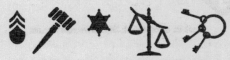

BRIDE'S BAY RESORT

UNLOCK THE DOOR TO GREAT ROMANCE AT BRIDE'S BAY RESORT

Join Harlequin's new across-the-lines series, set in an exclusive hotel on an island off the coast of South Carolina.

Seven of your favorite authors will bring you exciting stories about fascinating heroes and heroines discovering love at Bride's Bay Resort.

Look for these fabulous stories coming to a store near you beginning in January 1996.

Harlequin American Romance #613 in January
Matchmaking Baby by Cathy Gillen Thacker

Harlequin Presents #1794 in February
Indiscretions by Robyn Donald

Harlequin Intrigue #362 in March
Love and Lies by Dawn Stewardson

Harlequin Romance #3404 in April
Make Believe Engagement by Day Leclaire

Harlequin Temptation #588 in May
Stranger in the Night by Roseanne Williams

Harlequin Superromance #695 in June
Married to a Stranger by Connie Bennett

Harlequin Historicals #324 in July
Dulcie's Gift by Ruth Langan

Visit Bride's Bay Resort each month wherever Harlequin books are sold.

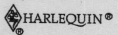

HARLEQUIN ®

BBAYG

You are cordially invited to a
HOMETOWN REUNION

September 1996—August 1997

Where can you find romance and adventure,
bad boys, cowboys, feuding families, and babies,
arson, mistaken identity, a mom on the run...?
Tyler, Wisconsin, that's where!

So join us in this not-so-sleepy little town and
experience the love, the laughter and the
tears of those who call it home.

WELCOME TO A
HOMETOWN REUNION

Twelve unforgettable stories, written for you by
some of Harlequin's finest authors. This fall,
begin a yearlong affair with America's favorite
hometown as **Marisa Carroll** brings you
Unexpected Son.

Available at your favorite retail store.

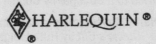

Look us up on-line at: http://www.romance.net

HTRG